God Help Us

SECOND EDITION

Arthur "Mac" McCaffry

GOD HELP US
SECOND EDITION

iUniverse books may be ordered through booksellers or by contacting:

iUniverse
1663 Liberty Drive
Bloomington, IN 47403
www.iuniverse.com
1-800-Authors (1-800-288-4677)

ISBN: 978-1-5320-4836-4 (sc)
ISBN: 978-1-5320-4838-8 (hc)
ISBN: 978-1-5320-4837-1 (e)

Library of Congress Control Number: 2018907069

Print information available on the last page.

iUniverse rev. date: 06/21/2018

And it shall come to pass in the last days, saith, God, 'I will pour out my Spirit upon all flesh; and your sons and your daughters shall prophesy, and your young men shall see visions, and your old men shall dream dreams:

Acts 2: 17

Contents

Authors Predictions

Prediction 1

I predict President Trump will orchestrate a treaty drawn for a period of 7 years between Jews and Palestinians living side by side in Jerusalem. I predict after the treaty takes place, a temple will be built for the Jewish people near the 'Holy Mount'; while on the other side of the Holy Mount, Palestinians will worship near the 'Dome of the Rock.'

Prediction 2

I predict there will be a weather change throughout the world: one greater than ever before. I predict this weather change will be as former President Obama predicted in 2015; before closing his speech in Paris before 150 nations. I quote his words ..." I believe this weather change will take place within the next 2 or 3 years."

Prediction 3

I predict sometime soon, 4 Cardinals at the Vatican will meet with Pope Francis, and the Catholic Church will split!

Prediction 4

I predict sometime in the future IS1S will attack our electrical grids in America: they've viewed them before!

Prediction 5

I predict the Euphrates River will soon run dry; ISIS has broken the lock!

Now, the last of them, not a prediction, but something Jesus warned us about as He sat upon the 'Mount of Olives' ... about to die upon a cross at a place called Calvary!"

"Mathew 24; 24 ... for there shall arise false Christ and false prophets and shew great signs and wonders; insomuch that, if it were possible ... "they shall deceive the very elect."

Yet another to make you think about; Daniel's vision of the 4 beasts ... interpreted by the angel Gabriel

Daniel 8: 25 ... And through his policy also he shall cause craft to prosper in his hand; and he shall magnify himself in his heart, and by peace he shall destroy many.

The author includes his prediction as part of his fiction novel *"God Help Us"*... but his true motive for this novel, is to make people aware the rapture of the *Church* is near; before a bugle sounds high in the heavens with our Lord Jesus appearing to gather His Church ... *"The Elect."*

INTRODUCTION

A couple of years ago I read Thomas Friedman's book, "The World is Flat," and I began to realize he might be writing something yet to come----something in line with "biblical prophecy." Things are changing as never before, and I'm beginning to wonder, "what's next" for us to see in this brave new world filled with knowledge beyond imagination."

Recently great tragedy struck the United States, and suddenly all peace- loving persons on earth were shocked: twenty of our most loved were brutally murdered, along with six of their protectors at a school in Connecticut.

I thought of other places the same took place; a movie theatre in Colorado, where six innocent persons met death by one of the same. And another place where Congress-woman, "Gabrielle Gifford," was shot without reason, except maybe someone with a deep troubled mind.

And I thought of another place, Las Vegas ... where a man went on killing spree injuring and killing people without known reason. He too, a man possessed by Satan: a man nobody seems to know about.

The world seemed to stop, searching for a reason. And I began to realize this isn't new, it has happened before. I asked myself the age-old question ... who in their right mind could commit such atrocities; the answer always comes up the same, only the devil and his demonic possessed followers.

Again, I ask myself, "who reaps benefits of these sick characters with beady-eyes, weirdo personalities ... filled with an unending desire to destroy the ones God loves the most? Is it the N R A, the ones who like to hunt, the ones who like to protect themselves from thieves or murderer's, *or could it be demonic forces taking over the hearts and minds of people here on earth?"*

I have a decision to make! I'm 91 years of age attempting to write something so great and wonderful upon my simple mind since childhood; Jesus our Lord and Savior returning to gather "His Church" before the greatest battle ever, "Armageddon." It's challenging for sure, but with His help ... I'll do it!"

Night after night I lie in bed remembering the words of "Moses!" I think of the words he said when the Lord told him he would deliver his people out of Egypt, but I'm no Moses---that's for sure! But I just might be one of, "**His Chosen**" ... perhaps the same as one of you. And the very thought of something so wonderful makes me think of my personal life; my greatest commitment ever ... my redemption!"

I guess I'm about like what the Apostle Paul called, "the least of the least" -----*a* sinner saved by the grace of God searching; never recognizing His almighty power with-in me."

Again, and again I contemplate the seriousness of something dwelling within my heart and soul; the power of the enemy I must face. I recognize from the very beginning I'm no match for the devil: my help lies in the hands of, "*The Father, Son, and Holy Ghost.*"

Acknowledgement

I humbly dedicate this novel to my good friend, Ethel Hamilton, now deceased at the age of one-hundred and two. She introduced me back into the Lord's Grace after years of absence. My disregard toward "The Church" has been erased, and through her love, patience, and devotion … I'm finally able to forgive my enemies as, Christ forgives me!"

I dedicate the same to my wonderful "Uncle Joe" … a poor man with riches beyond imagination, awaiting him in heaven.

I've never-ending thanks to the five most notable persons affecting my personal life; Billy Graham, John Hague, Dr. David Jeremiah, Greg Laurie … Hal Lindsey. Their message of dwelling with the Lord throughout eternity has given me faith and understanding beyond my wildest dreams. But, most important; their words of love and forgiveness never runs dry, even for a sinner saved by the grace of God … like me.

PRELUDE

Mike Cutler, a Vietnam vet returns home after two and a half years in and out of combat. His return is greeted by waiting protesters as he disembarks from a hospital ship in San Francisco. He's spat upon and cursed for serving in a war they refused to support. He's filled with bitterness but decides to move on with life.

He begins raising a family under the guidance of a *very* conservative church. Life moves on year after year as Mike and his wife become part of accepted church-life. Then it happened! His neighbors' daughter is sexually molested by a Deacon with-in the church! Cover-up and denial from the church, causes him to develop a never-lasting disregard for the church, and all it stands for.

"Friend," his Guardian Angel guides his way back to the church where he meets Ailene Brooks, a fiery fast-talking lady reporter for the, Indianapolis Star Newspaper, along with, "Brad Carso"; Pastor of "Morris Avenue Baptist Church" in Indianapolis. Their friendship proceeds as planned, and Brad describes Mike as … another John the Baptist, waiting in the wilderness for something from above to guide his life serving Jesus.

Mike's uncontrollable temper overcomes reason and hearing the word "Vietnam" causes it to erupt. The appearance of a

Satanic Bible, terror plotting in the Middle-East, turmoil and romance; all become part of an exciting story of Mike's new life within the church. Friend, his Guardian Angel reveals God's plan for the remainder of his days, but it's hard for him to understand. He considers himself a man without purpose, wandering in a strange new world looking for help, until, his Guardian Angel takes over; guiding him through a seemingly impossible mission. But … why he is one of *"The Chosen"*… is far beyond his wildest dreams, causing him to wonder.

The sudden appearance of a *Satanic Bible* at the famous "Eagles Nest," in the "Bavarian Alps" becomes his problem. He searches for an answer; asking himself … *"why me, Mr. Nobody, is selected for "Operation Un-Holy Ground."*

> **"Be not forgetful to entertain strangers; for thereby some have entertained angels unawares.**
>
> ***Hebrews 13: 2***

"I ask myself the question … 'is it possible I've met an angel maybe somewhere, sometime, during my life-time: the answer always comes up the same … "but why not me, they're God's messengers among us."

CHAPTER 1

Awakening

"Have mercy upon me, Oh Lord, for I am in Trouble.

Psalm 31: 9

Mike Cutler rises from bed after another night of sleeplessness. Rolling and tossing throughout the night becomes his way of life. His four-bedroom home on the west side of Indianapolis has become a prison, without promise of parole. He heads to the bathroom for his morning shave looking into the mirror, and it isn't pleasant for a man once considered handsome. His eyes show red and bleary ... his beard dark and crusty. Again, he looks in the mirror gazing at him-self, turning away disgusted. Wife has been dead ten long years, children married and gone; while old friends depart for heaven or hell, never noticed.

He returns to the dining room sipping coffee from a cup; remembering the good times, gone in the twinkling of an eye. He strolls across the dining room opening a sliding door leading out to a large wooden deck overlooking the back-yard.

He gazes around remembering grandchildren romping with his two big golden retrievers, Barney and Fred. He begins to mutter to himself, "Oh, wonderful memories, please never leave me. How do I find myself sixty-two, no wife, no kids, no friends, but lots of "buddies?" Has everyone deserted me? But Lord, why or why, are you doing this to me?"

He gazes out toward a high chain-link-fence surrounding his yard. Here he once gathered beautiful roses ... presenting them to his beautiful wife.

Walking to the farthest part of the yard he turns, gazing across the street noticing a building recently opened for business. He glances at the sign displaying, *"Nancy's Child Care Center"* seeing young women running in and out... heading for work.

He walks back inside ready to watch the morning news. ABC news anchors discuss a well-known politician caught cheating with numerous women. People express shock, want to forgive and forget ... others condemn and punish. Some call it sex addiction ... maybe a disease. He reads the newspaper noticing a small article at the very bottom; describing children dying by the thousands in places like Syria, Somalia, Kenya ... the world over.

Again, he switches channels hoping for something different. It shows a government spokesman from the "White House" addressing the press. He looks out over his audience announcing, they're dealing with persons in the "Security Exchange Commission" ... watching pornography while on duty. And from out of the crowd ... a reporter asks, "What will happen to those guilty watching porn, while our government heads into bankruptcy?"

Quickly, the spokesman shrugs his shoulders, looking

around his audience replying ... "We're dealing with it my friend, don't worry about it. We need to conduct a study to see if there's wrong-doing; this conference is over!"

He switches channels showing the president speaking in Berlin. Thousands stand before him shouting his praise as a new world leader; while television displays his speech globally to millions throughout.

He promises a world of change is about to come soon. He tells the world diplomacy is the answer to past American mistakes; his way solving problems in the future. He mentions America's mistakes in the past... future problems will be negotiated.

Disgusted, he switches to NBC--- more of the same. They show lawmakers and lobbyist walking from the "White House" smiling as angels; pleased with their days work... changing America forever!

He shakes his head looking away disgusted again!

Finally, ... he switches to Fox News hoping for something better. They show youth gangs beating and killing a fellow student with two-by-fours in Chicago, *murder capital of America.*

Politicians appear on the scene shouting to onlookers, "something needs to be done, but never a suggestion. And from the back of the crowd, someone yells, *"Call out the National Guard!"* ... bringing cheers well accepted.

The High School Principal appears, staring out over onlookers looking confused! He gazes over the crowd announcing ever so loudly, "Parents are the problem, don't blame the teachers."

Mike begins to ask himself, *What, Lord ... what is happening to my wonderful country: the country I love and adore is going to hell and nobody cares!"*

Chapter 2

Walk with an Angel

; and at the ninth hour I prayed in my house, and, behold, a man stood before me in bright clothing.

Acts 10: 30

Morning sun peaks through the clouds, and once again Mike Cutler awakens to the sound of chirping birds outside his bedroom window. It's a new day, and for the first time in months he's rested.

He moves to the living room listening to songs shared with his wife during days of wine and roses, dancing the night away. "Karen Carpenter" sings, "We've Only Just Begun," followed with "Eddie Arnold" singing, "Make the World Go Away"; beautiful, wonderful songs, gone forever. His 62 years are beginning to show, romance of youth is fading.

He moves outside walking to nowhere. His thoughts begin to ramble thinking differently; today… this very day, things will change for the better.

Houses appear unnoticed before, and he wonders what's happening. His thoughts run deep, searching for things from yester-years. He wonders if time remains on his side, what to do if it isn't. He begins to feel in a dream-world; not the happy world as it used to be.

Life for Mike has been interesting; real-estate, oil exploration, business ventures, Vietnam, come and gone ... memories forever.

His once blond hair turned silver, his six-foot frame dwindled. He struggles with his wife's absence remembering her final words before leaving him forever, "I love you, darling; we'll meet again tomorrow."

He mumbles words to himself, "What's going on in my miserable life, where are my friends: who can help a guy like me? *Why was I ever born Lord? Help me Lord ... please Lord help me!*"

Memories run wild, flooding his mind as only yesterday. He thinks of neighborhood friends, the "Indy Five-Hundred."

He wonders if ever again, children in school will have the privilege of singing *Amazing Grace or The Star-Spangled Banner*.

He stops abruptly wondering, "*is this the same America I was once proud to call ... "America the Beautiful, home of the brave, land of the free?*"

Again, he begins walking, remembering things from the past: standing in the hall-way at school, pledging allegiance under God before Old-Glory.

He remembers how he would look upon the wall at school, seeing, "The Ten Commandments" hanging beside it: now he's sad, disappointed again.

He stands gazing upward into nowhere barely muttering, "Where is the answer to my problems, Lord: where Is there a place of happiness for a guy like me, Lord…lead me wherever, Lord!"

Coming from out of nowhere a basketball rolls down the sidewalk beside him. He's startled, glancing to his side where a tall young man stands beside him, dressed in a white linen suit.

He looks him over, staring into eyes like never seen before; bright fiery eyes, causing him to shudder.

He watches him pick up the ball, twirling it around his fingers with ease; thinking, "one of the "Pacers," no doubt!

The new friend moves closer, speaking as someone past. "Good morning, Mike. Where are you headed?" he asks so pleasantly.

"Probably nowhere … just walking, thinking about things; didn't quite get your name."

"My name is Friend; feeling sad for your-self; aren't you Mike!"

Mike hesitates, looking him over again, thinking …" this new guy is different; his speech, his voice, all different."

He stops walking, looking at friend again … trying to remember.

"But why shouldn't I be sad … I've no friends, maybe a few buddies." He barely mutters.

Friend doesn't wait … moving beside him, "But, He will always love you, Mike. You remind me of Job, a guy my father knows."

Mike hesitates, wondering if it's the same guy he read about thirty years ago in a church he once attended.

"Anyone who calls him-self a Christian knows about Job," he says, smartly.

"Not everyone, but you do, Mike!" Friend says quickly, staring at him waiting …

Mike stops … looking again at him, speechless! He's never

met this guy, but somehow, someway; this guy knows things, secretive things.

"Friends deserted Job ... all his earthly treasures gone!" He says ... his eyes focused upon Mike.

Mike looks up at Friend differently ... staring at him, wondering, "But, what does Job have to do with me Friend ... I'm nobody?"

"He's haunting you Mike, night and day he's haunting you!"

Mike doesn't wait, backing away stunned again. He's talking Bible talk; something he doesn't want to talk about.

"You got to be joking, I've nothing left to fight over, Friend," he mumbles, turning away.

Friend moves even closer, barely whispering, "But he wants your very heart ... your very soul, Mike!"

"Bang!" Right out of the blue ... something shocking, causing Mike to look again; beginning to realize this guy is different! He knows things he and God know only!

His head hangs low, his heart pounds ... his eyes show worry. "But, who is this person you're talking about, Friend," ... he barely whispers.

"Satan, the devil, Mike!"

Mike is stunned, staring at Friend speechless...it's time to change the subject.

"Are you out for a morning stroll, or maybe out to meet people?" He asks, pleasantly.

"Business Mike!"

Mike turns gazing out into the street ..." Business with whom, Friend,"

Friend stops, placing the ball under his arm, while his other hand rests upon Mike's shoulder, barely whispering, *"You're my business, Mike! You're my business ... my agenda today,* tomorrow, *forever, Mike!"*

Again, Mike is speechless ... thinking, "This is a dream for sure! This never happens, he keeps telling himself over and over.

"You're joking of course," he finally can mutter.

"I don't joke ... I've a message for you, Mike!"

"A message for me ... Friend," he barely mutters.

Friend moves closer against him, whispering, "He heard your cry for help ... He heard your loneliness: I'm here to help you Mike!"

He's in trouble, deep trouble, and he knows it.

"And he ... who is he Friend," he can only mumble ... his heart pounding."

Friend grabs his hand squeezing it hard, bringing him alive... shouting, "Be serious and don't forget to whom you speak Mike!"

His hands tremble. His body goes limp, frightened again. "You mean Him ... Friend?"

"Him only Mike; the one who will never leave you, never forsake you!"

Mike turns ... looking away, "I've heard those words a thousand times Friend. I went all the way with, *Him*: we're talking about Jesus I suppose."

"You know we are. We're talking about *The Son of God ... Jesus; the one who gave His life for you at a place called Calvary, Mike!*"

His hands tremble, his heart beats faster, "My wife reminded me of "Him" till the day she died; holding her Bible looking up toward heaven smiling." he can barely mutter.

Friend moves even closer, beside him, "She did... and now it's time for you to come home Mike," he whispers close to his ear, barely breathing ...

His memory flashes before him thirty years past ... seeming

forever! A time he swore he would never listen to the words, "Jesus, our Lord, God and Savior."

He isn't satisfied. He wants to set the conversation his way, blunt words, driving away the best of them.

"You remind me of the ones who betrayed me, the ones who sent me away, lied about me!"

"But, he hasn't forgotten you; thirty years are nothing to *Him, Mike.*"

Wow! The very thought of it! Thirty long years ago, a time and a place, he can't forget.

"I don't know why you're here Friend, but it's over: you know nothing of my past!"

"Speak from your heart Mike. He sent me to bring you home… a new life awaits you!"

Along moment thinking back and, "Do you really want me to explain why I left the church?"

"But he knows… It's written in 'The Book of Life' to be opened on Judgment Day, Mike!"

"Stop it! Stop it! No more of that "Judgment Day" stuff: stop the rhetoric, Friend!" He's beginning to shout.

"But I'm here for you alone … I'm listening Mike."

"I'm glad you're listening…maybe now we can talk about the real problem."

"Tell me the real problem."

"Oh yes, I'll tell you the real problem …

"I'm waiting Mike."

"A 6-year-old neighbor's daughter was molested by a Sunday School bus driver in broad daylight, and the church denied it," he shouts, up in his face … angrily.

"Calm your-self Mike, we're just beginning!" Friend says, moving beside him.

"Don't try and stop me … don't try it Friend!" Mike shouts

up in his face; while Friend stands beside him smiling … waiting.

"But, it was the little girl's single mother… the one my wife and I invited to church hoping to convert her. But it didn't work … It didn't work because throughout the neighborhood everyone was saying it was because of my wife and I Friend."

"The rest of it Mike."

"I wanted to kill the miserable scum-bag, but my wife and the mother thought differently. They wanted to do it the good old church-way: turn it over to the church … let them be the judge and jury."

Friend stands beside Mike smiling, looking up waiting; while Mike stands pondering, finally moving before him.

"Why are you bothering me friend: I didn't ask for your advice. Get away from me… leave me, Friend!"

"But you asked for me: He heard your plea … he loves you Mike."

Mike's head lowers, gazing downward… worried again.

Again, they walk side besides never speaking … till Mike breaks the silence.

"My wife and neighbor insisted we bring the pervert before the Deacons and Elders, the good old church way!"

"And…

"He confessed his sin before Richard Blake, an innocent young preacher; while I stood beside the pedophile… accusing him in contempt forever! But, then it happened, the biggest mistake I made ever …

"Tell me your biggest mistake ever Mike."

"I trusted the church. I assumed the matter settled, but it wasn't. When it was over, my wife and I became victims; accused of causing the church trouble. It was terrible Friend, terrible! The only excuse the pervert had to offer ... the most despicable words ever!"

"But that was yesterday, your future lies ahead of you Mike."

"But, not over with me Friend ... never will it be over with me. He looked up at the preacher and said with his filthy mouth ... *"I just can't keep my hands off little girls, preacher... I'm guilty!"*

"Let it out, let all of it out Mike!"

"He showed no remorse Friend ... none whatever!"

Friend turns away, gazing upward toward heaven meditating ... till Mike explodes shouting, "Get away from me Friend...don't touch me! I hate the church and all the hypocrites within it!"

Moments of silence till, "Are you finished Mike?"

"No way I'm finished. Pastor Blake and I believed the case was over: time to send it to the deacons and elders... but boy, oh boy, was that ever a mistake?"

"A mistake ...

"The church did nothing, we became the problem. All I could hear was... 'protect the church, think of the families; always ending with those famous old words ...

"What famous old words Mike?"

"The Lord will take care of everything! Over and over they repeated the same... while our heart and mind bled endlessly. Yet today I ask myself ... why haven't they asked forgiveness Lord?"

"But you must forgive too ... as God forgives you Mike."

Mike stops ...staring upon him speechless. He tries to hide the tears, but useless.

"But Friend---- all I could feel was never ending hatred. It filled my soul, my heart forever. They stood before me looking righteous as a bunch of Pharisees, gazing down upon Mary

Magdalen: while she was lying upon the ground helpless. I just couldn't forgive them Friend."

"Mike stops, getting his breath… beginning again. "It was a nightmare for thirty long miserable years …I'm bitter, there's never an ending Friend!"

Friend moves even closer, listening.

"I wanted to die, but revenge I wanted more. I wanted a way to get even: make them suffer the way I've suffered Friend."

Friend walks beside him staring upward, searching the heavens; while Mike continues walking, stopping again and again.

"At the end of this sad painful story, my wife and I became known as untouchables…. turned away forever Friend."

Slowly, Friend moves ahead gazing upward toward heaven smiling, while Mike's anger continues, on and on.

"Don't walk away … listen to me Friend. My wife and I went through living-hell. I was snubbed, shunned by most everyone; except my Uncle Joe, a holy man among them. Listen to me Friend!"

Friend turns… facing him, "I've never stopped listening Mike."

"You're listening … then quit looking at me as if I'm nothing," he shouts up in his face, angry again.

"But you're wrong. You're someone he loves dearly: you're his forever, Mike!"

Stunned again … nothing like this ever! Mike is worried. His head lowers even further; thinking back to better days. Tears begin to show, pitiful looking tears … the kind he hopes Friend doesn't notice.

"Thank you, Friend, but I'm tired of listening … conversation over."

Friend takes his hand pulling him beside him … looking

into his eyes smiling, "Over, you say … your life is just beginning Mike!"

Mike looks up at him pitiful like, "I've had enough of this conversation. I'm tired of listening to you pretending to be someone holy. And something else, Friend …

"Yes Mike …

"You're no angel … not the kind of angel I've read about."

"But I am Mike! I'm your Guardian Angel: He sent me, Mike!"

Mike's body runs numb … speechless again! He runs his hand across his brow wiping sweat: caught up in something holy.

He stops… asking him-self over and over … *'can this be possible … can this truly be an angel of God: standing before the sinner of all sinners?"*

More silence, more thinking … "I need a plan to get rid of this guy. He's trying to tell me he's sent from God for someone like me; impossible, it has to be!"

"But … let me tell you the rest of my story Friend."

"I'm waiting Mike …

"The only person believing our story was my, *Uncle Joe* … a converted sinner; a person like Paul the Apostle…the least of the least!"

"He was … till he met Him, Mike!"

"But, my Uncle was an escaped convict from a Georgia chain-gang; a boot-lager: a whore-monger among the best of them."

"He was Mike!"

"My Uncle Joe did it all and I loved him … oh, how I loved him! He was saved from a life of sin; by far the greatest witness for Jesus I've ever met Friend!" Mike tries to explain, his voice changing, fighting back tears.

Friend moves even closer, looking up to him, "He was

Mike! He was a holy man, a believer in Christ; riches in heaven above many!"

Again, Mike is stunned; watching his every move as he moves away; gazing up into the morning sun... smiling.

"Well, if ever I've met a saint... it was my Uncle Joe, Friend!"

Friend's eyes dance in all their glory... pulling Mike beside him, "My Father has a message for you Mike!"

"Message from your father ... is that what you said Friend," He asks, standing before him motionless.

"Today's the day Mike, time to pay your debt!"

Again, he's speechless! Friend knows everything, all the way to the sad, dirty ending.

Chapter 3

The Chosen

**Because God has from the beginning chosen
you to salvation thru sanctification of the
Spirit and belief of the truth.**

2ⁿᵈ Thessalonians 2: 13

M ike is shattered! He looks down into the street, no desire
to talk about other events till, "I'm talking about today,
nothing else Friend. I'm fed up listening to Evangelists tell me
about the facts of life. I've tried their way … believe me I have."

Friend places the basketball in Mike's hand walking to
the edge of the side-walk, bowing upon his knees. His arms
raise upward, speaking words without meaning; while Mike's
imagination runs wild wondering … *'can this be real … a real
live angel.'*

Silence takes over … except for the sound of a few passing
cars heading to work unnoticed.

Friend rises, taking his hand, "Take a deep breath, stop and
listen. From this day forward, I'll guide you. You've a debt to

pay, a debt everyone must pay to enter His kingdom!" He says, bringing Mike alive, looking up to him.

His heart pounds, trying to remember... "But this debt ... where and when Friend," he asks, standing before Friend; arms and legs numb, hands shaking.

"Ashamed, aren't you. You know the answer better than anyone... you've been there Mike!"

Mike studies hard, wracking his brain forever, but never an answer. He's helpless, looking up at Friend pitiful like,

"I'm tired Friend... you win. I can't go on ... tell me my debt," he can barely utter.

Friend moves closer, up in his face smiling, *"But you've always known Mike; everything begins and ends at a place called, Calvary!"*

"Wow ... Calvary! A place, a time he'll never forget. His memory explodes, bringing back memories; peaceful, happy days all in the past.

"Leave me ... I can't stand any more of this, Friend. I need nobody; nobody needs me!" He's shouting, uncontrollably.

"But, Mike ... everyone needs someone, sometime."

Frustrated and exhausted ... he looks up at Friend pitiful like, while a couple of tears fall downward. He's thinking of a beautiful song he heard long ago ..." *He Touched Me."*

His thoughts go back to another time ... another place, the time he first met Jesus.

Friend's eyes begin to show their color, sparkling as diamonds. He moves close to Mike, looking deep into his eyes smiling ... "I touched you as our Lord up above told me to touch you Mike! From this moment forward, you will never forget the way I touched you; never again ... *till the day you die...lying beside me!!"*

Mike can only look up to Friend helpless, afraid to speak ... fearing the consequences!

"Ashamed aren't you. You've been there, you know better than all, Mike!"

"Now ... what are you talking about? Take your ball and go away, you're torturing me Friend!"

"I touched you Mike, and from this moment forward you will never forget the way I touched you!"

Mike's head slowly drops. pleading, "Have mercy upon me please Friend ... help me."

"I'll never leave you Mike ... never have, never will! *Think back to a time of war ... a filthy, bloody, unforgiving war!*"

He looks up staring at Friend, wondering where ... when ... "No! No! It can't be ... it can't be," he keeps telling himself over and over.

Friend moves against him touching him, "Yes, Mike ... ruthless never-ending war! It was war at its best, filled with unforgiven glory."

"I stood beside you in a rice paddy, while you lay helpless on your back praying: seeing your buddies and enemies covering the ground around you. Think Mike! Think!"

His heart pounds, numb from top to bottom. He can't remember the face, but oh ... that magic touch; so comforting, so overwhelming!

"But where does this guy come from? He asks himself over and over.

Suddenly his face turns pale; remembering the bloody days and nights in the killing fields... at a place called, "Nam!"

"You were with me *at* Phu Bai ... the landing strip ...

"I was with you Mike."

"The killing, the cursing, the yelling, the screaming ...

"That too Mike."

"The kid with his leg blown to bits …

"Joey … a farm boy from Indiana, Second Marines … Charley Company.

"And the crazy Colonel from the 101st Airborne …"

"I watched a Chopper take off through a hail of bullets on a rainy blood-soaked runway. I observed the one you call the crazy Colonel, as he dragged you and another marine inside a chopper. I listened to your cursing; while the young marine was telling you… 'shut your stupid mouth Mike; I'm going home … forget it!"

He lowers his head wanting to cry but can't. Memories, unforgettable memories; the screaming, the shouting, Corpsman! Corpsman; all through the night… in a hell-hole far away!

"But Friend, I've never deserted anyone! If only I could have moved my arms and legs. I would have crawled on my stomach to be with them. I felt paralyzed, wished I could die, but didn't. What else can you possibly ask of me Friend," He's pleading.

Friend comes to a halt, grasping his hand … stopping him, "But Joey didn't complain Mike! He suffered terribly; accepted war and death as a marine he was proud to be!"

"He asked for your Bible, the one you held in your hand… offering it to him. You remember the day, the time as only yesterday Mike!"

"Shut up Friend! I don't wanta hear any more of this," he shouts, up in his face … angrily.

"But it wasn't your friends you deserted, it was Jesus! You called his name … he heard your prayer, Mike!"

Friend reaches for his hand, but he draws away… staring up at him, pleading, "Don't touch me Friend … please don't touch me."

"But why Mike?"

"Don't ever believe I haven't wanted to be home with Jesus…but I'm not worthy Friend," he utters tearfully.

"But you are worthy Mike, all are worthy unto Him, Mike!"

He's puzzled … thinking back to the day, the time, the place: his buddies laying prone upon the ground, pleading for help … dying beside him.

And from nowhere, a message from above fills his mind and soul; Friend knows it all and then some, no doubt about it!

"I'm lost, nowhere to turn … help me Friend, help me," he's pleading.

Friend moves closer, placing his hand upon his shoulder, "I'm here for you. I'll guide you into a future beyond your wildest dreams ever, Mike!"

"My wildest dreams ever …"

"From here through eternity … wherever Mike!"

Mike looks again at Friend, smiling, "Your, father… the Lord our God I assume?"

"He is Mike. He's the one you once served faithfully. My Father knew you before you were born; before you lay in your mother's womb.

"I was there when your mother and father placed you upon the altar of God. I was there while Pastor Jeffrey anointed you with oil; holding you high over the altar, dedicating your life and service to Him only. You're one of the few Mike; you're one of **His Chosen!**"

Mike stops, looking again, "But this is impossible … I'm the most miserable person on earth, Friend!"

"But, it's over Mike. My father wants your consecration to Him alone!"

Wow … never anything like this … ever!

He continues, walking beside Friend never speaking. His thoughts wonder back to child-hood, another time, different places. thinking *... but what if just maybe, I am one of His Chosen.*

Friend moves beside him, taking his hand, looking up to him, whispering, "He loves you Mike. He shows His mercy unto you."

Again, his mind runs rampant; remembering his thoughts, his dreams, all filled with love for Him only.

"I know he loves me. I know his power, his greatness. I tremble, thinking about it, Friend."

"Tell me his greatness Mike."

Again, he's struggling ...

"It's your future Mike, His plans for you are priceless: tell me about Him!"

"His power is unthinkable! His grace is forever! He's my God ... there's none other!"

"Your name is written where Mike?"

"My name ...

"Your name is written in the book of life. It's there now and forever! It means everything Mike!"

"You mean ...

"Yes... "The Lambs Book of Life" His book!"

"But, why do I feel doomed forever, nothing but misery? Help me Friend ... help me," he's pleading over and over.

Friend moves closer beside him, grabbing his arm facing him, "But it's your future to think about... the past belongs to yesterday Mike!"

His face turns pale, staring at Friend traumatized! He pinches his arm till it hurts, slaps his face in disgust... staring up at Friend speechless ...

"Something bothering you Mike?"

A pitiful looking smile and, "There is something bothering me. I've been there before, you know the story. I know all about the "Lamb's book of life," Jesus, Judgment Day, and then some. I hate myself more than my enemies. But, when I think of those thirty miserable years of remorse ... I don't understand ... I cannot understand, Friend!"

"But, you forgot to ask another Mike ..."

"What are you trying to tell me?"

"It wasn't Him that caused your problem: It was Lucifer, Son of the Morning!"

"I've dreaded this moment forever, but I knew it would come someday Friend. I know all about Lucifer, the devil: but within my heart and soul ... I was afraid to even think about this day ... my confession!"

"He's waiting, tell me your confession. Today is the day Mike."

"It all started late one cold winter night. I was driving home from a poker-game with some buddies. I was tired, burned-out. I turned on the radio to keep me awake ... and suddenly, I was like in a trance listening to a song from happier days: unforgettable days, filled with love for Jesus. I loved it... oh how I loved it Friend!"

"But the song Mike, tell me the song."

"I'll never forget ... "Amazing Grace." I listened to the words thinking about it. I wanted to die but couldn't. I went to bed feeling guilty, waking up feeling guilty; when it was over... I fell upon my knees crying like a baby. Help me Friend ... help me!"

"But the words Mike, tell me the words."

"A wretch like me Friend; for someone like me ... it would take a miracle!"

"A miracle ...

"Nothing but a miracle Friend!"

Friend reaches out grabbing his arm looking up to him

shouting, "Is forgiving worth your soul in hell Mike? Think of John; think how John the slave trader felt!"

His memory goes blank. He's never heard of a guy called John …

"Search no more Mike. **His name is *John … John Newton, author of Amazing Grace; my father's son***

CHAPTER 4

And ... There's Angels

**For he shall give his angels charge over thee,
to keep thee in all thy ways.**

Psalm 91:11

"Oh yes, I remember reading about John Newton, the life he lived sailing over the ocean three-hundred years ago in the slave trade."

"John was like you Mike!"

Mike moves closer, looking up to him, "John ... the slave trader, like me ...?"

"John found a cure for his sin, Mike."

"You're losing me, my Friend. I'm not good solving riddles."

"You're one of the best. Think back to pleasant days; something you lost ... something most precious!"

"You mean His ...

"Yes Mike, His grace ... the most precious thing ever!"

"You know about my promise to God; the kid, the Colonel ... at the rice paddy-----

"I know it all Mike. I'm talking about the Bible; the book your uncle gave you before heading out for Nam."

"Oh yes … now I remember."

"I've a message for you Mike …

Mike pauses coming to a halt. "A message for me … about what?"

"There's a showdown coming: take it seriously, you're going to need it Mike!"

"A showdown about what?"

"He has a plan for you Mike. You will do His will as He pleases. When you're finished… your reward will be great: your long-sought question answered!"

Again, he's wondering if he's dreaming, shouting. "Now hold it a minute, Friend! It's time you use words I understand, plain and simple words."

"My Father has plans for you. You were anointed upon the altar of God as a baby: you belong to Him only, Mike!"

Mikes' body trembles, turning away, "But I'm nothing, I'm nobody Friend: go away and leave me!"

He stands motionless … staring at Friend waiting till… "Oh yes, now I remember … my grandmother told the same, one afternoon while going to a prayer- meeting."

"But little you know what lies ahead of you Mike Cutler! Our Father above has plans for you!"

Mike looks up at Friend, and back down again… barely mumbling, "I don't know why, but I believe Friend!"

"It's important you believe Mike. Your life is about to change, greater than anything you might ever imagine!"

Mike can only stare upon him, confused again He wonders how in just moments his life is changing. He wants to wake up from a bad dream and know it's nothing… but this is impossible:

this guy is real, a real live angel talking to him … the worst of the worst … Mr. Nobody.

He stares down at the ground and back up to heaven thinking; *this is reality time, time to start over.*

"Where are you headed Friend?"

"Morris Avenue Baptist Church."

"Oh yes, my wife went there."

"I know Mike."

Mike moves closer. He wants to be a nice guy and learn all about Friend. "Our meeting … quite a coincidence Friend."

"But, not a coincidence...."

Mike stops, facing him, "I've made a decision, a once and forever decision."

"Your decision is …

"His head bows low and back up again, "Whatever He wants, I'll do Friend!"

"But the rest of it Mike, the rest of it!"

"For Him … Him alone Friend!" Mike says, gazing up into Friend's sparkling eyes proudly."

"But there's something else for you Mike …

"For me …"

"You only Mike. From this day forward I'll be near you, protect you: I'll guide you into His presence throughout eternity!"

"But when Friend? When do I begin this journey throughout eternity?"

Friend grasps his hand, squeezing it hard, "Today Mike! This very day you begin your journey throughout eternity."

"But, how do I find Morris Avenue Baptist Church; you know… the church my wife belonged to serving Jesus?"

"Simple Mike. You go three blocks down, two blocks to the right, and …

"And what Friend?"

"Just around the corner you'll find the happiness you've been searching for Mike!"

Mike doesn't wait. He begins walking away humming a tune from childhood past ... *"And he walks with me, and he talks with me, and he tells me I am his own, and the joy we share, as we tarry there ... none other has ever known."*

CHAPTER 5

Trouble With-in

"God is our refuge and strength, a very present help in trouble

Psalm 46: 1

Hurriedly he returns home dressing in his best attire, and soon he's walking down Morris Avenue. He travels three blocks and stops looking around … no Friend.

He turns right two blocks, and just around the corner is a big white building: a church with a belfry, a bell, and a cross at the top.

His memory reflects to the past; his wife, her life with Friend, his father. He's wondering how some words Friend said so eloquently; *"dedicated, anointed when a baby."*

His mind runs rampant. Maybe this could be the day he has waited for … his day of redemption. Excitement builds; his pace grows faster, and now he's running to the building with a belfry and a bell at the top.

He stands outside gazing around before entering; it has been a while, a very long while ... perhaps a new beginning.

He remembers another time, another church; a time when he and his wife worshiped together, before all went so very, very wrong.

He thinks about Friend and whom he serves. Sweat appears upon his brow, causing him to wonder, 'can this be a day of reckoning? Surely, this new guy has to be my "Guardian Angel; the guy with answers about tomorrow.

He opens the door glancing around wondering if anyone recognizes him. It's the church, but where are all the people?" he asks himself over and over.

He hesitates, looking over the small group of persons: no youth, maybe thirty or forty throughout.

He stands, gazing around again and again, asking himself, "Can this be Morris Avenue Baptist Church: the church where my wife went every Sunday?"

From the front of the church comes an old, but spritely looking lady dressed in latest fashions. She's small in height, thin, head full of beautiful silver hair ... a heavenly smile ready to greet him.

He pauses, looking again; seeing a certain little twinkle in her eyes that catches his attention. *It's one of those good old mischievous twinkles, causing you to look again, wondering.*

"Hi Mike ... I'm Ethel. You've been taking your time getting here," she says, extending her hand greeting him loudly.

"We've ... met before Ethel?"

"Sure Mike, you remember me... your wife's friend, Ethel. I've watched you drop her off here on Sunday morning a hundred times over."

He doesn't recall the happening but remembers... Joyce did mention the name frequently.

She would smile and say, "Darling, when you go to church, and someday you will: look for the one who giggles and laughs a lot... the one with twinkling eyes always making you happy.'

"Oh yes, now I remember! She spoke of you many times Ethel."

"I'm sure she did. A hundred times over she told me you would be getting here when the time is right. And over and over I would ask her," But when will the time be right, Joyce?"

"And ...

Ethel turns her head to the side giggling, "Always she would say the same, 'when he gets ready to forgive he will be here, but only my husband will understand why.'

Mike hesitates, wondering what else she might know. Everything is happening so fast. First it was Friend, the guy whose eyes look straight into your heart: now here's another gazing at you giggling with twinkling eyes making you wonder.

"Come with me Mike, we'll sit up at the front, so I can hear better," she says, pulling him forward.

"You have a hearing problem Ethel?"

She stops, staring up at him surprised, "Maybe I do, but only slightly; does it bother you Mike?" She asks, firing back quickly.

"But you're getting up in years Ethel ... it's expected."

"Now remember this Mikey boy, I'm old in years, but young at heart. I've been there and done this and that; eighty-four years and I've never felt better. I'm what some call elderly... others call me feisty. And I'm ...

"I'm what, Ethel?" Mike asks, stopping her, again wishing he hadn't."

"I know what life all about is Sonny Boy, learned it the hard-way!"

Mike looks again at her thinking, 'she tells things right to the point, never withholding.'

Ethel pauses, thinking, "But I kind of figure everyone will have to answer for themselves when they stand before Jesus!"

Again, he looks down upon her, wondering if Joyce might have put her up to this moment: a grin and a smile appears quickly, 'Oh yes ... Joyce would have put her up to this moment," he's thinking.

A small choir begins to sing *"Amazing Grace,"* ... the song that brings the tears. His thoughts go back to days gone by; days of wine and roses ... good times gone forever.

From the corner of her eyes Ethel watches him cringe, looking desperate. She remembers what Joyce told her ten long years ago; 'when the time is right my husband will be here!'

Mike's head drops even further, seeing the cross hanging beyond the podium. More songs praising Jesus and an offering is given. He dabs his handkerchief, wiping away tears; thinking back to years gone past.

An elderly gentleman hair as silver, stands tall in the pulpit announcing his sermon, while Ethel moves next to Mike explaining his past.

"His name is "Brad Carson," once a Pastor and Missionary ...

"Something else, Ethel?"

"There is Mike ... there's something else I really admire about Brad ...

"Something else ...

"He tells it like it is Mike; no hedging around with Brad. I can't stand these modern-day "Peter Pan Preachers."

"Peter Pan Preachers ...

"You know what I mean, sure you do Mike; the ones pretending there's no hell ... everyone goes to heaven!"

Mike looks again at her wondering. He would love to burst out chuckling, but never in church.

"But you said he was retired ..."

"He was Mike. He wasn't busy preaching, so we asked him to do some preaching here at Morris Avenue Baptist Church."

Pastor Carson stands tall behind the podium glancing down upon his small crowd of worshipers beginning.

"This is amazing! For the first time in my career as a minister, I stand in bewilderment. Why, I don't know ... I simply don't know!" He shouts, looking out over his congregation.

Quietness reigns throughout till, "As I gaze out among you this morning ... I see something different among you. Someone here today is faced with a situation as the "Prodigal Son" once faced! I'm talking about someone in trouble, believing he or she stands at the gates of hell; nowhere to turn, lost forever!"

An eerie feeling begins to settle out and over the congregation quickly ... something is different!

Brad stops, peering over his audience, shouting, "Are you our "Prodigal Son" my unknown friend?"

Stone-cold expressions run throughout. but sitting next to Ethel ... Mike is different! He doesn't wait, moving slowly away. His head bows low, his eyes show tears unexpected.

Ethel punches Mike's side, while her blue eyes twinkle looking up to him whispering, "Now, you're about to see what it's all about, Sonny Boy."

It's invitation time! The pianist begins playing an old favorite: "At the Cross" ... a never to be forgotten song from the past.

Mike rises, moving to where Brad stands ready to greet him; it's confession time, time to face reality!"

Looking out over the small group of people Mike's broken voice rings out.

"Never in thirty years did I dream I would be standing before you are asking God to forgive my sins. I'm a sinner, I'm lost … I'm miserable! I'm the worst of the worst … as the Apostle Paul might say…he's the least of the least. I've read scripture from one end of the Bible to the other, but today… I'm different!"

"I stand before you, asking God to forgive me, be proud of me when He opens the greatest book ever …" The book of Life": His book alone, on Judgment Day!"

Brad holds Mike's hand looking out upon his audience announcing, "Let us stand and welcome home our "Prodigal son," our one and only … Mike Cutler!"

Morris Avenue Church comes alive! They remember his wife's words as only yesterday … 'when Mike is ready to forgive, he will be here Ethel.' All eyes turn gazing upon the cross … the place Friend calls, "Calvary."

Ethel moves beside him, her twinkling eyes shining. "You did good Mike, really good. I'm proud of you … you old-dirty-good-for-nothing scoundrel!" She whispers, her blue eyes dancing.

Mike turns looking up at the cross … time to think about tomorrow!

CHAPTER 6

Setting the Future

And when these things begin to come to pass, then look up, and lift your heads; for your redemption draweth nigh.

Luke 21: 28

Mike's life is changing. He studies scripture day and night, refreshing his memories. He can't forget Friend's startling remark, "anointed ... dedicated at the altar of God." He wonders if he's capable, what's in store for his future.

"He tries explaining his new life to old friends, but conversation ceases immediately, it's a different life, different friends, and Mike is deadly serious.

It's Sunday morning and he's headed for *Morris Avenue Baptist Church*. Fellowship with new friends becomes the love of his life. Brad's preaching stirs his lonely heart with a never-ending desire; a desire to learn *about the Lord's return ... overwhelming!*

He returns home opening his Bible. He reads the "*Book of*

Daniel," going forward to the *"Book of Ezekiel"* ... ending with *"The Book of Revelation."*

He compares it with daily news; frightening to even think about! Things are changing fast. Knowledge grows daily, while gloom and doom spreads like wild-fire ... *unnoticed.*

Mike remembers Pastor Jeffry's words from long ago; words about the second coming of the Lord Jesus.

"The world will be in great tribulation; time to get ready to meet the Lord." He remembers him shouting to his brothers and sisters in Christ ... 'You think World War 11 was bad; you haven't seen nothing ... yet!"

He settles at his desk reading scripture from the Bible. When he's finished, he gazes around the room asking himself ... "Was the world this way before the flood, during the time of Noah? Was it this way before Sodom Gomorrah; before God turned into a pillar of salt?"

He reads and reads, eyes grow tired, but never quitting. He's convinced the world is in trouble. But there's good news along with the bad; it's time to look upward toward heaven ... our Lord and Savior is coming!

He heads to his library searching for the Bible, a certain Bible with some history; the Bible Friend reminded him about.

He remembers how his uncle placed it in his hands just before heading out to war, telling him how holy it was. He removes dust, noting pages marked in red, the ones he's been looking for. And out from old pages falls an old crinkled note reading ...

Dear Nephew,

I leave you no money, but knowledge without end. This Bible is precious ... precious above all else, my loving nephew!

Use it well, search the scriptures, and understand. It's your passport to heaven with life never ending."

That's what it's all about Mike: a time to be born, a time to live, a time to die; being with Him … forever and forever.

Your loving Uncle Joe, as always …

P. S. And don't miss this, Mike …

> **For what has a man profited, if he shall gain the whole world, and lose his own soul? or what shall a man give in exchange for his soul?**
>
> **Matthew 16:26**

He walks out onto the deck looking up wondering, "But why underline certain scripture in red. Is it possible he thought I might witness the Lord's return?"

His mood changes quickly, troubling questions remain he's not sure about. It's time to call Brad, the guy with all the answers.

Pastor Carson greets him at the door, seeing eyes showing worry. "Tell me what brings you here Mike…a problem maybe?" He asks, smiling.

Mike stands gazing upon him speechless … wondering where to begin. "I'm confused Brad; more than confused would be a better term,"

"The whole world is confused Mike, sit here at the table and we'll talk about it."

Mike sits across from Brad reminiscing how he got here. He thinks of his conversion, his hunger to learn more. But most … his never-ending desire to think about the coming of Jesus.

Speechless moments, moving books from one end of the table to the other; talking about things to come later.

Brad moves closer, looking up to him, "Now tell me what we're talking about Mike."

"I'm in over my head Brad, way over my head would be a better way to say it. I can't think of anything but the return of Jesus. I'm beginning to wonder if I'm the only one believing Jesus is about to return. Tell me Brad ... is it just me wondering about these things ... or others?"

"You're only one of millions. Christians around the world are wondering the same. Tell me the rest of your thoughts and wonders."

Mike turns away, afraid to answer. "Call it what you want, but it seems like the world is turning up-side down ... going crazy over weird and filthy things. It's getting to me big-time, and I don't know how to stop it Brad!"

"This isn't news, we're all having the same problem. Sit back ... take a good breath and tell me the rest of your worries."

"I'm desperate and I don't know the reason. For the first time in my life, I just can't satisfy myself with what I've been reading. That's why I'm here with you, Brad."

"What does desperate mean ... tell me about it."

"I'm worried about the ones who are going to be left behind. I'm talking about friends ... the ones who can't see it coming."

Brad rubs his forehead ...wondering where to begin ... "Your desire is admirable, but sometimes I worry about you ..."

"What are you trying to tell me Brad?"

"I love you like a son, but sometimes you don't know how to quit!"

"I've been told the same a hundred times, believe me I have. But never in my life-time, have I experienced the feeling I have now. It's nothing compared to what's happening throughout the world today, Brad!"

"I agree. But tell me your real reason for this sudden interest in prophesy."

"It's because everything I read in the Bible shows up in newspaper headlines day after day; but the people I care for, can't see it, Brad!"

"I've been in churches where they don't talk about prophesy; more interested in the next basket-ball game, the next social affair: In the mean-time, I'm beginning to panic!"

"Panic about what?'

"I'm wondering why they can't see the Lord is just around the corner: as my friend Ethel told me only a week ago!"

"Calm yourself…we all wonder why they can't see it Mike!"

"I read the Bible hours upon hours, watching the signs He gave us come true. I want to shout it to the world: but I'm not sure about when He's coming back to earth again."

"But, it's about to end Mike! Things are happening faster than ever before; knowledge increases daily, sexual depravity, wars and rumors of wars all over; it's here Mike…it's time to get ready! Now, tell me your greatest desire … something that would make you stand up and shout His name before thousands."

"I would like to show people the things I think about. I would like them to feel the way I feel. I would let them hear the sound of a trumpet, watch dead people rise from their graves: all of us ready to meet the Lord in the sky going home forever and ever!" Mike says, a broad smile showing, looking up to Brad.

"You're talking about the rapture… right Mike------

Mike's face glows even brighter. "You know I am Brad …

all the way. But the big question ... the one everyone wants to know ...

"Yes Mike ......

"Tell me about "The Church"; the ones the Bible calls "The Elect." Will they be raptured before... "Armageddon," Brad?"

Brad turns, looking for Mary. She stands at the kitchen table shaking her head whispering ... *no, not me ... never ever Brad."*

He walks behind Mike, removing his Bible from a shelf placing it before him, "Read His words Mike ... no better place than the Bible!"

For the Lord himself shall descend from Heaven with a shout, and with the voice of the archangel, and with the trumpet of God; and the dead in Christ shall rise first;

Then we which are alive and remain shall be caught up together with them in the clouds, to meet the Lord in the air; and so, shall we ever be with the Lord.

1st Thessalonians 4:16-17

And except those days should be shortened, there should no flesh be saved: but for the elect's sake those days shall be shortened.

Matthew 24: 22

It's over, and Brad looks over at him grinning, "Does this satisfy you Mike?"

"It does for sure. I believe The Church... as referred to in the Bible, will be gone before the tribulation period begins. But there's something else Brad!"

"Yes Mike …

"My question remains …when will Jesus return: his second coming… you know what I'm talking about. I'm referring to when he actually plants his feet here on earth!" Mike tries to explain.

"You want an opinion … great! Move over here and take my seat; you tell me the time of his second coming!"

Mike turns his head looking away, concentrating, reflecting to Bible days; never to be forgotten Bible days. His mind is reeling. He's thinking of friends, preachers he will never forget.

"I believe this. I believe His second coming is soon, but only the Father in heaven knows the hour and the day. Let's read the book of Matthew; everything we need but the day and the hour, Brad."

Immediately after the tribulation of those days, shall the sun be darkened, and the moon shall not give her light, and the stars shall fall from heaven, and the power of the heavens shall be shaken.

And then shall appear the sign of the Son of man coming in the clouds of heaven with power and great glory.

Matthew 24: 29-30

"It's his second coming Brad … it has to be! Jesus tells us plain and simple his second coming is after the tribulation … not before."

"But a lot can take place in the meantime. Think about the signs Jesus gave to his followers foretelling his second-coming.

Many have come and gone, but there's more to come; preaching the gospel to all nations And the Fig-Tree parable ... a generation of Jews returning to Jerusalem before his coming."

> **Now learn a parable of the fig tree; When his branch is yet tender, and putteth forth leaves, yea know that summer is nigh:**
>
> **So likewise yea, when ye shall see all these things, know that it is near, even at the doors.**
>
> **Verily I say unto you, this generation shall not pass, till all these things be fulfilled.**
>
> **Matthew 24: 32-34**

"You're right Mike. The hand-writing is on the wall. Israel became a nation recognized by the United Nations in 1948. Count the years from 1948 till now; when you're finished ......

"Then what Brad?"

"We'll be near the end of the generation: the generation Jesus told us about. It's time to look up; no doubt about it!"

"You mean ...

"I do Mike. Soon the sky will open, a trumpet will sound, and the Lord with a host of angels will appear in the heavens!"

"Why the worried look, the smile upon your face is gone... what happened Brad?"

"It's the time element... time is running out and people can't see it!"

"But, what can we do about it Brad? We can't make them repent... that's for sure!"

"I think about a guy called Noah, building an ark way out in a desert hundreds of years ago. He was preaching to them about a flood to come, but they didn't listen Noah: why would they listen to us Mike?"

"That bad huh ...

"It is Mike, but we can try"

"Then what ... then what Brad?"

"Tell them this. Tell them all hell is about to break loose on this place called planet earth; it's time to get ready ... Jesus is coming!"

"And then what?"

"Tell them this too, Mike. When the time has come, run for the hills: The Lord is coming to gather "His Church" And tell them this too ...

"Yes Brad ... yes ...

"Tell them the truth as we know it. Make them understand if they're not one of His... they'll be left behind during the great tribulation!"

But there's something else: tell them now is the time to repent ... not tomorrow!" He's shouting.

"You really believe it, don't you Brad?"

"With all my heart, with all my soul ... I believe it!" He says ... pulling Mike next to him ... handing him a couple of envelopes before leaving.

Twenty minutes later Mike is home. From outside he hears the usual roar of motors, blowing horns; no longer a problem.

He glances up seeing a picture hanging on his office wall. It shows Jesus praying in the *Garden of Gethsemane*. His heart is touched ... he's thinking how Jesus must have felt; knowing his time here on earth was about to run out. He kneels to the floor, uttering his heart-felt prayer, "Come quickly Lord ... come quickly!"

He's tired, heading for the bedroom, but there's something

else … it's time to open the envelopes Brad handed him just before leaving.

He opens the first, displaying a note showing only the word … *immediately*. He opens the dictionary and there it is, *immediately* … "at once" the definition he asked for.

He sits in silence, thinking back to life before "Friend." He's not the same Mike; his life is changing … and he loves it.

And the other envelope Brad handed him … another message.

> **But thou, O Daniel, shut up the words, and seal the book, even to the time of the end; many shall run to and for, and knowledge shall be increased.**
>
> **Daniel 12: 4**

And … the mystery of all mysteries … it's over! Jesus is coming; time to get ready for bugles to sound far up in the heavens! And Mike is looking up smiling … his Lord and Savior is coming!

CHAPTER 7

Everything is Beautiful

"Be pleased O Lord to deliver me: make haste to help me."

Psalm 40: 1

M ike is awakened from a sound sleep early the following morning... the phone is ringing.

He picks up the phone recognizing the voice, but it's different ... hoarse and weak.

"Mike ...I haven't seen you around lately, what's going on partner?"

"I've been busy, but there's a noise in the back-ground ... what's going on Keith?"

"There's a noise for sure, I'm calling from one of our wells near Utica Kentucky, Mike. We had problems last night ... serious problems. Ashland Oil Company called about midnight wanting me down here immediately ... so here I am, pal."

"Just how serious," Mike asks, yawning.

"Real bad. One of the lines leaked spilling oil into a nearby lake ... as usual was looking for you, partner."

"1 Understand Keith."

"But, Mike ... there's another reason I called---

"Tell me about it."

"I'm hearing some crazy reports about you lately; something going on I need to know about?"

"Nothing you might be interested in Keith." Mike says, sleepily.

"You're probably right, but someone said you might be in love ... true or false?

"Maybe ...

"Now come on Mike, spill it out; tell me the change in your life ... your secret life!"

Mike pauses, thinking ... It's a little too early in the morning to start a long conversation, but this is Keith, his friend from way back.

"There's a lot going on. I'm no longer in the oil business: I sold my interest and made some changes in my life."

"But why now, where making big-time money ... getting ready to drill again."

"Not interested," he barely mutters, tired and sleepy.

"But this one is different Mike. There's plenty more oil nearby; we got it made pal," He says, persisting.

"Forget it Keith!"

"I'll never understand you Mike, but there's always a piece of the lease for you ... anytime."

Mike grows tired, wanting to end it ... "Thanks, for the invitation, but my life is changing Keith."

A long pause and, "Changing ... and what does changing mean?"

"I've become a Christian, a down and out Christian; one

of those Jesus worshipers, you're always laughing about." Mike says, hoping to bring him alive.

Long moments of silence and ... "But Mike ... Mike--

"I know what you're thinking Keith, but you're wrong...dead wrong this time!"

Another long pause and, "I don't know what to say, Mike ... except, good luck ...and I wish you the best!"

"I knew this would surprise you Keith, but I'll always remember the good-times we had."

"I know, but I'm a little confused...but I believe I heard you say you're a Christian," he mutters, weakly.

One more time ... "I'm a Christian and I'm going to church, and I love it Keith!"

A long pause, and a weak voice barely mumbles, "You got to be out of your cotton-picking mind! What in the hell ever brought you to this point in your life: are you losing your mind, Mike?"

"Maybe before Keith ... but not this time, I've never been more satisfied!"

"Mike Cutler a Christian ... never in my wildest, dreams ....

"I've heard the same before, but it's my life and my decision, guess what pal ...

"You tell me Christian!"

"I love it Keith ... I really and truly love it!"

Suddenly Keith is struggling, breathing intermittingly.

"My breathing isn't like it used to be Mike ... you probably can tell it."

"I can tell it, Keith ...

"But there's something else you should know------

"Tell me what I should know; something you've been holding back...a secret maybe?"

"It's a secret for sure, but not to you Mike!" a slow, weak voice barely mutters.

"That's good news, now tell me you're joking, partner."

"It's not a joke Mike, I have a problem ... a big problem."

"I'm beginning to believe you're serious, really serious for a change!"

"Serious as I can get Mike!"

"Tell me about it, Keith."

A long pause, till ... "It's my left carotid artery, the big one leading up from the back of my neck to the brain ... it's in trouble. My doctor said I might lose my voice ... whatever; it troubles me even to think about it Mike!"

"One more time ... and it better be the truth."

A long pause and ... "It's true Mike. It's hard for me to admit, but it's true this time! I know what you're thinking Mike: you're thinking I've lost my mind ... maybe I have. Maybe, it's time I own-up to something ...

"Own up to what Keith?"

Another long pause and... "Life hasn't been pretty to me; too many cigarettes, booze, pot, wild women. Just name it Mike... I'm guilty. Life has caught up with me; nothing I can do about it, partner!"

Mike's head drops, staring down at the floor, remorseful; wondering what a guy can do to make him feel better ...

"But don't ever give up Keith, there's always a way out."

A long pause and, "Not this time pal. I only want to ease the pain ... forget about things ... take things easy the rest of my life!"

"Tell me the rest of it... tell me what I'm missing."

"You wouldn't understand Mike. My life has been a mess; a game you've never played before!"

"Try me Keith ...

"Most days Rosy and I smoke some weed, get a little high!"

"Smoke weed, get high ...

"After being in the woods most of the day, she shows up over at my place covered with chiggers, raring to go...

"Then what Keith?"

"Oh ... the usual. I put her in the tub ... stick a joint between her lips, and she's happy. A couple of hours later she's wanting to sing songs from yesterday: the kind that blows my head away," he says, gasping for breath, resting.

"I'll bet it does! And then what?"

"Oh ... you know, some of the old stuff like, "Where Have All the Flowers Gone" ... Peter, Paul and Mary."

"Oh, yeah ... I remember Peter Paul and Mary ... how in the hell could I ever forget someone like Peter Paul and Mary," he's shouting, coming alive.

Another long wait and ... "Don't start it Mike, it's insulting; Rosy wasn't part of the sixties and seventies like I was."

"You're right about that pal ... she couldn't be; she was only a baby you idiot!" Mike says, angrier by the moment.

Long painful silence and, "Now hold it Mike: time we get serious ...

"I'm serious as I'll ever be, time for you to get serious, Keith!"

"But there's something more, something you got to know about Rosy; something between you and I alone Mike."

Mike's anger begins to subside, "Quit fooling around Keith ... tell me some more about Rosy."

"Another long pause, wheezing and coughing, "Well ... it's like this Mike ... she's twenty-years younger than me, easy to get along with ... always there for me when I need her."

"She's great Keith, the perfect woman for you. What else about Rosy?"

"I worry about her Mike. I worry about what might happen to Rosy if I wasn't around; you know ... just in case ...

"Sounds pitiful. Maybe now you can tell me how you came into her life ... the rest of it, Keith!"

"I met her at a restaurant where she was waiting tables, been with her since, Mike. I've feelings for her, but not love ... the way she wants it."

"I understand, but where do I come into her life Keith?"

Keith is struggling and it's showing, "She just might need some help, Mike. I was thinking maybe ... if I'm not around, she might need someone like you, to look out for her, Mike.

"You know what I mean ... someone to give her advice ... make her feel wanted," a broken voice is barely able to mutter.

"I understand. I've met Rosy a couple of times; maybe a little whacky, but she's a good person... I'm sure Keith."

"She is Mike ... she really is. She's the kind of person you can't help feeling sorry for; a heart of gold, ... always there when you need her. You know what I'm talking about Mike. All I want you to do is ...

"Is what Keith?"

Another long pause and ..." Do what's gotta be done Mike ... that's all I can ask of you," a weak, pitiful voice barely can utter.

"Whatever Keith ... but, there's something else to talk about ...

"Talk about what?"

"Drugs ... mind breakers!"

"I know how you feel about drugs, but for me ... the stuff works Mike. It eases my pain... when I think of my past."

"What's next ... tried quitting?"

"A thousand times. But this is different ... a different kind of ball game....

Mike pauses again, "But it's never too late Keith, believe me it is!"

"But it is for me Mike. Time has run out … the game is over. I can barely breathe … I'm hopeless!"

Another long pause and, "I understand, time we get serious."

"You're talking about the Bible, going to church … all that kind of stuff … right pal?"

"Nothing but Keith."

Another long moment of wheezing and gasping and, "I've tried everything … why not the church, Mike!"

"Maybe, I'm just one of those doped-up happy persons from the sixties and seventies … you know what I'm talking about … the hippie generation; drugs, parties …"

His words strike a sore spot with Mike … something that never goes away. Vietnam, demonstrations in the streets back home; while other young Americans gave their all … dying in rice paddies far away at a place called, Nam!

"Don't try being funny Keith. I still remember a gang of "Flower Children," … spitting in my face for fighting a war they refused to fight."

"I remember more than sixty thousand brave Americans fighting, dying in a land far away; while your doped-up friends with faces painted like scare-crows paraded down the streets of San Francisco. Oh yes … it bothers me a hell of a lot to even think about it!"

Long moments of silence and, "But it's over. Vietnam is over … a thing of the past…Mike," a pitiful weak voice, barely can reply.

Mike is tested to the core. He wants to throw the phone at Keith: spit in his face like his friends did to him. But something's different; he's changed by the grace of God he's changed.

"Yesterday … I would be cursing you Keith … today I'll

be praying for you. I'll be praying that somehow, someday … you'll meet a guy like I did; a guy named, Friend … someone who cared for me… introducing me to his father!"

Another long pause … a faint muttering of scrabbled words, and … "Someone praying for me … Is that what you said, Mike?"

"That's what I said Keith … praying for you. I've been in your shoes, felt the pain; hated every moment, partner!"

"But for me… life is over. I've nothing left … what's a guy like me to do, Mike?"

"It's never over Keith. I've been there, did it all and then some… believe me it isn't over."

"But I'm hooked. I'm hooked for the rest of my miserable life … no way out…" Keith is barely able to mutter, as his voice drifts in and out barely breathing.

"Are you alright, Keith?"

"I suppose. What else is there for a guy like me to do?" He barely can whisper.

Mike takes his time … thinking back to his own situation; a time when he felt the same.

"But there is something you can do Keith; it's something called repentance! Its what life is all about, Keith. It's the same for all of us… believe me it is!"

"But I've other problems Mike … insurmountable problems …

"You're putting me on… right Keith." Mike asks, hoping.

"Not this time, I'm serious as I'll ever be-----

"Tell me about it Keith."

"I'll tell you the only way I know how to tell you."

"I'm listening Keith, out with it."

A never-ending pause and, "The party is over Mike; It's half-past midnight … time to go home!"

Boom! It resounds into Mike's mind like a death sentence, shocked again!

"Use your breathing apparatus Keith, you're struggling!" He's shouting.

"I'm trying Mike ... really I am. I need more time. We need to talk ... get down to serious business." Keith can barely mumble.

Mike sits alone wondering, "What's Keith talking about ... serious business," he mutters to himself, settling back ... waiting.

CHAPTER 8

Daddy Keith

**For mine iniquities are gone over mine head:
as a heavy burden they are too heavy for me.**

Psalm 38: 4

Two hours since Keith called promising to call back, and the phone rings.

"Sorry the delay Mike, but back to Nam. I've wished a hundred times I could go back and apologize to some of your friends, but didn't,"

"Forget it, Keith. It's a problem from the past... I lead the pack."

"I don't know what's happening to me Mike ... for the first time in my life I don't have an answer."

"You're not alone, it happens to all of us, my friend."

A long time waiting, and, "But for me it's different, Mike ... my time has run out ... nothing I can do about it," he barely can utter.

Mike struggles, searching for words. Keith … his partner from way back is in trouble… serious trouble.

"But, you're different Keith, you've something going for you …

"I have something going for me …Mike!"

"Sure, you do. "I'll always be here for you; always have and always will; count it, partner!"

A lot of gasping, wheezing, and… "I've always known it Mike … time you hear my confession!"

Mike sits straight up in bed coming alive … "Confession … did I hear you say, confession Keith … or am I dreaming?"

"I did say confession. Everyone has something to confess … when there's no other way out: now … it's my time Mike …

"Take your time … tell me about it."

"I was in England a month ago with my daughter; had the time of my life. It was like being in heaven Mike!"

"Am I dreaming, or did I hear you say *daughter*?" Keith asks, coming alive…waiting.

"You're not dreaming. I'll tell you my secretive life; the part you don't know about, Mike!"

"Your secretive life, let it all out; it's about to get interesting!"

"I've a daughter… a beautiful, wonderful blue-eyed daughter. I was married thirty years ago in London to a well-known socialite. She had it all Mike; wealth, beauty, everything a guy could want… everything a guy would pray for…

"Get your breath … keep going Keith!"

"She was out of my class … way out my class, Mike." he says, struggling.

"Take it easy Keith … we've plenty of time for the rest of it."

"I'm trying, really I am Mike!" He's barely able to mutter.

"I know you're trying, but tell me the rest of it, Keith."

"The marriage went down in about a year, but I've always

loved them, Mike. My daughter's name is Brittany Ann Lincoln: a beautiful young lady, always pursuing her ambition."

"And ... her ambition Keith... tell me about it."

"She's big-time ... a super-model, pretty as her mother. That means something; it really means something, Mike!" He can barely mutter, his voice growing weaker by the moment.

"But, I don't understand, why are you telling me this; it doesn't make sense Keith!"

Another long pause and, "Who else Mike ... you're my friend ... I trust you. Brittany knows our friendship, how I've always depended upon you."

Again, he's puzzled, "But you're the father, you're the man of her life, Keith!"

"Her father for sure ... but it just isn't probable I'll be able to be there," a weak voice is barely able to mutter.

"What are you trying to tell me?"

"Well, it means ... I might not be around very much longer, Mike!"

Mike's beginning to get the message: Keith's in trouble, it's reality time!

"Stop it ... quit talking that way Keith ... it's senseless!" Mike is beginning to shout, hoping to bring him alive again.

"But I need you ... I need you now more than ever, Mike," Keith can barely mutter ... his voice growing weaker by the moment.

Mike's head lowers ... his voice barely audible, "I'll be there for you ... you know I will Keith."

Quietness all over, till ... "Having trouble speaking; don't worry about it, Keith."

A long pause, getting his breathe and, "Hang with me partner, please don't leave me ...

"You know I will ... I'll never leave you, Keith."

"After you meet her … tell her about the oil wells, the fun we had, but more than all … tell her how much I've always loved her."

"And what else Keith?"

"Tell her how I've missed her … always wishing things had been different. Tell her to inform her mother … I always loved her too; missed her terribly!" Keith can barely utter, as his voice grows weaker and weaker.

"I'll do it, I promise you I will. But don't ever give up … keep fighting, Keith."

"Tell Brittany the lake and house you sold me … it's hers …hers alone Mike. Above all tell her some good news … something that might make her happy. And what else Keith?"

"Tell her, I've just made right with the Lord … everything is well between the two of us!"

"That's the best news ever Keith, but why did you wait so long making your decision?"

"It was something you said to me long ago; before you went back to the church, Mike."

"What was that, Keith?"

"You said something about where we go from here …

"And---

"You said … something about being in heaven or hell throughout eternity …

"And, …

"Well … last night …when I was feeling a little bit sorry for myself; I got to thinking about what you said to me about eternity … hell fire and brimstone, forever and forever …

"Yes Keith …. yes …

"I began to think about the other place you told me about; heaven, being with Jesus, walking down streets shining as gold … forever and forever …

"Keep going Keith …

"I thought about you … my wife and Britany being in heaven without me; thought about burning in hell with the devil and his disciples throughout eternity"

"And …

A long pause and …" I sure don't want to be that gang; I want to be with you, my wife, my daughter and Jesus … Mike!" He barely can mutter, fading away …

Mike's imagination runs wild thinking about it. He can imagine a tear or two dropping down upon Keith's pillow, while he's trying desperately to get his breath again.

He thinks of the last words he uttered … *my wife, my daughter, myself with Jesus in heaven throughout eternity.*

And now he's smiling, thinking …" it's just like Keith, that dear old rascal; holding back forever, coming to his senses… finally.

Pauses grow longer, while Mike worries even more.

He's putting all the pieces together adding up to one big surprise; Keith's a daddy with a beautiful daughter living abroad; about to die… leaving her forever.

The room around him goes deathly silent, while Mike sits alone shaking his head … wondering how it all happened.

He remembers the good-times, their week in New York watching the Broadway hit-show "Annie."

He remembers how they partied the night away; laughing, singing till dawn and then some. He leaves his bed heading for his desk finding some sheet-music …

'*Tomorrow.*'

Oh! The sun-----will come out tomorrow
Oh! I got to hang on till tomorrow-------come what may!
Tomorrow, tomorrow, I love ye tomorrow,

You're always a day away--------
The tomorrow------tomorrow
Only! -----------tomorrow.

He wants to cry but can't. *Its' reality time!*

CHAPTER 9

Home Coming

**He shall call upon me, and I will answer Him:
I will be with him in trouble; I will deliver him
and honor him.**

Psalms 91:15

Early the next morning Mike sits thinking back to his past,
and the phone rings.

"Uncle Mike, this is Doug your nephew. Martha and I just
arrived at the Airport. We'll be on our way to your place right
away. We're here on business for one day only!"

"But one day only ... why Doug?"

"I'll explain later, but right now Martha's putting our
luggage in the cab, and if I don't get moving, she'll leave me
for sure Uncle Mike."

Twenty minutes later a cab arrives in front of Mike's house...
and "wow", how they've changed!

They're no longer kids, nothing like the same newly-weds
six years back. Martha's no longer the tall blond statuesque

blue-eyed beauty, he remembers strolling down the aisle at "Trinity Methodist Church." Today she's nothing but a beautiful business-like young lady: hanging onto a brief-case close to her side.

Doug, too, has changed: shoulders wide as the front door, six foot-two--- tall and handsome. He's no longer the little freckle-faced kid running around in the back-yard chasing his puppies... "Fred and Barney."

They head for the nearest bedroom, and back again in moments.

Doug stands beside Martha gazing out toward the large back-yard, reminiscing his past. He's thinking of Joyce, his aunt ... and the stories she put into his mind: all about Jesus coming back to earth again.

His head bows low and up again; looking upward toward heaven mumbling words only He and she would understand. Moments later he's finished ... walking away with a smile on his face, satisfied.

Mike can't wait ... moving up close, "Before we begin other conversation, there's something the two of you must know about me ...

"And what might that be, Mike?" Martha asks, looking back to Doug...turning his head, grinning.

"You've learned about my past for sure, but I've changed, Martha. My desire to get even with the church is over; today I'm back where I started...serving the Lord again!"

"We know Mike----believe me we know!" Martha says, looking over at Doug...still grinning.

"But there's something else Martha ...

"Yes, Mike ...

"Things are happening in my life; impossible, wonderful, exciting, things ...

"What does wonderful, exciting things mean, Mike ... tell me about it."

"It's hard to believe things ... things I try to explain, but never find an answer." He tries to explain, but useless.

"Try again, we've business to handle."

"I wish I could, but I can't Martha. It's something never ending. It's something ... maybe I'll never find the answer for!" Mike says, his voice breaking ...

She moves beside him, looking up at him smiling "Rest easy Mike, your worries are over. We've enough excitement to last you forever; that's why we're here, Mike."

Doug moves beside them interrupting ... "Martha's telling you straight out. We're here to talk about the future... your future Mike!"

Mikes eagerness turns sour, facing him, "Then ... what are you here for, Doug?"

Doug takes his time, trying to explain, "Something radically different is about to take place in your life: It's something completely different than ever before, Uncle Mike!"

"Then ... tell me about it nephew; don't hedge around with it, spill it out lad!"

"For some unexplainable reason your future is being planned for you; might sound hard to believe, but it's true Mike!" Doug says, waiting.

Mike moves closer, up in his face, "It's time you quit worrying about me, tell me all of it ... get it over with Doug!"

Doug moves next to him, looking up to him, "This is hard to explain, but somehow ... someway, you're about to be a major player in something beyond reality. Your destiny, your future is set, but the sad part is ...

"The sad part is what nephew?"

"I don't know why this is happening to you only. But somewhere ... sometime, you will know the reason, Mike!"

Mike can't wait, "But me, me a major player, you gotta be kidding, nephew!"

"But you're wrong, we're here strictly for business. I'm talking about business you've never heard like anything before; beyond your wildest imagination completely, Uncle Mike! Doug says, up in his face, waiting ...

"You better start thinking about someone else nephew. I'm one of those "over the hill guys" ... you hear people talk about. But a major player ... never in a life-time!"

"I told you before ... we don't have a lot of time to get our message over, but we will, Uncle Mike!"

"That's not enough nephew ... let it all hang out, tell me about it!"

Doug takes his time, hard to say the words, but does, "We want your service for something beyond your wildest imagination. We want your soul, your mind, your heart ... everything that goes with it, Uncle Mike!"

Mike lowers his head thinking ...'how is this all happening? They come saying things fast and furious; things I know nothing about. But they're my people, the ones I love dearly.

"Get it over with ... I'm waiting, Doug!"

"Now we understand one another Uncle Mike. Get your breath ... sit back and listen for a change!"

Mike sits staring at Doug, wondering. He's wondering ... 'what ever happened to that little kid I once saw running wild in the back yard a few years ago. This can't be real; this just isn't happening. Why, would anyone want me for anything ... impossible ... it has to be!"

Martha moves beside Mike taking his hand looking up to

him, "There's a lot to talk about Mike; maybe hard to sell you upon, but there's one thing you can be sure of …

"Sure, of what Martha?" Mike asks. quickly.

"You're the one we came for. Only a guy like you could fit the bill for something we're about to discuss; nobody but you, Mike!"

His head drops, looking up at Martha pitiful like, "But of all the people in the world … why me, Martha … I'm nobody!"

Doug moves beside him, taking his hand, looking up to him, "You're going on a journey. You're going on a journey greater than anything you've ever dreamed about; beyond human imagination, Uncle Mike!"

"Stop it Doug, I don't wanta hear it," suddenly, he's shouting.

"I've told you straight out, we're here on business. We might need the entire night getting through to you, but we will Mike!"

"I've listened to this crazy talk long enough … out with it, Nephew."

Martha moves beside Doug, looking up at Mike taking over.

"You're either in … or your out Mike. There's no in between in this game: that's the way it is… all or nothing!"

Wham! He looks hard at her, tired eyes blazing … "I trust the two of you more than anyone; more than you could ever imagine. But it's time we get something straight … Martha!"

"Then go ahead, now's the time, this is the place … get it over with!"

"It's about time the two of you get it in your head that I'm no five-year-old kid you can play with, Martha! I'm the same guy you met the last time, but a hell of a lot smarter. Now … it's about time you tell me the real purpose your being here!"

Doug moves beside her, taking over, "You're right, Uncle

Mike. It's time you know the whole story; a story like none other!"

"Keep going nephew!"

"We're here because of you Mike. We're here to set the stage for the return of Jesus! It's important: it's more important today than ever before, Mike!"

"What's more important than ever before, nephew," he asks, looking up at Doug … waiting.

"We're heading home, Jesus is coming back again! We're the fore-runners … preparing people to meet the Lord in the sky, Mike!"

Mike pauses … shaking his head, thinking … 'this is my nephew, the little one in my back-yard; boy oh boy … what a surprise this is!"

Martha moves beside him, pulling up a chair… ready for business.

"It's time we move on. It's time we tell you everything; the good, the bad, whatever. Are you ready for it, Mike?" She asks, up in his face, grinning.

"Ready as I'll ever be Martha," he says, moving closer… waiting.

"But, there's something else, something I forgot to mention …"

"Yes Martha …

"Once you agree with our proposal you're in for good; no backing out later… agreed Mike?"

"Agreed Martha … now out with it!"

"We want your participation in something out of your realm of thought … something you could never imagine!"

He rubs his hand across his brow, looking again at the two of them, "But first hear me out, the both of you … please Martha."

"We're waiting Mike. Take the floor and tell us all about your problem." Doug says, moving beside him.

"From the moment you arrived I felt something inside of me ... something different; something like I've never felt before. It was a wonderful feeling. It was as if you came for me ... me alone, Doug."

"You're right, we are here for you alone; we've told you so before Mike." Martha says, pushing papers before him, ending the conversation quickly.

A quick glance and Mike shoves the papers back in her face, angry again!

"Now what's bothering you Mike?" She asks, disgustedly.

"Bother me ... sure it bothers me. When I see the words "Military Intelligence" spread out before me ... I don't look twice... dearie!"

Doug moves beside him placing his hand upon his shoulder, "But you're wrong Mike ... dead wrong this time. Sit back ... hold your breath and listen for a change."

"But just for the record nephew I've traveled this route before, and it was anything but pleasant!"

"I'm aware of it Mike. I'm aware of a lot of things, including your military history."

"Then ... let it all hang out!"

"I would love to, but this isn't the time or the place. But, you can rest assured when we're done with you: you'll be changed forever! You'll be looking at things you've never dreamed about: a world different than anything you could ever imagined!"

Mike sits listening, eyes wide-open ... never speaking; while Doug keeps pressing him over and over ...

"Everything has a place with a purpose Mike. Don't say a word ... just sit be quiet and listen!"

"I'm listening ... believe me I'm listening, nephew."

"I know you're listening. But there's matters you know nothing about. I told you we didn't come hear to sit and chatter; we're here on business only, Uncle Mike!"

"Then tell me what kind of business your here for; let it all out!"

"Important business; things that will blow your head off thinking about."

"But just for the record ... I don't give a crap who ordered you here. I'm the one who will make the decision about me... me alone nephew!" Mike is beginning to shout.

"I know you don't give a crap, but you just might be interested in knowing I'm working with Military Intelligence: assigned to be here with you only, Mike!"

Slowly he rises from his chair, moving over to Doug extending his hand... "I'm sorry Doug ... I'm really sorry, what else can I say?"

"Just sit back and quit your arguing, were only beginning. I'll explain more of the same later; not everything, but important ... pressing things, Uncle Mike."

"But before we go further ... there's something else you need to know Mike ...

"Yes Doug ...

"I'm with Military Intelligence..., but not Military Intelligence alone ...

"Now what are you about to tell me?"

"I'll be working with whoever benefits our country! Were in trouble as never before, and people are finally beginning to open their eyes and recognize it!

"Just for the record, we agree upon something for the first time; anything else you would like to tell me, Doug?"

"Glad you asked Uncle Mike. Soon, I'll begin a short vacation. Later I'll be heading for the Middle East."

"But why the Middle East?"

"The Middle East is the hottest place in the universe, Mike. It's closer to hell than anything ever," Doug says, causing Mike to come alive … speechless again.

CHAPTER 10

Something to Worry About

Lord, make me to know mine end, and the measure of my days, what it is ...

Psalm: 39: 4

Again, Mike wonders where to begin. He moves closer. pulling the two close to him, "I'll be rooting for you Doug, but when you talk about Military Intelligence ... you're far beyond my class."

"But not this time Mike ... no more of your excuses: the world is changing and it's time you get with it!"

Mike moves closer ... worried, "But, what's the real reason you're here Doug? I know you better than you know yourself. There has to be something driving you!"

"Your right Uncle Mike! The country we love next to our God... is in trouble as never before. I go to bed every night wondering if there's a way out of this mess."

"But there has to be something else driving you Doug?"

"Your right Mike, there is something else: I'm sure people

in our own government are working against us. I didn't want to say the words, but it's true!"

"This is serious, it's more than serious... it's treason! But the big question is ... 'who they are working for?'"

"I'm not positive ... nobody is positive. But things are happening fast ... hard to believe how fast. It's like Bible predictions coming to life right before our very eyes, Mike!"

"But there must be someone ... somewhere, knowing the answer to this ... there has to be!"

"No doubt about it Mike. But what are we to do in the mean-time is the question. You're afraid of your friends, you know your enemies ... but you don't know who the traitors are!"

"Are you positive about this Doug?"

"I'm only sure of one thing Mike... the government is taking sides with people wanting to destroy us. The sad part is people in high places are going along with it: afraid to asks questions to the ones they once trusted."

"That bad...huh?"

"It is Mike. I worry about fanatical Muslim terrorist groups wanting to change the world...while our government is doing nothing to stop it. It frightens me to even think about, Mike!"

"I believe I know what you're saying Doug; to hell with your view, our way only!"

"I'm beginning to feel as if I'm living in another world, a new world: not the world I knew only a couple of years ago. People don't know where to turn ... people don't know who to trust; It's all here, Mike!"

"And the Bible Doug, what about the Bible, when does it come into play?" Mike asks, waiting.

"All the things the Disciples and Prophets warned us about a couple of thousands of years ago ... it's finally here, Mike!"

"Tell me some more...I'm loving it, nephew!"

"They told what would come in the latter days, but most of the people can't see it: preachers don't preach it! That's the only way I know how to say it, but it's true, Mike!"

"Maybe... it's time we look in the Bible for the big question Doug; have you thought about it?"

"You're referring to the antichrist, the false prophet: is that what you're asking me, Mike?"

"You bet I am! The signs the prophets wrote about in the Bible ... they're here, but nobody mentions it Mike."

Martha moves closer taking over, "But, that's not everything Mike. They're coming after Christians, the ones who are brave enough to stand up against them."

"I've always believed this day would come, but never dreamed I would be here to witness it, Martha," Mike says, moving beside her.

"But there's a bright side to everything. There's always something from the Bible telling the story better. It's something we can lean on when times get rough ... never forgetting where it's coming from."

"Tell me about it Martha."

She hands him a tract of paper, "It's straight from Jesus Mike, there's nothing better. its something He told us before he was crucified. Read it and contemplate the meaning!"

When you're finished ... think of someone powerful, professing to be a holy man; a great religious leader coming from out of nowhere!"

Mike holds the tract in his hands reading it carefully ... a moment later, a smile crosses his face satisfied!

"Beware of false prophets, which come to you in sheep's clothing, but inwardly they are ravening wolves.

"Ye shall know them by their fruits ......

Matthew 7; 15,16

"Ring a bell, Mike?"

"It does Martha. But I'm thinking about another one

And then many shall be offended, and shall betray one another, and hate one another.

Matthew 24: 10

Mike shoves the paper back, glancing down seeing other papers, "But, where does all this other literature come from Martha?""

"It comes from my office, and it doesn't get any better Mike-------.

"Something bothering you, Martha?"

"Oh yes, something bothers me a lot. Things are growing more frightening every day, every hour: my friends say we're in turmoil, and they're right Mike!"

"Think about what fills our newspapers, our television, nothing but wars, rumors of wars, greed, deceit, political unfaithfulness: all of it... take your pick, Mike!"

She stops, getting her breath, beginning again, "But after a lot of prayer, reading the Bible ... I've finally found the answer ...

"And ... the answer is what, Martha?"

"Add the pros and the cons, there's only one conclusion; were headed for *"One World Order" ... no doubt about it Mike!"*

"You really it, don't you, Maratha!"

"Sure, I do! Think about what Jesus told us about, just before he was crucified: He told us he would come as a thief in the night, Mike!"

Mike looks up at her shocked again ... waiting.

"People running our government are deceiving us big-time. They're good at it ... the best-ever, Mike!

"When they're caught, they look at you innocently changing the subject. But the sad part comes last ... the most frightening part ...

"The sad part ... the most frightening part, Martha------

She lowers her head, "People actually accept it! It's hard to believe, but they do. The devil has them hook, line, and sinker, Mike!"

Doug moves beside her, taking over.

"I'll make it simple, Mike. They want to change the "Constitution", destroy our heritage, make anything acceptable."

"Today as we speak, hundreds of Christians are being killed throughout the world. In North Korea, Iraq, Africa all over the Middle East; while thousands wait starving to death for announcing the Gospel of Jesus."

Look at this Mike, something to make every Christian shout about," he says ... handing him a tract.

He that findeth his life shall lose it: and he that loseth his life for my sake shall find it.

Matthew 10: 39

"It's all coming to an end, frightening to think about Mike... unless----

"Unless what, Doug?"

"We're moving out. The man is here! *The man with the mark: no doubt about it Mike! He's here on earth today walking among us!*"

"But the Bible Doug ... the Bible!"

"Read the book of Revelation. Once he comes in power ... once he has their mark; they're his throughout eternity!"

> *... for it is a number of a man; and his number is*
> *Six hundred threescore and six.*
>
> *Revelation 13: 18*

Again, Martha takes over, her voice serious. "I'll wrap it up for you Mike. We're in trouble financially, militarily and morally. History has proven one thing for sure ...

Yes Martha----

"When we lose our morality, we lose it all Mike! People like Billy Graham, and a host of others; they've warned us about it."

"Think back to the flood in Noah's time, think back to Sodom Gomorra! We've become like them ...it's scary to even think about, Mike!"

"But, if we don't change our ways Martha ...

"We'll be the same as Sodom Gomorra, lost in a cloud of salt,...gone forever, Mike!"

Mike moves close to her ... waiting.

"But that's only part of it Mike. There's a cyber-space war going on every minute; a war that can blow this planet to hell and back!"

"It's serious as it gets; time we wake up and see it as it really is. It's not what the newspaper and television people try to make you think it is, Mike!" She's beginning to shout.

"Now what are you trying to tell me?"

"Think again Mike! The whole world is out in no mans' land searching for a leader ...

"You mean ..."

"None yet, but the world stands waiting. They're hoping for

someone to get us out of this mess; someone, anyone … they're crying for help like nothing ever before, Mike!"

Mike turns away, remembering something he heard long ago in a little country church.

"Now, you're in my league Martha."

"What league is that, Mike?"

"I'm thinking about something I heard from way-back: back when I was only a kid sitting on an old wooden bench in a country church about to go to sleep."

"Tell me about it."

"I'll do even better Martha, I'll quote it to you."

> **For there shall arise false Christs, and false prophets, and shall show great signs and wonders; insomuch that, *if it were possible … they shall deceive the very elect.***
>
> *Matthew 24: 24*

She's caught, staring up at Mike, thinking … "Mike of all people … maybe he's right!"

Again, she gets her breath, continuing, "But, the important part is the part you're about to play, Mike!"

"Me, important, you gotta be kidding …

"Stop it Mike! I'm fed up listening to your whining. Time's getting short, and it's about time you step up to the plate and forget all the sad stuff that happened thirty years ago," she's shouting, watching his eyes gazing down at the floor … back up again waiting.

She points her finger in his face, moving closer … "Now look straight into my eyes and remember what I tell you once again, Mike Cutler!"

"You mean something like this Martha," he asks, grinning, taunting her,

"Don't try to be funny, it doesn't work with me. You're part of us all the way to the sweet bitter end ... like it or not, Mike Cutler!"

Again, Mike lowers his head, looking up at her," Tell me some more Martha ... I'm listening."

"It's not only our country I'm talking about: I'm talking about the whole stinking world! I'm talking about a world governed by the devil himself!"

"He's been walking this earth since God threw him out of heaven thousands of years ago: He's prepared to do battle ... think about it Mike!"

She stops, wiping her brow, "This is hard to speak this way, but there's only way I know how to tell you how serious it is!"

"But, time you do, Martha...I'm loving it." he barely mumbles ... waiting.

"We're living in a different world, a different time. We're engaged in a war you're not aware of: a war of angels and demonic forces."

"We're fighting a battle like none before. They're waiting to do battle Mike! Its' a winner takes all kind of battle at a place called "Armageddon!"

A long pause and... "I'm aware of it, really I am Martha." He's finally able to mutter, looking up to her.

A lovely smile appears upon her face, "But don't be so sad Mike, the game isn't over!"

"Isn't over Martha ... is that what you said?"

"It is Mike. Remember Yogi Berra the baseball catcher, the guy you might have read about or heard about."

"Sure, I remember what Yogi said ... *"It ain't over till it's over"* ... *right Martha?"*

"You're right partner. Grab hold of something and hold on tight; it's time we play hard-ball--- *"Yogi's game!"*

"I'm waiting Martha."

"Good! We're a little behind with only a couple of innings left, time to get our signals straight. We come to bat in the last of the ninth, time-out to decide. The stakes are high, souls hang in the balance ...

"Yes Martha, yes...

"Baseball is like life on the field Mike, but with us, the stakes are higher!"

"Higher!" Like what Martha?"

"It's either heaven or hell, no other way I can say it, Mike!"

CHAPTER 11

Assignment ... Unknown

"Bless the Lord, ye his angels, that excel in strength, that do his commandments, harkening to the voice of his word."

Psalm 103: 20

It's time for a break. Conversation has been fast and furious, leaving a bundle of unanswered questions. Mike is reeling from one question after another. He's the guy ready for anything, but this is different ... growing deeper by the moment.

"We've explained minor things to you, now it's time we get down to details. I've been instructed by Nate to move forward; set our course with you in the middle of it, Mike," Doug says, causing Mike to move closer.

"But, I've never heard of Nate."

"You will ... depend upon it. When Nate speaks people listen, ... we all do, Mike!" Martha adds.

"I'll explain Martha's part. Nate put her in her position

because she's not only good … she's really good, and everyone knows it."

Martha moves between them, "This is the way it is, Mike. I'm tough---maybe a little, "hard-nosed at times." It isn't not because I love the job; I do what it takes to get the job done and over, Mike."

"You're amazing Martha, but maybe it's time I tell you something about Mike Cutler … the guy you've been grilling for the last couple of hours."

"I've been waiting for this moment … let it all out, Mike Cutler!"

"It's this certain feeling I have, Martha. It's unexplainable, hard to talk about. It's like I'm lost … searching for something, never finding it. It goes on and on, never ending!"

"You'll know someday … believe me you will. But there are other things to think about, things you alone must find out before we leave this place. I've told you before we're here for you only Mike!"

Mike lowers his head, thinking back again … "But why are you saying these things to me, Martha?" He asks, looking up to her … waiting

"I suppose every time I read the Bible, I can't help but compare what lies ahead of you; something the *Apostle Paul* warned us about 2000 years ago!"

"Then please tell me about it Martha."

"Paul told us what would come in the latter days and, with all my heart and soul I believe those days are upon us. Think about this …

"This what, Martha?"

She reaches out grasping his hand, smiling, "Maybe someday, sooner than you can imagine… we'll be standing before Jesus, our Lord and Savior, Mike!"

Again, Mike looks up at her wondering …

She places a small tract in his hand, looking up at him, "Read this Mike … something that could help all of us … you specially, Mike!"

> **"Put on the full armor of God that you may be able to stand against the wiles of the devil.**
>
> ### *Ephesians 6: 11*

His face turns pale, worried again. "Tell me something I don't know Martha. I believe the Lord is coming. But when I think of my life, the wasted years … I wonder if I'm worthy for anything!"

She takes his hand, bringing him alive, "But you are worthy Mike, time for you to get over it. There's a future for you somewhere, someplace; there has to be!"

"Please don't do this to me Martha, please don't------

She takes his hand, guiding him to an open window, looking deep into his tired looking eyes, "Look beyond Mike … set your sight upon tomorrow; your sins are forgiven as far as the east to the west!"

A moment of silence and, "Tomorrow … explain it to me, Martha."

"You're the recipient of something greater than anything you've ever imagined … your chance of a life-time! Maybe it's something you've always dreamed about Mike; something to ease your pain … your suffering,"

"But Martha, how do I fit the pattern for any kind of service; my life has changed, but there are other problems …

"Like what, Mike?"

He looks up at her wondering how to explain, "But, there's

something else Martha, look at me and when you're finished ... I'll tell you what happened to me, who I really am!"

"Tell me what happened to you Mike."

He takes her hand, looking up to her wanting to cry, but doesn't, "He touched me, and my life has never been the same, Martha!" He barely can mutter ... while a couple of tear drops appear unnoticed.

She moves beside him, embracing him. "Calm yourself Mike. We know your history, everything about you and then some."

"You know about me ... the church, and-------

"Everyone knows about you and the church Mike; we're family ... remember."

Mike's head hangs low while he gazes up at her barely muttering, "Night after night, I lie awake wondering about myself ... my past, my future. I try to hide my feelings, but there's no place to hide them Martha ...

"But you fail to understand-----

"Understand what, Martha?"

"You're different Mike. You have a life ahead ... a new life; a life of service to Him only. From the moment your name was mentioned the issue was settled!"

He glances down at the table, and back to Doug ... "Are you sure about this ... absolutely sure, Doug?" He asks, waiting.

"I'm sure of it ... no doubt about it. It's time you forget your past; time to open your eyes and look up. You have a service to do for Him alone Mike!"

"My service to Him ... is that what you said?"

"That's what I said, meant every word of it. Something waits for you that only the Lord up in heaven knows the outcome. Think about this Mike; Jesus, angels, throughout the universe ... all looking down upon the three of us waiting; sounds unbelievable but isn't!"

"Get over with it Doug ... tell me the rest of it," he mutters, his head hanging low waiting---

"It's about you alone Mike. You've been given the honor of participating in something great that God alone knows why; that's the only way I know how to explain it, Mike!"

"Please don't play games with me Doug, my name is Mike, not Paul; the guy who gave it all for Jesus. I'm not like Peter, the fisherman, or Mary the one who waited for Him at the grave. They were His picks ... all different people. They were chosen for a purpose Doug. I knew all about them till ...

Doug places his hand upon his chest shoving him against the wall without warning ... shouting, "Don't say it Mike ... I warn you again Mike, don't say it," He says looking down at Mike grinning----

"Now what's so funny Doug?"

"It's you Mike, It's all about you."

"Now what are talking about?"

"You answered your own question. You're one of "His Chosen", but haven't recognized it, Mike!"

Mike's face brightens. He remembers Friend ... the words he said to him, "You're chosen to do His will, Mike!"

His body goes limp ...thinking about it. Slowly, he moves seating himself across from Doug, looking up to him,

"Your boss in Washington, the one called Nate ... he told you this, Doug?"

"He did Mike. When your name appeared, I wondered if maybe he knew you. I asked him the question, but he didn't answer. He just sat in his chair looking up at me smoking a cigar turning his head away. Then he got up and walked to the window looking out, leaving me sitting. It was weird … never saw anything like it before, Mike!"

Again, Mike runs his hand across his brow thinking … 'Not too many people give me a recommendation for helping Christians; more of the opposite might be more appropriate," he barely mutters, his head looking downward.

"That … I don't know, but Nate isn't the kind of person I wish to question. I'm warning you now Mike: never, ever … question Nate's authority. He has enough authority for the both of us!"

Doug looks toward Martha waiting … "It's time we take a break, sweetheart. Let's go someplace, clear our minds before we get down to some real business!"

Mike's puzzled again, wondering … 'get down to some real business' … what's he talking about now, he asks himself over and over.

Thirty minutes later they're seated at a fashionable restaurant in down-town Indy. Conversation is open … limited to family. Inquiries of whereabouts, who married who is enjoyable; but the look upon Mike's face displays no interest, till he turns, facing Martha … "Tell me something Martha …

"Yes Mike …

"Are you about to tell me what you're really here for or … must I drag it out of you the rest of the evening?"

"This isn't the place for business. We're heading home, and once we're home we'll make you an offer you can't refuse, Mike!"

"Can't refuse … did I hear you right?"

"You did. It's a chance in a life time offer, Mike!"

Again, his mind runs wild. He wonders if this is another bad dream … one of those crazy heart-breaking dreams; the kind that never goes away, leaving you wondering.

CHAPTER 12

Setting the Stage

Therefore, if anyone is in Christ, he is a new creation; the old has passed away, behold, the new has come.

2nd Corinthians 5: 17

Thirty minutes later they're home with Martha leading the way to the living-room.

"Sit down and make yourself comfortable Mike. This could get interesting …real interesting maybe. Prepare for something in today's world; the world you're about to see more and more of Mike," she says, seating herself across the table before him.

"Today … listening to you and Doug is the biggest surprise of my life, Martha. I'm ready for anything that doesn't kill me," Mike says, causing her to look again at him … grinning.

"Great, Mike … you just said the magic words!"

"What words, Martha?"

"*Kill me … words* that might describe the next chapter of your life! How do you feel now Mike Cutler?"

He can only stare at her coldly … afraid to answer.

"You're about to be part of the real-world Mike … a world you've never been told about: now do you understand what I'm trying to say to you, Mike?"

Mike shakes his head looking toward Doug … waiting … hoping, but nothing …

"Evidently you can't Mike. You're not the first one to look at me that way … nobody can! To understand the world, I'm talking about you must be one of them; no other way to tell you, Mike!" Martha says, causing Mike to sit up, his eyes upon her only----

"Anything you would like to say at this point, Mike?" She asks, looking again at him expecting … but only a surly glance stares up at her … waiting.

"What's the matter … something bothering you Mike?" She asks, down in his face taunting.

Mike gazes over toward Doug and back to Martha, "You're talking tough Martha … real tough to a sixty-two-year-old guy whose only real asset is my undying faith in Jesus Christ. I've changed Martha … time you get used to it!"

"Anything else you might want to say, Mike?"

"Oh yes … maybe, it's time you tell me who we're dealing with, so I can play the game with you!"

"Well praise the Lord, you're finally getting it. Listen carefully, this … you don't wanta miss …"

"I've been listening … get with it!"

"But you don't understand. You don't have the slightest idea what you're about to move into. We're dealing with the supernatural. We're dealing with a different kind of world; a world of evil … filled with nothing but darkness!" She says, down in his face shouting.

Again, he's stunned ... hearing nothing like this before. His eyes stay glued to hers ... missing nothing, waiting ...

Martha stops, turning to face him, shouting up in his face, "It's because of Satan ... the devil himself Mike! He walks among us on earth this very moment. His time is growing short and he knows it. He's the most dangerous creature ever, Mike. He'll do anything there is to do ... knowing----

"Knowing what, Martha?" He asks quickly, interrupting.

"He knows his time on earth is running out: he knows the war that began in heaven is about to end for good, Mike!"

"But what then ... Martha?"

"He's going to rot in hell, Mike! He's gonna burn, burn, burn, Mike; he's gonna burn forever and ever Mike! Now's the time to get ready; Jesus is coming to gather *His Elect* ... ones like you, Doug and me, Mike. It's time to get happy ... let the whole world know about it, Mike!" She's shouting hysterically.

Again, he's stunned! Martha tells it like is and he loves it.

"Think back Mike, think about something I told you moments ago."

He wonders, but useless ... "Tell me again Martha."

"We can't lose Mike! He's with us always; all the way to the bitter end," She reminds him, moving beside him.

"And the rest of it ... Martha ...

She stops ... looking up at him differently. "Sorry Mike, but I can't. This is different; it's out of my realm of knowledge completely!"

Mike studies her every word; tired eyes looking down and back up to her feeling desperate, "I don't know how much more of this I can handle Martha. I'm lost, I'm tired ... but why Martha ... why?"

"We all are Mike ... but this is what it's all about!"

His head drops, looking down … worried, "But this guy Nate … what about him Martha?"

She takes his hand looking up at him smiling," Who cares about Nate, this must be God's will … that's all that matters Mike!"

"It has to be His will, but the purpose of the mission … is that too much to ask for Martha," He asks, looking up to her … waiting.

Martha turns pointing upward. "It's all about angels and demons, Mike! It's about a war that began in heaven; a war that's about to end here on earth."

"It's a war that we're a part of … like it or not. They're waiting for you, Mike," She shouts, rising from her chair … walking away, leaving him thinking.

"But, Martha! Martha! Come back … please come back. You don't understand. I love angels; without angels I'm lost … nowhere to turn to …

They stop … staring back at him, "But, why this sudden change Mike … why?"

"I've had help Martha … help beyond your wildest imagination. Help from Friend … my Guardian Angel. He knows everything, my thoughts, my weaknesses … the path I'm heading, Martha."

"Where are you heading Mike?"

"Wherever Martha. I'm heading wherever He sends me, Martha!"

They stop, looking back at Mike amazed. "We've been waiting to hear you say those words Mike. We're moving on … a lot to do … a lot to explain."

"Doug calls Martha to the side taking her hand, "But did you ever think this might be Nate's decision Martha … did you ever think about----

"I did for sure Doug ... who else could it be?"

"I'm not sure, but remember who Mike's Guardian Angel works for." he says, grinning.

"You mean ...

"There's no doubt about it sweetheart, it has to be ... Him only Martha!"

CHAPTER 13

Preparing for Battle

For his anger *endureth* but a moment; in his favor is life:

Psalm 30: 5

Martha opens her brief case removing a book filled with papers, beginning, "I'm satisfied the way things are going so far Mike, but now the question is … 'are you ready for something big … your assignment I'm talking about?"

A smile crosses his face, looking up her, "I'm ready as I'll ever be, Martha."

"That's good to know… I'll give you a schedule for things to come. Pay close attention. Keep track of times and dates, they're important … very important. And something else to remember … anything I submit to you today can be changed in a moment's notice. Go to your note-book, look it over … I'll give you dates, times, places and schedules; still with me Mike?"

"I'm with you Martha!"

She begins again …talking slowly; stopping to emphasize things to worry about, things never to talk about. On and on it goes, time to make appointments.

"Forty-five days from today you will show up in Washington. After you arrive … you'll grab a taxi and proceed downtown to the "Mark Twain Hotel" … registering immediately." She says, getting her breathe, moving on.

"Your room will be paid for … reserved for two days only. Ask for your mail at the desk, where you'll find a cashier's check waiting to cover expenses---whatever. You will remain at the hotel the rest of the day, but making no contact … still with me Mike," She asks, catching her breath again, waiting.

"I'm with you Martha."

"You'll receive a call at midnight on the first night of your arrival … you'll be told where and when to be on Monday morning. Still with me Mike?" she asks persisting.

Mike hesitates, "I'm with you but, the day I arrive is Sunday … two weeks before Halloween."

She stops, looking up at him, "Just shut up and don't argue with me … just be there Mike!" She shouts up in his face.

"Sure … I'll be there, but why the secrecy?"

She takes his hand pulling him against her … "Just shut-up and listen for once Mike! I've told you the kind of people we deal with over and over: just sit … be quiet and listen for a change!"

His temper runs high feeling scolded, but no reply.

"From the moment you embark from the plane … you'll be watched; maybe by us … maybe not by us. Do you understand what I'm telling you, Mike?"

"I do …sure I do Martha!" He shouts back at her for the first time, waiting.

"Then don't look up at me stupid: just write it down and do

what you're told to do!" She says, lashing out at him again ... turning away, showing a smile on her face... *It's temper- testing-time; he's at her mercy.*

"Once you arrive in Washington, pay close attention to what surrounds you; don't make yourself noticeable! Act normal as those around you... perhaps a business person, someone important ... are you getting it, Mike?"

Mike isn't happy, he's growing tired, "I'm getting it Martha!" He barely mumbles, dropping his head down, looking disgusted.

"I'm aware you're waiting Mike, but as I told you before ... this is different; a matter of life or death ... no in-betweens to make you happy. The world you're about to enter is a different world; a spiritual world filled with good and evil."

"They're fighting for your very soul Mike. It's a world-humans like you and I know nothing about. It's a world where only God, the devil, demons and angels are aware!"

"It's an unseen spiritual world told about in the Bible. Very soon you're going to be part of doing things you never dreamed about, Mike!"

"It's a world you could have never imagined! It's a whole new ball-game, with you the middle of it, Mike!" She's beginning to shout.

Mike looks up at her ... and back to the wall staring blankly ... still wondering ...

"You'll be dealing with forces beyond your wildest nightmare ... satanic forces; ready to face anything, guided by the devil himself. I'm talking about the 'occult,' deadly forces you know nothing about. We pray for you Mike ... we pray and pray again for you." She's shouting up in his face again ...

"But you haven't the slightest idea what I've faced... you never will Martha!"

"You're right for sure, but get this through that thick brain of yours, this isn't Nam ... buddy boy! This is warfare beyond warfare, deadlier than anything you've ever dreamed about!"

"Now, what are you talking about?"

"Think back to a grade-school in Connecticut, Mike. Think about a place where innocent school children were murdered by a wild, beady eyed young man devil possessed. He went on a "Killing spree" over and over; never looking back. He was one of them Mike ... devil possessed!"

Mike listens, on and on ... speechless.

"It's still the same old war ... God against Satan... nothing changing. It's like the days when Jesus walked the earth, Jesus taking you to heaven: the devil promising you wine and roses sending you to hell with him forever and ever, Mike!"

Bells begin to ring immediately! Mike is thinking ... remembering things he heard in church thirty long years ago; demons, witches, false prophets, antichrist, all of them serving the devil."

"She moves against him, bringing him alive, "Do you believe you're up to the task Mike: or time we say good-by and farewell...letting another do it later?" She asks, not so pleasant ... threatening.

"Sure, I'm up to the task; and it's about time you quit worrying about me and get on with it, Martha!"

"I know you're up to the task, Mike, from the very beginning I've never doubted you. We care about you; we care more than you'll ever know. It's possible Doug or I could be with you meeting Nate; if not, you're on your own ... God bless you Mike!"

She turns, glancing over at Doug, smiling, "But, I may have forgotten to mention ...

"Mention what, Martha?"

"You're not going alone ... you're about to have a partner!"

"That's something new ... who's my partner?"

"I've no idea, but it has to be someone with an established record!"

Briefing is ending, while Mike sits thinking about their visit; so short, painful at times, changing his life completely.

"But... one more question Martha ...

"Yes Mike ...

"Is there something special or specific I should know before meeting Nate? I don't know why, but I've a feeling this is one time I need to be sharp ... really sharp might be more like it!"

Doug moves beside him, "There just might be something special Mike. Just before I departed, he said something odd; something that caused me to take notice!"

"Yes, Doug-----

"He looked up at me while puffing on a big old black cigar, and with an old gruff, gravel-coated voice I'll never forget: he said, 'Oh, by the way Doug---tell Mike to watch a television mini-series, it just might help someone like him!"

"Nate, said that ...?"

"He did Mike ... he sure did. But I had no idea what he was talking about. I asked him "what series are you talking about, Nate ... and he yelled back at me, "A Band of Brothers" ---- you know, the old blood and guts type, the kind Mike likes!"

Mike is puzzled, thinking back, "Something else he might have said maybe ... Doug?"

"Nothing for sure. But 1 had a feeling he knew more: maybe your assignment has something to do with WW11 ... something we talked about earlier. Do your-self a favor, and watch it twice ... you might need it, Mike!"

"That, you can be sure of. I'll watch it till I can picture it in my dreams, Doug!"

Martha begins to move on, stopping suddenly looking back at Mike shouting ... "Oh, but there's something else I might mention Mike ...

"Yes Martha ...

"Doug and I are heading to Hawaii for a week vacation!"

"Something special in Hawaii, maybe?"

"There is indeed Mike; the largest observatory in the world at the foot of "Mauna Kea." It's there waiting for us; now's the time we go see it!"

"Wonderful Martha ... wonderful! But maybe another reason ...a secret reason?"

"No secret Mike. It's all about *Mauna Kea*, a volcano melting pot ready to explode most anytime. It's the hot-spot for the world's best astronomers; a playhouse for the rich and famous!"

"And ... you'll be searching for what Martha?"

She pauses, taking her time ... *"Oh! Maybe----- a trumpet to sound, the heavens to part ... while Doug and I stand gazing upward; watching Him and His angles coming to greet us."*

"Oh yes ... there're out there by the ten thousand, Martha!"

"Who Mike--who is out there?" She's yelling, waving her arms frantically.

"Angels ... God's holy angels. They're over the prairies, the oceans, the mountain tops, the land; they're everywhere Martha!" He's shouting, walking away smiling.

CHAPTER 14

No Way Out

"Cast your burden on the Lord, and He will sustain you; He will never suffer the righteous to be moved.

Psalm 55: 22

Mike hits the sheets near midnight, but sleep doesn't come. He tosses and turns, same as he did before meeting Friend. Things have changed … he's serving a different master, yet … something is missing. He wonders if he's capable of serving his creator, and it bothers him greatly; but his biggest problem comes when Friend says---"there's no way-out Mike … no way out!"

He dreads the thought of failure. His bedroom becomes his prison. He considers himself nobody; nothing but worry day and night. He gazes into the mirror, turning away in disgust. He mumbles the words of *Moses*, *"Who am I … that I should go!"*

There's a soft knock at his bedroom door. He gazes at the clock … showing an hour past midnight; wondering if something is wrong with Doug or Martha. Another soft knock and the door opens: before him stands Doug, looking down into his uncle's eyes … worried.

He seats himself at the side of Mike's bed, "I don't know why, but I just couldn't sleep, Uncle Mike."

"You're not the only one, I've been lying here for hours doing the same. My mind is running wild … imagining everything that might be ahead of me; it's driving me crazy, Doug!"

"Tell me about it."

"I worry if I'm capable of anything; especially what I hear from you and Martha. Can you possibly understand what I'm trying to explain, Doug?"

Doug looks at him, thinking maybe it's time I tell him some of my problems."

"You're not the only one who worries Mike. I worry about my own capabilities. Maybe this is what they call … the human side of us ordinary people. But you Mike … only you, have something going most people would envy … maybe die for. It's something special for you only. I've never doubted it, Mike!"

Mike points to a nearby table, wanting to explain. They sit quietly thinking … studying … and finally, Mike breaks the silence.

"I wrack my brain over and over: I search and search forever, but never an answer. I plead over and over words from the Bible, "why me Lord … why send me?"

"When I'm finished … I go on pleading the same; anything, Lord … anything to make me feel better, but never an answer."

Doug moves close to him. "I don't have the answer either, but there's one thing I know for sure …

"Then tell me something for sure Doug," he mutters, hopelessly.

"You're not alone Mike. Everything was set up before we arrived here at your place."

"I understand, but the hardest part to understand is why me, of all people … doesn't make sense, Doug!"

Doug looks up at him grinning, shaking his head wondering … 'how can I ever make him understand this is something beyond all reason; maybe something between God and Mike only."

"But you don't understand Mike. You haven't the slightest idea what might be ahead of you. It's the chance of a lifetime … something far above reason. You're going on a trip; a trip that only He knows where. I envy you … I really and truly envy you," Doug says, placing his hand upon his shoulder … waiting.

"You make me feel proud, but humble, Doug. But never did I believe I would be here sitting beside you talking about a journey to nowhere: it frightens me to even think about it," he says, rising from his chair going to the window, looking out into a sea of darkness.

"But I can tell you this for sure Mike---

"Anything Doug…tell me how to soothe my crazy thoughts and mind."

Doug looks up at him reminding him, "Your selection wasn't done by simply picking a name and number … it had to be something far greater!"

"It had to be something myself and others will never know why it was you, Mike! But someone, someplace … knows you for sure: knows you better than you know yourself!"

Again, Mike pauses … thinking back to other times … other places. "There has to be, but who or where… maybe I'll never know the reason Doug."

Doug walks to the window standing beside him. He places his arms upon his shoulders comforting him, "But you'll get over it, believe me you will. I've been in some bad spots for sure, but nothing ever like this Mike. It baffles me to even think what lies ahead of you Mike!"

Mike gazes out the window speechless … thinking and thinking … waiting.

"But there's always good news to go along with the uncertain, Mike. Think about something Martha told you, something important …

"You mean we win … is that what you're saying, Doug?"

"It is… we always win, were on His side, Mike!"

Complete silence, till Mike looks up to him lost again, "But, I'm an expert at failure, Doug, believe me I am."

"You're not alone, so were others… people we like to read about. People like Mary Magdalene, the biggest prostitute in Palestine, Paul, the Apostle … the guy who persecuted Christians. And another … someone called Peter, the guy with the short fuse; denied the Lord three times before his crucifixion. Does this remind you of someone, Mike?"

"But I don't … understand, I can't understand …

"They were like you Mike; they were *His Chosen*, but only the Lord knows why they were chosen!"

"People like me-----is that what you said, Doug?"

"Yes…they were like you. When your mission is completed you'll never be the same … never ever, Mike!"

Doug turns away, walking to the other side of the room looking out toward the highway; seeing an occasional car whizzing by in both directions.

"But, there's more to talk about Mike."

"Talk about what?"

"I've analyzed every possibility for your selection down to the last hilt and then some. I've put all the pieces together… coming to one conclusion …

"And your conclusion is …

"When there's no other way out … stop, look around and turn to the Bible!"

Again, Mike looks at Doug, worried … "But not for me Doug … I'm nobody, a very simple person!"

"We all are Mike. God created a lot of us simple persons. There's times when logic doesn't make sense, but with *Him* … never question! The Lord is looking over you Mike. Everything is falling in place like clock-work, *and* you're in the thick of it!"

Mike can only stare at Doug … trying to speak, but useless.

"It's time you forget about your wants and plans, Mike. If the Lord wants you to serve Him … the issue is settled! With all your past troubles … you should be the proudest of the proudest … the happiest man ever, Mike!"

"But Doug … can you really believe this is happening to a guy like me? I'm the guy who hated the church as much as I hated the devil. How can I ever get over it, Doug?" he asks, looking downward … tears falling, unnoticed.

"But your sins are forgiven. Jesus, died on a cross for you and millions of others like you, Mike," Doug says, taking his hand… waiting.

Mike moves away, staring downward, barely mumbling, "But, Doug … of all the people in this wide, wide world … how can it be someone like me?"

"I don't know … I just don't know! But someday, somewhere with God's help … you'll know for sure. Where or when … only He knows, but you will know, Mike."

His message is over, and Doug is tired. "It's time we get some rest… if the Lord wants you to know, you'll know in His time. In the mean-time … get ready to serve Him, Mike!"

An hour goes by and Mike still lays awake thinking back to his youth. He remembers what Friend told him … his dedication to God. He remembers what his mother told him as a child at six, but never understood. And … suddenly it hits him! He remembers the first time she called him Mike … not the usual childish name, "Mikey Boy."

"You were placed on the altar as a baby. You were anointed with oil by the minister as your father and I submitted your life to God. Your life is dedicated to Him, and someday … somewhere; you'll understand why. Mike!"

CHAPTER 15

Farewell, Oh, my Captain

*"For as the heaven is high above the earth, so
great is his mercy toward them who fear him.*

Psalm 103: 11

A week has passed and no word from Keith with all his troubles. And just at the break of dawn on Sunday morning, there's a loud rap on the front door. Before Mike can get to it, he hears more loud raps. He looks through the peep-hole and there's Rosy, Keith's woman standing outside, crying alone.

He opens the door inviting her inside, and still … she cries uncontrollably. She's hardly dressed, around thirty-five to forty; about five-foot tall with flaming red hair down to her neckline, dirt and mud all over.

She wears only a pair of skimpy red shorts, a shirt covered with mud, sandals held together with a single strap. Mike has seen her in different attire, but never nothing as this. He places his hand over her mouth, and she stops her crying.

"Quite Rosy, get hold of yourself," he says, trying to calm her.

She continues sobbing, trying to speak. A moment later, she's staring up at Mike, pleading, "Help me Mike … Help me! "I'm desperate … you alone can help me," she barely can utter.

Mike takes his time, looking her over again. He wants her under control, his control only. Police … he doesn't need hanging around asking questions. But, there's only one way with Rosy, 'get tough, real tough' … the only way Rosy knows it.

"Shut up for a moment Rosy! Get your breath and we'll go from there. Now … before we go further, take your time and tell me about the police!"

"I will … I will! Please don't yell at me … please don't Mike. I called them from the house but didn't wait till they arrived. I was mixed up-- scared to death … still frightened Mike!" Rosy says, panicking.

"You didn't wait … why didn't you wait?" He shouts, up in her face. "Are you nuts, stoned, or just plain crazy, Rosy?"

"The very first thing they're going to think is you had something to do with it," he's yelling up in her face, causing her to draw away frightened.

Rosy begins crying again … till Mike grabs her, pulling her closer. He puts his hand over her mouth, calming her,

"Straighten-up and pull yourself together Rosy! Any more of this crying all over the place, you'll be going on a trip alone, think about it… Rosy girl!"

More sobbing and crying … finally looking up at Mike, tears showing … waiting.

"Sit at the table and drink this Rosy," he says, handing her a can of coke.

She walks to the dining room table gulping it down without stopping. A couple of minutes later, the sobbing and crying comes to an end, looking up at him, barely muttering, "I'll be alright for now Mike. But I'm scared ... frightened more than I've ever been frightened."

Mike stands behind her, his arms placed upon her shoulders comforting her. "Tell it all Rosy. Right now, I'm the only friend you have. Don't lie to me and I'll help you: one lie and I'm history with you forever. And remember this Rosy ---

Again, tears begin to show ... looking up at him pitiful like asking, "What Mike---what must I remember?"

"I'm all you got ... and don't you ever forget it! Now, do we understand each other Rosy?"

She turns, staring hard at him, her body still quivers. She watches his look of disgust ... knowing he has reason.

"I understand Mike ... really I do. Keith always told me I could depend upon you above anyone ... you alone Mike."

"I'm still scared. scared as I've never been ... I'll begin with this ..." she says, fighting back tears.

Mike looks hard at her again...his voice threatening, "It better be nothing but the truth, so help you Rosy!"

"Every word I say is true, I swear it, Mike."

"Now tell me everything that happened... leave nothing out."

She gets her breath, looking up at Mike, "He and I were getting ready to have a party as usual, but suddenly everything went wrong----

"Whatta you mean ... went wrong?"

"Well ... the drugs we had lying on the table ...

"Keep going Rosy ... I'm listening----

"It's really hard to explain, but I'll try."

"I'm waiting Rosy."

Rosy looks up at Mike ... her head bowing low. I don't know how to explain it Mike, but for the first time ever ... Keith looked like a different Keith!"

He looked at me smiling as I've never seen him smile before. And suddenly ... he grabbed the drugs off the table and threw them on the floor, stomping on them."

"He seemed like a completely different Keith ... a Keith I had never seen before. He was happy ... he wasn't the same Keith I knew before!"

"Keep going Rosy, I'm listening!"

"I was shocked as never before. I didn't know what to do. He never did anything like this: he loved getting high. But he had changed completely ... he wasn't the same Keith I knew," she says, shaking her head, staring downward.

"Don't stop Rosy, it's getting interesting."

"Before I could ask him why he got rid of the drugs ... he put his arms around me ... kissed me as I've never been kissed before Mike."

"I love it Rosy ... keep going!"

A long pause and, "Before I could get my breath he took off running to the back-door heading down to the board-walk in the middle of the lake. He didn't look back... till he stopped at edge of the water. And then... he began looking upward toward heaven spreading his arms out ..."

"And then what Rosy.?"

A long pause and ..." I don't know why, but Keith was smiling as I've never seen him smile before. He seemed to be happy, Mike!"

"And then what Rosy?"

"There was a long moment of silence, and Keith jumped into the water ... nothing I could do about it Mike. That's all I can tell you ... I'm sorry!"

"It's over and I believe you Rosy. Keith had changed, he told me about it. But this isn't exactly the time for all the crying and sobbing."

"It's only going to be a while till the cops come looking for you; when that happens, you better have your story straight. But in the mean-time … pray your heart out like you've never done before Rosy!"

"Pray for what Mike?"

"Pray they don't take you in for further questioning Rosy."

"I know … I know Mike."

"Now listen to me, this is a onetime only."

She peers up at him, sobbing again, "I am listening…really I am Mike."

His eyes turn away from her, showing pity; a moment later, he's facing her explaining.

"There's no use letting the police think you had anything to do with any part of this. Now stand up and pull yourself together; think back and answer my questions. Do you understand what I'm trying to tell you, Rosy?"

"I do understand Mike … I'm just upset. Please don't be angry with me---guess I just wasn't thinking good…maybe I panicked." She says, her voice broken, sobbing again.

"You're doing fine Rosy. Just take it easy and answer my questions. I understand why you might have panicked; but tell me about the dirt covering your body top to bottom."

"Yes Mike, yes… I'll try to explain. I was running around like mad trying to get rid of the drugs off the floor. I gathered it all up and put it in a big old sack and hauled it across the road to an empty lot."

"I looked around trying to find a way to get rid of the stuff. I was beginning to panic till I found a spade and buried it about two or three feet down." She says, stopping to get her breath again.

"And then, what?"

She takes her time, thinking back. "Oh yes, now I remember!

I ran back to the house and called the cops before coming here. That's the truth ... every word of it is the truth, so help me, Mike!"

Mike walks around the kitchen slow and calm, occasionally glancing over at Rosy.

He's thinking of every possible angle to cover her: knowing the police will be asking questions fast and furious. He glances over at the clock looking satisfied ... time to give her the word.

He moves beside her, staring down at her, speaking softly for a change, "Now ... here's what I want you to do Rosy...

She looks up at him pitiful like, "Yes Mike ... yes ...

"Go into the bedroom and find some clothes of mine to wear. Leave nothing lying around. Take a shower to make your-self more presentable: not too presentable, I hope you understand."

"I do understand Mike!"

"Later go back to the house ... walk boldly inside where police and emergency people will be waiting. Take your time and tell them the same story you're telling me... except hiding the drugs of course!"

She heads for the bedroom to prepare herself. A quick shower, an assessment of her other parts ... coming back into the living room.

She's dressed in a pair of loose fitting jeans, a shirt looking half-way presentable, standing before him posing, shouting, "How does this look Mike?" She asks, turning herself around before him.

Mike grabs hold of her hand, turns her around a couple of more times looking back at her, "Better---much better Rosy," he says, giving his final approval.

Rosy returns his smile looking up at him, while he's guiding her to the door, waiting. Rosy hugs and kisses him, and off she goes to the lake-house, a smile on her face, showing.

A couple of days later there's a short story in the newspaper obituary Colom explaining ... Keith was of ill health without cure; the funeral service will be at *Raccoon State Park* on Wednesday morning at eight, a short distance from Indy.

CHAPTER 16

Someone for Rosy

**The Lord is nigh unto them that are of a
broken heart:**

Psalm 34: 18

Days waiting for Keith's daughter to arrive from England
are miserable for Mike. Friends call and ask if he's
attending the funeral, if some of his pals might be needed for
pall-bearers; but he doesn't want to be reminded, shutting them
off quickly.

Sleep doesn't come easy the night before Keith's burial.
Again, his mind runs wild ... thinking of the good times; ...
hiding the bad times.

Morning comes and Mike drives to *Raccoon Lake* alone ...
feeling miserable. Arriving ... he glances around seeing the
scenery at the entrance gate; a small sign showing Keith's name
and area of the ceremony about to take place.

He heads into the camping area noticing a gathering around
a small pond, where about twenty or thirty people sit upon the

ground near the water. He parks his car, walking over near the pond becoming one of the participants; all waiting to honor Keith … praising him as one of their own.

Morning sun has arrived, and a warm breeze blows briskly, causing a couple of trees with over-hanging branches to bend slightly. In the middle of the gathering Mike can see Rosy sitting with a small crowd, waiting for the ceremony to begin.

She's dressed in a flowered white silk dress reaching down past her knees, and a blue silk bandana wrapped neatly around her neck. Rosy doesn't look like the same Rosy he met the last time. She waves at Mike displaying a lovely smile; a faraway different looking Rosy … just a couple of days ago.

Men participants wear garb of the sixties and seventies, displaying red and white bandanas tied around their forehead. Women wear skin-tight shorts barely hiding their butts, low cut blouses hiding little or nothing. Mike doesn't like the style, but this is for Keith; Keith only … he keeps telling himself over and over. Looking further he notices a couple of men off toward the back dressed in business suits … different from most.

But he doesn't notice someone moving up from behind: Keith's daughter, Brittany Ann … the love of Keith's life from England.

She doesn't wait, moving next to him blurting out loudly with an ever so pretty Brit accent," Hi, Mike … I'm Brittany Ann Lincoln, from London!"

Shock and more shock … and finally it hits him. His arms reach up pulling her to him, hugging her as a long-lost daughter. Another quick glance looking her over, and he begins to realize… she's as Keith perfectly described her; beautiful … a super model, top to bottom. Heads turn, looking to where Mike and Brittany stand dressed differently, not their usual.

Mike is different … peaceful for a change; forgetting his

anger from the past: seeing "Flower-Children" from the sixties and seventies, seated on the ground at the other side of the pond waiting.

Someone begins humming a song of the sixties and seventies, while Mike and Brittany stand holding hands, watching from across the pond, wondering ... 'what's next for these friends of Daddy?"

Brittany squeezes Mike's hand, whispering, "I suppose they all knew Daddy ... right Mike?"

"They did Brittany, but none knew Daddy like I knew Daddy," Mike says, turning his head away, grinning.

A couple more songs of the sixties and seventies ring out, and there's a sudden halt; it's time for Keith's eulogy.

An elderly hippy-looking guy rises from the grass taking off his cap ... raising his arms high in the air beginning ...

"I knew Keith well, knew him thirty years, and never a better guy have I yet to meet. We had a friendship, a deep respect for one another. Keith was like a brother ... he trusted me, and I trusted him. Sometimes we argued ... sometimes we laughed; when it was all over ... we never looked back. That's the way it was folks ... everything was beautiful!"

Mike sits at Brittany's side when a slightly greying lady, about Keith's age rises, offering her eulogy.

She tells of Keith's love of nature and all the hidden beauty from the soil they once enjoyed. A recording begins to play, and she waves her outstretched arms looking upward toward heaven listening: while Peter, Paul and Mary sing an oldie ... "Where Have All the Flowers Gone." ... finishing with ..." The Age of Aquarius."

Music from the sixties and seventies fills the morning air, while the distinct smell of marijuana comes blowing in from across the pond ... making them happy.

Brittany pulls hard on Mike's arm looking up to him asking, "Is that what I think it is, Mike?"

"It is for sure darling, I'm sorry to say," he says, turning away hoping she doesn't see the grin upon his face.

From across the pond another gentleman about Keith's age dressed in full hippie attire rises slowly to his feet. He wears a bandana wrapped around his forehead, no shirt, bare to the waist; walking slowly toward the water with a large silver metal urn filled with Keith's ashes.

Suddenly … he's gazing upward hurling Keith's ashes high into the cool morning air above the pond, watching them drifting downward into the still water.

A moment of silence, still looking in awe, cheers ring out praising Keith's life of happiness during the sixties and seventies: when suddenly from out from nowhere, a beautiful 'Robin Red Breast' appears, landing on an over-hanging branch of an elm tree.

A breeze begins to blow, while branches bend downward touching the still water; causing the audience below to rise standing looking upward staring in awe, shouting, "A miracle! A miracle!" … Keith looks down from heaven upon us!"

An older lady wearing a long white skirt, a red thin blouse and a blue bandana raises her arms pointing upward yelling hysterically … "Look … look everyone, It's Keith… his spirit parts the branches before us."

Standing far off at the other side Mike laughs without end, while Brittany hangs onto his arm shaking her head wondering… what's next with these old friends of Daddy's?"

Proceedings are over, and people begin to leave, while Keith's ashes become part of the mud and water. Mike and Brittany hold hands heading for the car … when suddenly from afar; Rosy comes running with arms out-stretched shouting, "Brittany! Brittany darling!"

Mike watches surprised as she greets Brittany like an old friend with hugs and kisses; making him feel proud and happy for the ones Keith loved so dearly.

And ... a couple of days later Brittany calls Mike expressing her gratitude...announcing so proudly, "I have a new friend Mike, a loyal most charming friend Rosy ... my personal maid from America!"

CHAPTER 17

Person of Interest

"Rejoice with me, for I have found the coin which I had lost."

Luke 15: 9

It's nine a. m on a beautiful Sunday morning and Mike heads off to church once again. He remembers only a month ago he gave his life back to the Lord after thirty years of hatred. Life is great, though lonely for companionship. Financial problems plague the church, but no worry about the future.

He's about to enter when suddenly a sound from above causes him to stop, looking up; seeing an old wooden belfry with an iron cross at the top.

He looks again seeing a beautiful "Mourning Dove" sitting alone chirping away, looking downward gazing upon him. He shrugs his shoulders, moving inside looking around as usual.

Ethel and Marie sit waiting as usual. He passes the center pew noticing someone sitting alone; not just someone, but a very attractive lady looking up at him, smiling.

He doesn't wait, approaching her with a smile upon his face announcing, "Good morning ... my name is Mike Cutler, we're pleased to have your presence this Sunday morning,"

"And, I'm Ailene Brooks, reporter from "The Indianapolis Star Newspaper," Mike Cutler."

"You're a reporter ... wow! This is something new for "Morris Avenue Baptist Church." Make your-self comfortable and If I can be of help ...just call my name and I'll answer," he says, turning away.

She reaches out stopping him. "But hold it a moment Mike; don't walk away ... maybe you can help."

Another casual look back and, "Then, tell me how I can help Ms. Brooks."

"I'm looking for a story Mike; something like a human-interest story!"

"A human-interest story ... Ms. Brooks?"

"Oh, you know ... a kind of story that makes you wonder, what life is all about is: tearing your heart out, making you want to sit up and think about!"

Mike looks up at her surprised. "But why here Ms. Brooks ... nothing unusual happens at "Morris Avenue Baptist Church.""

She looks up at him again, pausing briefly, "Well--- here's the way it is Mike---plain and simple. I'm here to find out what's happening in America ... what's happening to our churches all over this nation of ours. You know what I'm talking about; whatever happened to the old Billy Graham, George Beverly Shea type of meetings; the ones that made you stand up and shout... ready to pray your heart out!"

Wow, what a statement, he's thinking. Here sitting beside him is a reporter from the "Indianapolis Star newspaper," asking a question he's afraid to answer.

"But why important Ms. Brooks, everyone knows churches

are having a hard time watching their speech: preachers or priest afraid to say things they truly believe. It's all because of something called "Political Correctness." It's a brand-new world Ailene, a brand-new culture."

Ailene looks up again at him, "Well … that was quite a speech Mike. But I'll give some credit for …

"Credit for what Ailene?"

"You're sure not afraid to speak the truth about how you feel partner! In my book you hit it right on the head. But let me explain something Mike …

"Please do."

"I'm a reporter first: it's my job and I'm proud of it. But there are other things … important things that matter. I've made some notes, things of interest, and … surprisingly "Morris Avenue Baptist Church" is what I'm searching for," she says, moving beside him, looking up smiling.

Again, he looks her over, hesitant to say something he's thinking.

"I know what you're thinking Mike … but I don't mince words. I'm what people call a straight-out person; others call me a little more than aggressive person. I'm the kind of person that isn't afraid to call a spade a spade, no matter who it hurts!"

"That's good to know Ms. Brooks…you're different for sure," he barely mutters.

"But there's something else Mike …

"Tell me something else … I'm interested!"

"She looks up at him ever so pleasantly, "I'm crowding sixty Mike … and I'm still waiting!"

"Waiting for what Ms. Brooks?"

"Oh, you know Mike, every reporters dream; a big story, one that never goes away… making you wonder!"

His eyes roam looking her over again; her dress, her eyes,

her hair … he loves it. She wears a navy-blue business suit trimmed in white, about 5'5" in height, a figure fit for a model. She's a dream woman for sure … something special for a guy like Mike Cutler, he's thinking.

"But you look so young … so vibrant, never sixty Ms. Brooks; never would I have never guessed it."

She likes it! She likes the way he says things … someone she might like to know better; a friend for sure she's thinking.

"I'm aware I don't look sixty Mike. Tell me you're not interested in what you're gazing upon: I'll stand up before everyone and call you a dirty no-good for nothing liar right here in church!" She says, shrugging her shoulders, brushing back her dark long hair … flirtatiously.

Again, he likes it! He likes the way she talks, a fast talking right to the point kind of person.

She leans hard against him, taking his hand, smiling, "But the best part is---

"Yes, Ailene …

"I have dreams yet to come Mike. Maybe something wild, something different … who knows where or when!"

Mike can't wait, interrupting … "Tell me some more Ailene … the rest of your dreams."

She turns her head, looking up at him smiling," But the best part is … life isn't over, it's just beginning! I've a long way to go … dreams and more dreams…all about tomorrow!"

"You mean dreams yet to be filled … is that it Ailene?"

"I suppose you could call it that. There's always something you hope for: you know the kind of story every reporter dreams about!"

Again, he's speechless. It's the way she says things; things that make you think … maybe they're some of your own dreams, he's thinking.

Ailene moves even closer, grinning mischievously," But now, you tell me your hidden dreams, your desires, everything Mike," she whispers, touching his side playfully.

His face turns pale! He's caught in her trap with no way out. Maybe this is the time and the place to tell another, he's thinking. Tell his long-hidden secret; one that never goes away ... still haunting him.

"We all have dreams Ailene. Dreams of things to come ... fantasies of faraway places; places like somewhere I once read about ... or maybe dreamed about," he says, leaving her guessing.

"I like it, tell me the rest of it ... sounds interesting!"

He pauses, thinking of his never-ending dream, "I call it my, Shangri-La" ... my make-believe-place far away, somewhere over the mountain tops; but somehow ... I never find an ending. My dream always ends as suddenly as it began ... leaving me wondering and wondering, Ailene."

"Wondering about what Mike?"

He gazes up at her starry-eyed ... thinking back, "I always end-up wondering what else might be waiting for me somewhere on the other side of the mountain top!"

"But, that's good Mike! Its' called human interest at its best ... keeps you wondering. But there's one thing for sure Mike ...

"What's for sure Ailene?"

"You're definitely not the kind of person I ever expected to meet in church!" She says, leaving him guessing.

Mike looks again at her, waiting to hear more from someone so pretty.

"But, what are you truly looking for Ailene ... maybe something special, something you might be proud of. ...

She takes her time, gazing out elsewhere ..." You got me pal,

I really don't know! But ... maybe I'm looking for something simple... a person with a story worth telling."

"It's not me for sure, but maybe---

"Maybe what Mike? Now come on... open and tell me all about it," she says ... her dark blue eyes looking into his waiting ...

"It's my seemingly, wonderful, impossible friend; he saved me ... he really and truly saved me, Ailene!"

She comes against him hard, nudging him forward whispering, "Don't stop Mike! Tell me the rest of it; you know ... how, where, and when he saved you!"

"But this is different ... completely different!"

"How different? Now come on now Mike, tell me the rest of the story," she says, punching his side, urging him on.

Mike begins to stammer, searching for words ... "But how do you tell someone about an angel Ailene?" He asks, looking up to her waiting---

"Then ... tell me about other things; tell me what's happening at "Morris Avenue Baptist Church." I need a story bad ... something different for sure. If I find the right story ... it's Sunday morning front page story!"

"Oh, nothing special, but there is one thing ...

"Keep going ... all of it; tell me the one thing, Mike."

"Today as I was about to enter the church, I noticed a beautiful "Mourning Dove" sitting at the top of the belfry perched upon a cross."

"A Mourning Dove ... is that what you said?"

"Yes, Ailene ... a "Mourning Dove." But this "Mourning Dove" was different!"

"Different ... just how different, tell me Mike."

"The poor little thing just wouldn't quit chirping, on and on and on... staring down at me, causing me to wonder."

"Wonder about what Mike!"

"Oh! … I don't know for sure, but he never turned his head: he kept gazing down upon me as if I was somebody different, Ailene!"

"Then let's talk about something different Mike."

"Like what?"

"Like … what has happened to all the young people … are they so perfect they've all gone to heaven?"

"A thousand times I've asked myself the same Ailene … but never an answer."

She takes his hand, stopping him, "Then … let's talk about you, Mike---what's happening in your life; maybe a love affair hiding in the closet?" She asks, teasingly.

He wants to chuckle but doesn't. "Take a look at the one sitting in the front row waiting for me Ms. Brooks. Her name is Ethel---and boy, oh boy---- can she tell some stories?"

"Your lady friend … perhaps?"

Mike can't hold back, "Look again Ailene … she's twenty years my elder, my dearest friend ever!"

"Tell me some more … this might get interesting."

"She alone knew my loneliness, my sorrow. She alone invited me back to church after thirty miserable years going nowhere," he tries to explain … remembering how it all began, how it all happened.

"Wanta talk about it Mike?"

"Sometime maybe, but not today Ms. Brooks. It's a long story, hard to talk about."

"But, I'm a reporter, that's what I do. I listen to stories … if they're good I write the stories; that's the way it is Mike!"

Mike turns, looking away, "But I was bad Ailene … bad, lost without hope," he says, fighting back emotions.

She looks again at Mike. thinking … 'the guy is honest even if it hurts; maybe something to write about!"

"You're interesting for sure. Perhaps when the service is finished we'll talk outside … agreed Mike?"

"Agreed … I was thinking the same."

Her thoughts and mind move quickly; no time to say hello, no time to say good-bye. It's time to write the story, a human-interest story … a story for everyone!"

She opens her briefcase… taking off running toward the entrance, reaching a small wooden table near the doorway.

A moment later she's at her best … her very best; pecking away on something she calls … "the story of all stories" …" *The Dove That Never Stopped Chirping!"*

A week goes by … still nothing from Ailene. Mike can't help thinking of her. It's Sunday … time to find out.

Mike rushes to the newspaper box; seeing something spread out in bold letters across the front-page newspaper … "A *Miracle from Above … The Dove That Wouldn't Stop Chirping.*

The phone rings and Mike's heart begins to pound, waiting …

"Hello Mike … I've been wondering if my story pleased you. I wanted to write something about you; something touching … something that would that would soothe your troubled mind!"

"It was great, beyond my wildest expectations … better than anything I've ever read, Ailene!"

"I'm glad you liked it Mike … really I am. I've been thinking about you … I truly have been thinking about you Mike," she says warmly, making his heart flutter.

"What's on your schedule next Ailene--maybe some more of this human-interest material?" He asks, jokingly,

"Only the Lord knows. Maybe something different;

someplace crazy---like your dreams of Shangri-La ... or perhaps someplace high on a windy hill... sound exciting partner?" She asks, hanging up ... looking in the mirror, watching herself grinning mischievously.

CHAPTER 18

Someone to Think About

"The Lord is my light and my salvation; whom shall I fear?"

Psalm 27: 1

Days pass and still no word from anyone concerning the mission. Time has run out and Mike's anxiety runs high ... it's the night before D-Day.

He sits at home thinking of tomorrow, a day he has waited for so long. It reminds him of Nam ... heading out on a mission. But this is a different kind of enemy; an enemy warned about thousands of years ago. He tries to sleep but can't.

He thinks of David ... what he might do. He opens his Bible reading the Twenty-Third Psalm; his mind is soothed ... his worries are over.

Sunday church services are over, and Mike bids farewell to Ailene, Ethel, Marie, Brad and Mary. He discusses nothing, talks about taking care of some overdue business in Washington. They ask no questions, and he drives to the airport alone, wondering, "what lies ahead for someone like me ..." Mr. Nobody."

He sits alone inside the concourse at the "Indianapolis International Airport" thinking of his past ... unable to comprehend the reason for his selection. To Mike, it sounds like something unattainable. He thinks about Friend, his Guardian Angel. He thinks about Nate, the mystery guy he's yet to meet ... and he wonders and wonders, never stopping.

There's no rest during the trip. He watches a young couple holding hands across the aisle ... sneaking a kiss or two when none are watching. It reminds him of his own young love ... his great expectations. But now, his life is suddenly turned around without known reason. He only knows he's been selected to do God's work. keep the faith ... keep the faith, he tells himself over and over.

Time passes quickly, and soon he arrives at "Dulles International Airport," a few miles out of Washington; the city where laws are made governing the nation he loves so well.

He thinks of George Washington, Abraham Lincoln, Franklin Roosevelt and his hero, Ronald Reagan: all presidents ... residing here in the "White House."

He feels proud to be a part of a nation so great in history, but now he's beginning to worry; wondering if the nation he adores is the same-- a nation proud, blessed by God.

He stands outside the airport entrance waiting for a cab to deliver him to the "Mark Twain Hotel," ... until one stops in front of him. The driver gets out, grabs his baggage, and off they go whizzing by an endless crowd of traffic.

"Where to Buddy?" The driver asks, nonchalantly.

"The Mark Twain Hotel, please."

"Washington new to you friend?"

Mike pauses before answering, "It's been a while," he says, remembering Martha's words … friendly with the unknown."

He watches the scenery as they speed away without conversation. Twenty minutes later they pull up in front of the "Mark Twain Hotel," … where a bell-hop stands waiting. His baggage is placed on the curb and another bell-hop grabs it … taking off before Mike can say "hello or good by" … causing Mike to begin to realize … this is Washington, one of the busiest cities in the world … it isn't Indy.

Mike walks inside the hotel heading to register, where an older grey-haired gentleman greets him at the counter with a smile, politely asking, "And your name … please, sir?"

"I'm Mike Cutler. I have reservations for tonight and tomorrow night. Will you please check to see if I have mail waiting?"

The clerk hands him the card to room 217 … while checking his mail over and over … "Only this Mr. Cutler," he says, handing him an envelope with his name only.

Turning to move on, he stops suddenly, "Oh, by the way Mr. Cutler, I do remember several phone calls asking for you … you only, sir. They left no messages, but another couple called back again and again. Enjoy your stay at the Mark Twain, Mr. Cutler."

Mike heads for the elevator, while the bell-hop places his luggage in another elevator near-by. He tears open the envelope, finding a cashier's check bearing his name as the payee for five thousand dollars. This is a surprise, a welcome one for sure.

Soon, he's unlocking the door hearing the phone ringing. But, before he reaches it … the phone stops ringing.

The message light is lit, and Mike hears what sounds like a man's voice saying, 'glad you made it Mike,' … suddenly going dead, without leaving a name.

He gazes around the room, seeing it looks comfortable; maybe elaborate for someone like me … he's thinking. It's a well-maintained room with a Jacuzzi big enough for four, a bar with booze, a bath room with shower, an excellent view of the outside from the second floor.

"It's everything a guy like Mike could want, except the booze he no longer needs. He watches television the rest of the evening, heading to bed about eight.

So far everything is going smooth, as he begins to ask himself …" what's ahead for me tomorrow?"

The phone rings at midnight, as Martha said it would. "This is Mike Cutler, to whom I am speaking," he asks sleepily.

A female sounding voice responds quickly, "I'm Grace, your contact here in Washington. Be at the "Sampson Building" on Massachusetts Avenue at ten A. M. tomorrow morning."

"Any cabbie knows the place. You'll be able to recognize it by the four large marble pillars showing at the front. Go to the tenth floor, room seven, ring the buzzer; someone will answer."

"They will ask for your identity, have it with you. After your identity has been cleared … you will meet your representative and receive your indoctrination … clear enough Mr. Cutler?"

"Clear enough, look for me Grace."

The phone rings at six … "This is the front desk, Mr. Cutler; it's six in the morning as you requested sir," a sleepy voice announces, lowly.

"Thank you so much my friend," Mike replies … wondering who made the request; assuring himself it wasn't him, Mike Cutler.

A quick breakfast and he heads to the "Sampson Building" … ready for action. Minutes later he stands outside looking up admiring four huge pillars of stone; what a work of art he's thinking, but what lies inside waiting for him … he's beginning to worry about.

Mike begins to think about another "Sampson" … the one in the Bible he's read about so often; the one who lost his long dark hair succumbing to his earthly desires and pleasures; with a raging beauty called, "Delilah."

He carries only his briefcase loaded with papers. And, soon he's standing inside the seeing a magnificent work of art; but not a single soul waiting to greet him.

He looks upward seeing cameras pointing downward, viewing the large entrance near the elevator. His eyes roam— encasing his surroundings, wondering … 'what's next for me to see in this great city called *Washington*.'

Up, up, travels the elevator reaching the tenth floor, where he's supposed to be. He steps outside glancing around seeing cameras posted everywhere, but still, not a soul nowhere!

Down the long marble hallway, he sees room seven… his place of destiny.

He touches the outside buzzer and a voice from inside answers quickly … '*Come inside, Mr. Cutler: its' indoctrination time!*"

Mike opens the door and from atop the ceiling some light shines brightly, displaying a drawing of Moses covering the eastern wall. Hanging further down upon the wall is an ancient looking scroll displaying the "Ten Commandments" in big shining letters.

Row after row of metal filing cabinets are lined against the wall. At the far end of the eastern wall; another entrance leading into an office area … without human presence.

He continues … following bold marked arrows along the path until … far off to the western end of the large room is an enclosed area; what looks like an office designed to withstand an earthquake. Looking ahead, a large poster outside displays the words, "Enter Friend."

He pauses, wondering…

"Is it possible it could be someone like my Guardian Angel, or maybe someone like me … a guy alone in Washington searching for the unknown I'm about to meet somewhere."

He makes his move, pressing the buzzer … standing outside waiting …

"Enter and take a seat," a rough graveled voice bellows loudly from inside somewhere.

Slowly, Mike opens the door confronting something unexpected; a large decorated room with picture after picture of famous scenes of history.

On the far side of the room is a large mahogany desk, where someone sits in a huge swivel chair turned backward.

Smoke rises from the chair … indicating someone is smoking more than normal. And suddenly … the swivel chair turns facing Mike directly.

Wow! Right in his face, staring at him sits former Colonel Nathaniel P Roberts,"101st Airborne; someone he can never forget.

His heart begins to flutter, staring up at him, noticing a change; once a massive figure that could tear you apart, but now the once blond hair turned silver. That's Nate … a man destined for a place in military history.

A big Cuban cigar protrudes from the corner of his mouth; his face, a grin he'll never forget. He wears a dark suit, open white shirt, a golden necklace with two large diamonds … fitted tightly around his huge bull-like neck; causing Mike to look again, wondering …

"Semper-fi Mike Cutler!" He bellows, clearing the air around him. "I've heard some scuttle-butt about you lad …

but the biggest shock of all was when I learned you've finally decided to get your act together. Am I right," he asks, puffing away ... looking up to him chuckling.

Mike can only look up at Nate, unable to speak ... still wondering. Never did he dream he would be facing the guy who helped load him into a chopper thirty years ago in Nam; a place of memories ... all of them bad!

He stiffens, standing at attention saluting ... without thinking, "Colonel sir!" He bellows, loud and clear ... gazing into his eyes still wondering ...

Nate stands gazing up at him, placing his left hand upon Mike's shoulder, "None of that kind of stuff Mike ... Nam is over. From this moment forward, I'm Nate; no saluting necessary."

Mike breathes easy ... facing him directly, "Thank you Nate ... expected no less," he says, relaxing at ease.

Nate glances up toward the clock pointing to a chair across from him, "Time, we get started Mike, the best part will come later."

"What's the best part Nate?"

A grin covers his face, "The part you could never understand Jar-head ... taking orders; that's the best part!"

Mike lowers his head ... never replying, thinking, "this is the Nate ... the Nate I once knew; it's him all over, God help me!

"We're moving out, things are happening all over Mike. I'm not sure what you know, but you're in the middle of it... believe me you are!" He says, trying to hold back, but can't, chuckling.

Mike looks again at him ... hard as usual, "That's news ... not the kind of news I had hoped for ... but it's news sir!"

A big grin crosses Nate's face immediately. "Don't worry lad, I've got some more good news for you."

"Now, what are you talking about Nate?"

"Only this lad, you're part of us like it or not! Now do we understand each other Jarhead?"

Mike stiffens … staring hard at him, "We understand each other Nate; always have and always will. But in case you're interested, I've heard the same before … remember Nate."

"What words, Mike?"

"You know what I mean … like it or not Jarhead" … the same words I was tired of hearing in Nam!"

Nate watches him stiffen, standing before him as he once did in Nam; wanting to spout back … something to hurt him, but can't find the words.

Nate looks up at him, grinning, "You know Jar-head … you're lucky I wasn't permanently assigned to your outfit!"

"Just what does that mean sir?"

"I would have straightened your butt out for sure lad. I can't believe it … I just can't believe it! You're the same old Mike I left in Nam. You're never going to change … never Mike!" He's shouting, moving from his chair, chuckling even louder.

Mike's head lowers. He wants to be angry, but can't … "I'm sorry to show my anger Nate."

"But, there's something about you I'll never forget Mike; it never changes … always the same …

"What's always the same Nate?"

"Your short-fuse lad, you were born with it: It's gonna haunt you till, the day you die lad!"

Mike lowers his head, looking down, "But I'm trying to stop Nate---really I am," he barely mumbles.

Nate walks from around his desk, placing his hand upon Mike's shoulder, smiling, "But never worry Mike … everything works for the best on this team," he says, surprisingly.

And … what a shock it is! He was expecting a few curse

words, a few insults; maybe a quick good-bye with a final pat on the back: all from a guy he once feared more than the enemy.

Nate stands rigid, gazing down at the floor ... searching for something different; maybe soothing words ...

"Let's start over Mike. Time is precious, and your about to find out just how precious. There's information coming with you in the middle of it. I'll put it to you plain and simple ... the way you always wanted it."

"I'm waiting sir."

"Our mission is the same. We work as a team for the same leader! We're brothers in Christ ... looking forward to His coming. You know who "Him" is I hope!"

Mike's grin turns to a smile. Nate is human after all; not the same guy he last saw in Nam threatening to have him court-martialed; but always defending him in trouble.

His thoughts ramble on, searching for words he might understand.

"Yes, I know "Him" ... I know Him personally Nate," Mike says, humbly standing before him ... waiting!"

His words ring loud and clear, causing Nate take notice, thinking ... 'maybe he is a different Mike; not the Mike I remember crawling into a chopper cursing me with the vilest language ever!"

"We don't have time for the past Mike; time we talk about tomorrow!"

"I'm ready sir."

"I'm with you today only, orders can change in a moment. We live in one crazy world Mike; no longer a happy world like it once was. And Nam ... it's hard for me to say the words, but time we get over it... Jarhead!"

"But not forgotten Nate!"

"Agreed! From this day forward, till the day we die … ok marine?"

"It's ok with me, we'll do it your way till the day we die Nate."

"You'll be here only a couple of days … plan your time well. You're about to get an education you'll remember the rest of your life. When your mission is completed … there's one thing for sure …

"Sure … about what Nate?"

He rises from his chair, moving around his desk confronting him. "Never again will you be the same person standing here before me today. You'll be changed … changed forever Mike!" Nate says, leaving him guessing.

"But, there's something else Nate, something important …

"I'm listening … a pleasure I've never enjoyed with you before Mike."

"This may sound difficult for you to believe sir, but I've no ambition to be the same person you remember from Nam. I'm the least of the least, the worst of the worst … but I've changed Nate!"

"Nate holds his breath waiting for him to laugh, but he doesn't. He can only stare at him, beholding something different. He's not the same foul mouth marine wanting to kill 'em all and then some; he's sounding like a "down-to-earth-born-again Christian."

"I'm proud of you Mike. No matter where our paths may turn, I'll remember Phu Bai; your unrelenting will to win. I loathed you … despised you as a dangerous animal: when it was over … I was always wishing I had a dozen more like you," he says, causing Mike to back away, looking again wondering … 'can this be the same Nate I knew back in Nam … wanting to choke me to death before the entire company?'

They sit gazing at one another … till Nate breaks the silence, pointing to the chair next to him. "It's time for business… serious business Mike!"

"I'm ready Nate."

"Everything you're told within the concept of this building is critical. There's things you must be able to recite in a second; life threatening matters … death in a moment! Do you understand what I'm saying Mike?"

"I do understand what you're saying Nate."

Nate moves closer, reading something from a paper … "But there's something else Mike … something I just became aware of …

Mike looks up at him smiling … "Whatever it is, just name it!"

"Neither you or your partner will contact anyone back home till your mission is completed … questions Mike?"

"Well----there is this one question Nate … I'd like to know who assigned me to this mission?"

Nate wants to laugh but doesn't: he's choking on the big Cuban cigar, enjoying the moment.

"Well Mike … it wasn't me for sure, but I notice you quote some words like Paul the Apostle might have said."

Mike begins to smile, *"I'm reading your mind. I know what you're thinking. I'm the least of the least, the worst of the worst; that was me* and then some Nate!"

"How's that Mike?"

"Paul was nobody before he met Jesus. I was nobody till I met the same. But this talk about a journey to no-where … it's driving me nuts thinking about it!"

"But don't forget the prize when it's over Mike!"

"Now what are you trying to tell me?"

Nate turns facing Mike, "*It means a life in heaven forever Mike … what better deal could anyone have?*"

Mike can only stare at him, looking again at him stunned.

"But tell me Mike …

"Tell you what?"

"Your secret … you gotta have a secret!"

"But I don't have a secret Nate … honest I don't," he barely mutters.

"Sure, you do Mike … everyone has a secret of some kind. Tell me what happened in your miserable life. The last time I saw you … you hated everyone. You carried a chip on your shoulder like I've never seen before!"

Mike lowers his head thinking back to Nam again … "You're right again Nate. I hated the world and everything within it. But I met an angel … my "Guardian Angel" He helped me Nate … oh, how he helped me!" Mike says … as his voice drifts away … ending.

"I believe you. It had to be a miracle; a real down to earth-shaking-miracle to change a guy like you Mike!"

Mike's head lowers even further … "I know what Friend told me and I believed Nate. He looked me in the eye and told me I was one of "His Chosen" … and it frightened me as I've never been frightened before. Just imagine, me … the worst of the worst, one of His Chosen!"

Nate moves slowly to the other side of the office picking up his briefcase, turning to face Mike, "But I remind you again Mike, it took a miracle … an absolute miracle to change a wild and crazy marine like you, my Lad!"

"You're right again … nothing but a miracle to save a guy like me; but He really and truly did Nate!"

"Take a break, it's time for you to travel!"

"Travel where Nate?"

"Wherever Mike. But I'd bet my last cigar it's bound to be interesting wherever you are!"

"But you Nate … what about you?" He shouts, as Nate heads for the door leaving.

"God only knows, but now it's time to say good-by and God bless you, till we meet again … Jar-head!"

CHAPTER 19

Thirty-Nine Steps to the Upper Room

For their stood beside me this night the angel of God, whose I am, and whom I serve,

Acts 27: 23

Thirty minutes pass and back to work ... but not with Nate. Another person, about six feet three or four sits in the big swivel chair dressed in a long white shining robe ready to take his place.

From first glance it shows this person is different; far and away different! His long dark hair hangs down to his shoulder, teeth shine as pearls ... eyes burning as fire. Mike is taken ... looking up at him wondering ...

Slowly, he rises from his big swivel chair, "My name is Reuben Mike. I've good news for you; words to make you happy," he says, ever so pleasantly.

Mike is shocked again; nothing but angels everywhere. His

mind is reeling with questions, but afraid to ask, 'what this be, maybe another episode like the first, meeting Friend?"

He moves closer, looking up to Rueben, "You have something to please me Rueben ... some good news maybe...

"I do. It's time you meet your partner, someone you'll pleased to see... someone you're familiar with Mike!"

Quickly he turns pushing a buzzer announcing, "Mike is here, bring forth his partner."

"Yes Reuben ... a sweet voice from the other side says, making Mike wonder ...

Mike rises from his chair waiting, and suddenly ... the door burst open causing him to get his breath; he's gazing into the dark blue eyes of Ailene Brooks ... *reporter for the Indianapolis Star newspaper.*

"This is an unexpected pleasure Ms. Brooks ... a pleasant one for sure," he says, regaining his composure.

"It's a pleasure for me too Mike. We'll talk about it later," she barely mutters.

A couple of quick glances toward Reuben, and they're settled at his desk ready for business.

"I'll inform you of things ahead of you, details and places you'll learn later," he says bluntly, causing them to look again at him, wondering ...

He hesitates, wiping his brow, beginning again, "The mission you're about to participate is special: it comes from Him up above ... I'm the messenger!" He says, with a voice, like nothing they've never heard before.

Suddenly...it's nothing but silence between the three of them... till he picks up papers lying upon his desk reading them: finally wiping his brow again ... facing them. ...

Ailene doesn't wait, moving close to him, "Don't hold back Reuben ... tell us what's ahead of us."

His eyes turn fiery red, facing Ailene. "But there's something that must be said …

"Yes Reuben …

Reuben moves from his chair guiding Ailene to the window, staring upward, beginning to speak, "Jesus … The Son of God will never leave you or forsake you Ailene: he will watch over you, protect you throughout eternity!"

She can only stare at Reuben, afraid to speak, moving even closer touching his robe, "But you sound as if you're about to leave us for good Reuben …

"You're correct my dear, I am leaving you. It's time we say good-by and farewell, till we meet again … tomorrow!"

"But Reuben, what about us and tomorrow; when is tomorrow Rueben?" Ailene shouts.

Rueben turns glancing back, and with a wave of his hand and a big smile she's never shown before, he's shouting, "Oh yes, to mortals it's always tomorrow; to ones looking down from above … it's forever and ever. But now … the candle-light blinks for me alone; farewell till we meet again … forever and forever, my darling!"

Mike can't wait, running to him, asking, "But … where do we go from here Rueben?"

"I thought you knew Mike. When you're finished step outside to the "Upper Room."

"But the "Upper Room" … is where Reuben?" Ailene asks, quickly.

"Follow the cross darling … follow it thirty-nine steps to the "Upper Room"; there you'll find the answer waiting for you," Reuben shouts, never looking back.

He's gone, and they move together, never talking. A quick backward glance and they head for the door ready to find the cross leading upward; thirty-nine steps to the "Upper Room."

Outside, looking around it's empty, except far over to the side some lights blink; sending a streak of light displaying a golden cross pointing the way upward.

They move near the cross nervously expecting anything, whatever. Numbers begin to flash upon the long narrow wall. They stop, gazing around nervously, joining hands, counting steps. They ascend upward to the very top; where an arrow shows room 39 … their flight up the stairs over.

From out of nowhere … another majestic structure of stone appears just ahead waiting. They stop---gazing upon a sign at the door in bold letters; "Remove your shoes … I'm waiting."

Only a moment, till they're sitting on the floor removing their shoes ready to enter. Their heart pounds, faster and faster as they move forward searching … stopping abruptly; staring before an altar without blemish … made from mahogany … the finest wood ever.

At the center of the altar sits a huge golden candelabrum with seven candles: the middle candle looks to be gold, shaped as a cross … spreading light throughout the area around them.

Hanging down from the large marble ceiling, a beautiful silver chain dangles up and over the altar; while a beautiful silver dish holding sweet smelling, incense burns throughout. They stop …glancing at one another wondering; 'who or what they're about to encounter.'

Again …their thoughts run wild wondering …" could this be a holy-place … a place like the *"Holy of Holies,"* or maybe a place like the *"Inner-Sanctuary,"* a place they've read about in the Bible!" They bend downward kneeling in fullest of reverence without going further.

And from out of no-where there's a loud resounding bang, followed with a thumping sound from the other end of the long mahogany table.

Quickly, they stand gazing throughout, seeing Friend; sitting alone in a huge golden chair waiting. He's dressed in a long bright white linen robe; arms wide open... beckoning them come closer.

Slowly, he rises from his chair confronting Mike, shouting, "Mike Cutler, the eye of the Lord dwelleth upon you... time you prepare to serve Him!"

Mike's body goes numb ... looking up at Friend speechless.

Quietness reigns throughout, till Friend turns facing Ailene, smiling, "Ailene Brooks, the eye of the Lord dwells upon you; time you prepare to serve Him," he shouts, causing Ailene's body to tremble all over.

His eyes close, hardly breathing, whispering, "Quiet, Ailene, quiet ... His holy presence is among us. Stand ... the both of you stand. Bow your head, make the sign of the cross; show your reverence to Him only. You're standing upon holy ground, about to receive His protection for the remainder of your days upon earth ... serving our Lord and God only!"

Wow! Magnificent words, spoken by an angel; strong and powerful words, sending a message about their future.

Still they listen and listen ... finally understanding the words; all is well within God's most holy of sanctums.

Bowing his head reverently, Friend moves slowly toward the front of the altar speaking solemnly, *"Bow-down upon your knees Chosen Ones, you're standing upon holy ground: His presence is among you!"*

His words are cutting ... digging deep into their heart and soul; words never dreamed about; coming strong and fast from an angel.

They glance at one another wondering; while their bodies shake ... uncontrollably. His words sink deep and deeper into their very mind; reminding them of something Jesus might have said to his Disciples at the "Last Supper"; or maybe before His crucifixion at a place called "Calvary."

All is silent within the "Samson Building", till Friend stands gazing upon them … his fiery eyes blazing.

"I carry a message to the both of you from Him … our God up above looking down up us," he announces, with a voice booming … rocking the "Sampson Building."

Again, Ailene's body turns life-less, while Mike holds her hand afraid to look, where Friend stands over them, smiling.

Mike turns again … seeing the candelabrum's seven candles burning brightly; while the smell of sweet smelling incense grows stronger by the moment.

They move near the altar, performing the sign of the cross; while Friend stands over them removing a beautiful mahogany box from a golden case, … kissing it … adoringly. Slowly he opens the box removing two golden necklaces, sparkling as diamonds.

It's silence … deadly silence throughout; except for the ticking of an ancient looking clock hanging upon the wall … formed in the shape of a cross. They wait, and they wait … while Friend yet stands before the cross, his face glowing … showing his reverence.

And suddenly, a booming voice echoes throughout… "Bow your head and remain kneeling most honored ones, I'm about to fit each of you with this golden necklace I hold up before you; touched by our Lord in heaven, looking down upon us!"

But still … they wonder! They wonder if they're in another world, a world they've often dreamed about. They wonder if maybe another heaven, the third heaven; the one Paul the Apostle talked about. They think and think again, beginning to recognize … "This is the time, this is the place, there's no way out!"

They're spellbound … kneeling in awe in the presence of God; praying their very heart and soul out!

They want to contain themselves, but useless. It's their moment of all moments, as tears drip downward exposing their very heart, their very soul; everything for the love they have for the one above; they're God in heaven looking down upon them.

Slowly Friend bends downward removing one of the golden necklaces, placing it gently around Ailene's neck bowing, kissing the cross: thinking back to a place where he and ten thousand other angels, stood watching and waiting … for the "Son of God" to call upon them at a place called Calvary!

Friend repeats the ceremony the same with Mike. His hands rest softly upon his head, speaking loud and clear…

"You, Mike Cutler, and you, Ailene Brooks are His Chosen Ones: you're kneeling before the altar in the presence of "God Almighty." Therefore, in the name of the Father, Son and Holy Spirit… I commend you to do His will: perform His work from this moment forward. Wear the cross as your sword against evil; never remove it … till your mission is over!"

Again, Friend stands above them at the altar, beginning, "Arise and place your hand upon the altar of God Ailene!"

His words are strong, spoken magnificently. Never in their wildest dreams could they behold a ceremony so great; filled with sacredness beyond human comprehension.

Frightened, still kneeling beside Ailene, Mike waits to hear his name called. His head remains bowing, listening, never moving.

A brief pause and Friend places his hand upon Mike, his head bowing downward before the altar of God speaking softly and reverently, "Mike Cutler, look into my eyes but say nothing, I've a message for you … *With His will …, I release you from your burden!*"

Again…Mike's body shutters, confused, left wondering! He doesn't know the meaning. He peers upward looking at Friend barely muttering, "With His will … I release you…what does this mean, Friend?"

"It means the burden you placed upon yourself the day you left the church; it's over and forgotten. From this moment forward … you will never refer to yourself as, "Mr. Nobody": you're one of His Chosen Mike!"

Again, long moments of silence. Moments to think; erase the shock! Tears fall from tired looking eyes pleading, "I understand Friend: I do understand! Thank God … I do understand!"

Mike moves close to Ailene grasping her hand. Legs and arms once weak and trembling… now firm and strong waiting.

They begin to smile, gazing upon something sacred; the neckless from God … something with wonder-working-power, filled with love and grace beyond human comparison!

CHAPTER 20

Finals

; and at the ninth hour I prayed in my house, and, behold, a man stood before me in bright clothing ...

Acts 10: 30

A thirty-minute break and back to work in what used to be Reuben's office, but now, someone new sits behind the desk; a manly figure dressed in a shining solid white linen suit prepared for business.

He's a massive figure with long silver hair dropping down to his shoulder ... eyes sparkling, burning as fire.

He looks across the table, introducing himself as "Raymond ... messenger of the highest"

Raymond removes folders from a brief-case, spreading them out before them, speaking softly, "Ailene ... Mike, tell me what you're seeing."

"It's the village Berchtesgaden, Hitler's home away from

home in the Bavarian Alps during WW11," Mike says, without waiting.

They open folder after folder, viewing atrocities never imagined; gas chambers, naked dead bodies thrown one upon one into holes of dirt. All of it during the time of Hitler and his reign of terror upon Jews, the world over. An hour goes by ... still they sit looking at pictures inside the "Eagles Nest."

Another hour goes by and the showing is over.

Again, Raymond begins lecturing. "Moving further into your mission you will observe and learn; miss something ... will cost you dearly. You'll learn the history, the torment, the people; all who occupied the "Eagles Nest" ...a time of war ... hell on earth, never to be forgotten!"

"But, why the "Eagles Nest?" ...Ailene asks, interrupting.

Raymond rises from the big swivel chair, his fiery eyes blazing ... "The "Eagles Nest" is a never lasting symbol of horror unimaginable...filled with the occult, demons, all that goes with it. When your mission is completed, the "Eagles Nest" will no longer exist! He's shouting, causing them to shudder.

Ailene can only stare at him wondering ... asking, "But the mission ... tell us when it begins Raymond."

"But Ailene my most beloved one ... you and Mike are the ones who will guide "Operation Un-Holy Ground", it's your mission my darling!"

She rises slowly, feeling scolded without reason, "But, please Raymond ... help me. I was thinking as a mortal, not someone special as you Raymond!" She says, humbly, causing Raymond's eyes to drop, focusing downward.

"Your move out time from "Dulles International Airport" is scheduled for tomorrow night," he says, pointing his finger toward Mike, sitting beside Ailene waiting ...

"A question ... Mike?"

"Berlin ... what about Berlin, Raymond?"

"Move out time is the night after arrival. From Berlin you will be moved to the village, "Berchtesgaden" ... near the foot of "Kalkstein Mountain.""

"You will stay the night at a local inn. Your mission will move into action twenty-four hours later: ending when the clock strikes twelve, midnight!"

A moment of silence, while Mike and Ailene sit lost in a sea of questions, meditating, searching for answers... while Raymond continues ... never ending.

"Prepare for the worse! Pray without ceasing! When your mission is over: our Lord and his angels will look down upon you rejoicing in heaven!"

Again, they exchange glances, marveling the way Raymond says things; heavenly things, 'God ... angels rejoicing forever.

"But ... Halloween, Berchtesgaden, why Raymond?" Ailene asks, nervously.

Raymond's face is different, his eyes no longer sparkling. He's looking down upon her barely uttering, "It's Satan's holiday Ailene. It's a time to celebrate the killing of millions of Jews ... God's chosen people! It's a holiday filled with blood, murder, debauchery; a place remembered for devil-worship ... along with Hitler and the occult!"

Silence all over, till "But, my job Raymond, my obligation to the Star newspaper," Ailene asks.

He moves toward her, holding his arms out stopping her, "You will never write the story! Your memory will wilt, disappear as blades of grass; grass that never was to be ... never will be Ailene!"

Again, she stares at Raymond, looking toward Mike

shocked again. She sits quietly wondering, *"How something so great, so historical, will be lost… never heard from again."*

She glances away to the side searching … till, "But why can't I write the story Raymond?" She asks lowly.

"It's the history my dear: a dreadful most evil history!" He announces loudly, knowing her thoughts … waiting,

"Understand Ailene, no you don't understand; you or the world around you will never understand the killing, the raping, the dying… begging for mercy!"

Ailene has struck a point with Raymond, a painful point she wishes she could take back. She joins her hands with his… wondering if she has offended him.

"I'm sorry Raymond, truly I'm sorry," she says again and again, wishing she could take back her question.

"But the mystery … the reverence, why Raymond, why?" Mike asks.

"Step outside with me, the both of you," he says … beckoning them to follow.

Outside in an open area he joins their hands with his, raising their arms upward; while deadly silence reigns throughout.

Raymond raises his arms upward speaking words only he can understand; words they've never heard before, holy words with mountains of reverence.

Moments of tenseness … till Raymond lowers his arms smiling, "Your mission stands ready, all is clear, problem over," he says, heading back to his desk sitting … waiting.

Mike follows Raymond, his mind reeling, "You mean it was Him … He told you this Raymond?"

Raymond doesn't wait, looking down upon them smiling, "The both of you will be at your post on the night of Halloween, ready to destroy the one and only …" *Satanic Bible!*

Shock and more shock, till ... "You mean Ailene and I only Raymond?"

"The two of you together. You'll lead the way ... stopping them from performing their mission. Your mission is under the guidance of our Father in heaven ... Jehovah: their mission is under Satan ... and all who follow him."

"When your mission is over ... a thousand legions of angels will sing glory to God in the highest; praising his name forever and ever!"

Again, they're frightened! Something far beyond their wildest dreams is about to take place. They're about to be part of the other world----the unknown world; a world of demons and principalities, told by Paul the Apostle 2000 years ago.

They move inside and again Ailene floods Raymond with question after question.

"But Raymond, a Satanic Bible ... our Holy Bible says nothing about a devil's Bible: sounds like something Satan himself might come up with!"

"Stop as you are ... say no more; there's no need to, Ailene!" Raymond shouts, raising his hand, stopping her.

"But, I don't understand Raymond ... I can't understand!"

His fiery eyes sparkle. "But Ailene, you've found the secret; the answer to your very own question!"

"Impossible Raymond, impossible," she's barely able to mutter.

"Raymond moves close to her, "But possible when the devil authors his own Bible Ailene," he says, causing her to back away, trembling, thinking of it.

Silence, deadly silence all over, meditating the consequences of something so evil; the devil himself writing the future.

"The success of your mission has never been doubted. We've come a long way, the easy part over. Prepare yourselves for an adventure into the unknown: a view into darkness only messengers of God are privy to view," Raymond says, gazing upward toward heaven, praying.

Long moments of wondering, wishing, hoping, and it's over! Raymond stands tall looking down upon them as someone holy; while they begin moving away, afraid to stand closer.

Suddenly, they stop ... gazing upon one another, beginning to realize ... Raymond's world is a different world: it's a world filled with angels, demons, still fighting a war that began in heaven thousands of years ago.

Ailene moves close to Raymond, bowing before him. She holds out her hands before him, pleading, "I'm sorry Raymond, truly I'm sorry. We're not as you Raymond, we're only mortals sent by Him to serve you," she says sadly, looking up again at him ... waiting.

Raymond looks down upon her smiling, "All is well Ailene, we serve the same master. This very moment the Satanic Bible lies hidden within a vault at the "National Library in Stockholm Sweden!"

Mike's hands begin to tremble, thinking of it, "Stockholm Sweden ... is that what I heard you say Raymond?", he barely can mumble.

"Yes Mike ..." Stockholm Sweden!" But, it's about to be moved to the "Eagles Nest," atop Kalkstein Mountain" ... near the village "Berchtesgaden."

"But Raymond, it can't be; it doesn't make sense! Why expose the Bible now Raymond?"

"Open your mind Mike! Think of history ... Bible history. There's a place called heaven, a place called earth!"

"But why here on earth Raymond, that's what I wanta know ... just why here on earth?"

"It's only part of it Mike. The war in heaven is over: here on earth it's never ending!"

"Mike doesn't wait, moving close to him, asking politely, "But now you're smiling Raymond, what makes you so happy?"

"Things are looking up! It's coming to an end, about to be over Mike!"

"But when Raymond, when...

"Only our God in heaven knows the answer Mike. But it's about to be over; Jesus ... The Son of God is about to come back to earth again!"

Mike is smiling as never before, beginning to understand; Jesus, the Son of God, will soon be splitting the heavens, coming back again: just as he promised his disciples 2000 years ago upon the "Mount of Olives."

On and on it continues; information flowing from an angel about another time, another place; a place they hardly know about.

Mike looks up at Raymond confused again. "Now tell us the rest of it ... all of it Raymond."

"Your mission is here. No longer must you wait for an enemy to appear. Satan's disciples stand waiting for his call; a call to perform a ceremony of allegiance to him only. They're prepared to follow him into the pits of hell, Mike!"

Mike sits staggered, wiping his brow again and again, bewildered; still wondering ..." how can this be, a guy like me talking to an angel ... as if I'm one of them ... the most holy ones!"

Raymond watches Mike staring downward bewildered again. He moves beside him, tapping his shoulder, "But you will understand Mike. You're one of His Chosen! You're a player on a mission; a mission that only our God in heaven knows the reason!"

"But Raymond! Raymond! Please tell me more," Mike is pleading, begging.

"Everything is falling in place, the clock-work is perfect Mike!" Raymond is shouting joyfully, raising his arms upward toward heaven.

Ailene moves even closer to Raymond; a worried look clouds her dark blue eyes, "But tell us more Raymond ... please tell us more."

"You're about to view the destruction of the once famous "Eagles Nest" in the village of Berchtesgaden. A celebration is planned; planned for the most hideous Halloween ever. It will be the Halloween of all Halloweens, planned by the devil himself Ailene!"

Long ... frightening moments, and Mike regains his poise, "But why so important Raymond, there has to be a reason!"

"Maybe not important to you, but to Satan it's everything ... It's the timing, Mike!"

"But the timing ... I don't understand! What's timing got to do with now Raymond?" Ailene asks, confused again.

His eyes begin to sparkle, staring down upon her, "The time has come Ailene, it's time to look up. Soon the earth will shake, mountains will tumble. His mighty power will be known to all, throughout eternity!"

Ailene moves close to him, her tender voice shaking, barely muttering, "Blessed be our Lord above Raymond ... we've waited for this day forever!"

Raymond gazes down upon her, placing his hand upon her shoulder, saying so pleasantly, "Ailene darling, it's time you prepare yourself, time to get ready. Open your eyes ... hold the necklace against your heart: it's power unthinkable, your life-line to heaven," he says, heading for the door at break-time.

CHAPTER 21

And Then ... There's Grace

If I have told you of earthly things, and ye believe not, how shall ye believe, if I tell ye of heavenly things?"

John 3: 12

A ten-minute break and they're back seated with Raymond beginning again

"False prophets will come displaying love and affection; learn to discern them, avoid them bitterly."

"But how do we recognize them Raymond?" Ailene asks quickly.

"Think Ailene! Remember your teaching, your Bible teaching!"

"You mean... within they're nothing but ravenous wolves ready to devour you?"

"Yes dear, along with government traitors betraying they're very own."

"But the part I'll play in this mission... Raymond?" Mike asks, moving beside her.

"Oh yes ... your part, Mike! You'll be among them ready to greet them... armed like nobody ever!"

"Ready to greet them with what Raymond?" Mike asks, quickly. ...

He takes his hand, pulling him closer, "You'll greet them with the neck-less dangling down from around your neck: it's power unthinkable, Mike!"

Again, he wipes sweat from brow ... hands cold as ice shaking. He runs his hand over the necklace feeling its' power, magnifying its' beauty; while his eyes open widely, gazing upward toward heaven marveling its' wonders.

Raymond watches him waiting until, "Use the necklace only when necessary Mike. You're living at the end of the age... about to witness history in the making!"

"End of the age ... about to witness history ... Raymond," ... he can barely mutter.

"Yes Mike. The fulfilment of "The Book of Revelation" ... the coming of the devils most fearsome; false prophets, antichrist ... millions of followers waiting!"

They sit mesmerized even thinking about it, till ..." "Then what Raymond?" Mike asks, holding his breath, waiting.

"It's debauchery at its worst, beyond human imagination; Satan's last hurrah ... his final party. Mike!"

Ailene moves closer, looking up to him, "But Mike and I together ... our part Raymond?" She barely can mumble.

His arms open wide, a smile shows unnoticed, "Smile and be proud "Chosen Ones". ... you're about to deliver the first blow!"

Silence! Nothing, but silence all over till, "But when will all this end Raymond?" Ailene asks. nervously.

"The day you meet Jesus my dear, the day you're home forever!"

On and on it goes, Raymond showing the way explaining, "Devil worshipers by the hundreds, all at the "Eagles Nest" waiting; ready to proclaim their allegiance to Satan.

Raymond stops, moving to the window peering upward toward heaven. Long tense moments, and he returns standing before them smiling.

"But, all praise unto God up above … they'll never leave the mountain top: the party of all parties will be over, forever and ever," he says smiling.

Mike pulls Ailene close to him" Does this mean what I think it does pretty lady?"

"It has to be Mike, no other way to say it!"

They remember Martha's words, "we win," and the thought of it rings home: knowing the outcome before it begins.

Ailene holds her hand outward joining Raymond's hand, "But, Raymond … Oh how I love Him! I feel His love, the beauty He brings me, but why do I fear tomorrow," she asks, begging.

"But you're mortal my dear! You're blessed by the one who has conquered hell and all beyond. But, tell me your weapon Ailene … the most powerful weapon ever!"

He waits … but never an answer.

"It's the cross Ailene! It's power unthinkable, filled with love and glory," he shouts, causing her to move away, frightened again.

Time passes without notice, both tired, never resting. They wonder if they're in another world, maybe a dream-world; one they've read about, but never want to see.

The very thought of something so evil… a Satanic Bible

written by the devil himself: unbelievable to mortals upon earth, but not to ones up above … waiting.

"But the others … the ones were yet to meet Raymond," Mike asks, growing more and more weary.

"Yes, the others … they too are Chosen, Mike!"

"But when Raymond?"

"As you were chosen, from the very beginning; before you lay in your mother's womb, Mike."

"And my final question Raymond, a question I dream about hoping it's true. I want to believe it will happen, but if I could only be sure ….

"Yes Mike …

"You tell me you were with me from the beginning and I believe you. You tell me you're an angel sent by God, and I believe you. But, the one everyone desires to know …

"Yes Mike …

"I've read about angels, how they serve God here on earth …

"Yes, Mike …

"But, Ailene and I, it must be different, Raymond … It's just gotta be different----

"Brilliant Mike, brilliant! You see things others wonder about; it pleases me greatly!"

"But the answer Raymond… please Raymond please---

Again, he gazes upward searching the heavens. His eyes close, wiping sweat from his brow meditating … turning to face them.

"But soon, very soon things will begin to move; the earth will shake, mountains will tumble: only then will you know what you've been searching for, Mike!"

Mike waits thinking" …another mystery to worry about, but when is soon," he keeps asking himself over and over, but never an answer.

Raymond rises from his chair walking to the window, staring back, facing Ailene, "Return to the hotel and be here tomorrow for finals Ailene. After finals, you will leave for Berlin; problems ... contact Grace," he says, his eyes never blinking.

Again, she stands glaring at him dumbfounded! Raymond reads her mind, before she can tell him her problem.

"But Raymond ... I've yet to meet Grace! "She shouts, frantically.

Raymond stands at the door ready to leave looking back ..." But Grace is with you always Ailene ... even to the end, my darling!"

And over at the window the candle is out ... no longer blinking.

CHAPTER 22

Ready to Roll

"The Lord knows those who are his."

2nd Timothy 2: 19

It is six AM on a cool clear autumn morning and the phone rings in room 217 at the "Mark Twain" ... it's Grace.

"Be at the "Sampson Building" at eight AM--- the both of you. Today's the final day before departing ... understand----

"I understand." Mike says, placing the phone down never questioning.

A quick shower, a shave, and he phones Ailene asking, "Are you ready for breakfast, Ailene?"

"Meet you in the dining room in ten minutes."

"Ten minutes later they're seated in a large dining room just off the front entrance of the "Mark Twain."

A briefcase lies beside each, prepared for business; no shaking hands, no pleasantries. nothing but business.

Ailene breaks the silence ... "Are you worried about

something Mike … maybe something we need to talk about?" She asks, pleasantly.

He looks up at her puzzled, "I'll put it to you this way, "I'm happy about this trip to the mountain top, nothing could make me feel better, Ailene," he says, jokingly.

Moments of silence, no looking around and, "But, I've a question for you Ailene!"

"A question for me----

"Oh yes, a very important question!"

"Then spill it out "dearie," she says, never looking back at him.

"Many nights I've lay awake wondering about something, but never an answer---

She looks at him grinning, "Quit your hedging around Mike …fire away. Tell me what keeps you awake wondering."

"But, I've gotta know the truth for sure, it's important … understand …

"Then don't take all day, out with it, time is wasting!"

"Did you come to "Morris Avenue Baptist Church" by the wishes of the "Star" … or was it Friend Ailene?"

"Does it bother you Mikey Boy?" She asks, taunting.

"Sure, it does; bothers me a lot. Last night I lay in bed thinking about you … how we first met."

"Now, you got me interested, tell me about it."

"Well, it just might be … that's why we're here together!", he says, nervously, looking away.

"Guess Mike… guess!"

Mike looks away, his temper begins to flare. He isn't about to guess. He picks up the newspaper pretending to read, wait another day … if ever.

Breakfast is over, and they head back to the "Sampson

Building,", where Raymond sits alone inside the office waiting at his desk.

No greeting, nothing; just business with Raymond taking over beginning again.

"Before you leave here today my part will be over. Later today you will leave for Berlin; expect a last-minute briefing while traveling. Make notes of nothing, remembering everything."

"I explained to you perfectly and I reiterate once again … 'the enemies you're about to face are soldiers of Satan: sent to destroy you… carry out his willing only!"

His eyes close, studying, beginning again, "But most important is …

"Ailene can't wait shouting, "Most important is what, Raymond?"

"The power of the devil, Ailene. It's frightening beyond your imagination. Thousands upon thousands of unseen demonic forces wait for the day he proclaims himself God: God of heaven and earth, all beyond we aren't privy to!"

They sit wondering, while Raymond stares hard at them, finally asking … "Questions, anyone …?"

"No questions Raymond," Mike responds quickly.

"Before you leave Washington get rid of everything written, every note, every notation. Store it in your mind, like money in your pocket. Check your room again and again… but don't check out."

"But why … why not check out Raymond?" Ailene asks, quickly.

Raymond moves closer, whispering, "Let them do the worrying where you've moved. I'm talking about unseen forces, the kind of forces the Apostle Paul warned you about.

"I'm talking about unknown principalities, demonic,

evil forces watching; waiting to destroy your soul, your body Ailene!" He says, leaving her hands and body shaking.

"Sometime in the next twenty-four hours you'll be notified by Grace to leave the hotel; grab your bags, move out quickly. Leave everything except the clothes you carry on your back. Outside the hotel … you'll meet "Rainbow …

"And … who is Rainbow?" Mike asks quickly.

"Rainbow is your pilot, Mike. She will deliver you to the airport where you'll meet "Golden," … her fellow pilot."

"Leaving Dulles airport, you'll move to Berlin. Later, you'll continue by helicopter to the village "Berchtesgaden" … a small village in the Bavarian Alps. … waiting for you."

"Berchtesgaden …tell us about it, Raymond," Ailene says, quickly.

"A place in history, home of the greatest devil worshiper ever; Adolph Hitler, killer of Jews, leader of the occult!"

A short pause and, "Watch your surroundings … take nothing for granted …

Over and over it goes. Grilling on and on … never letting up.

"Arriving at Berchtesgaden things will pick-up drastically."

Again, Mike wipes sweat from his brow, looking up to Raymond, "But our part … when does the real action begin, Raymond?"

"Raymond rises from his chair, standing before him, looking down upon him, "You will begin the night of Halloween: move over to the window and look out … the both of you!"

They move to the window gazing out, seeing a hundred strange figures dressed in white: protectors from above, waiting. Mike turns quickly, looking back … no Raymond!

CHAPTER 23

Berchtesgaden: A Place in History

"The chariots of God are twenty thousand, even thousands of angels: The Lord is among them, as in Sinai, in the holy place."

Psalm 68: 17

Ailene and Mike sit waiting for someone taking Raymond's place, and from out of nowhere-- an unknown voice from behind breaks the silence, shouting, "Mike--Ailene, I'm Golden, your pilot; Rainbow isn't coming!"

They glance toward the door and back to the swivel chair, where a beautiful young lady with long blond hair sits alone.

She's wearing a white linen pilot's uniform strikingly adorned; fitted with gold buttons, red stripes running down to her black leather shoes. Covering her head, she wears a matching cap displaying a small, but noticeable golden cross."

Anxiously-- they wait for her to speak, but she only stares back at them smiling, settling back in the big swivel chair beside her. And … they begin to realize; they're in a different kind of world, the kind of world Raymond knows; a world of angels only.

"Prepare for excitement, "Chosen Ones", things are happening fast and furious, I'll brief you later. Once we land at the village Berchtesgaden, you'll be briefed again and again. You'll learn your part, your every move, what's expected of you!"

"Questions?" She asks, catching her breath, waiting.

"But, the remainder of our schedule Golden?" Mike asks.

"Within the next twenty-four hours you'll move on; prepare for it Mike!" Three nights from now will be Halloween, the night of all nights; a time when the action begins. When the clock strikes midnight in the village of Berchtesgaden … your mission will be over, completed!"

"But, when the mission is over Golden … what then?" Mike asks, moving closer.

"You'll be going home Mike; the Eagles Nest will be only a hole in the ground … a playhouse for the devil no longer!"

"But, Berchtesgaden … the children, the people, the homes Golden--- Ailene asks, quickly.

Golden places her hand upon her mouth hushing her, "The "Eagles Nest" only Ailene… nothing more; but I must warn you …

"Warn me about what, Golden?"

"It's all about prayer Ailene. Prayer and more prayer; only He has the answer for everything!"

Golden opens a briefcase spreading maps across her desk, motioning them come forward,

"Placed before you something to read before departing for Washington. Read every detail, memorize every hallway, stairwell, elevator: whatever strikes your eye important."

"Once you leave the motel in Berchtesgaden … things will

begin to happen, frightening things: things only He above knows. In minutes ... you'll be on your way to an elevator at the base of Kalkstein Mountain. From the base of the elevator you'll zoom upward ... reaching the top of the mountain."

She stops, waiting briefly, looking around, continuing,

"When you arrive at the top of the mountain, stop and look around you: you're inside the notoriously famous 'Eagle's Nest" ... a place where things get busy, time becomes critical!"

Their eyes stay focused upon her only, missing nothing, waiting. ...

"You'll be given three hours to complete your mission. Evil ... unseen satanic forces will surround you, but there's nothing to fear, nothing to harm you!"

Ailene can't wait, breaking the silence," Yes! Yes! Golden ... tell us more Golden!"

Golden looks down upon her smiling, "But always remember this Ailene--

"Yes—yes Golden!" Ailene mutters.

"Our Lord above is with you always Ailene: He will never leave you ... He will never forsake you...

Time is moving fast, and again Golden opens her briefcase spreading maps, diagrams on the table before them.

"Check every nook, every cranny within the "Eagles Nest" And ... the Great Room, a place of pleasure unlimited for Hitler's best; the Gestapo, the most feared killers of Jews ever imagined!"

She mentions "Joseph Goebbels" ---the Nazi madman, Hermann Goering, the political leader who hung himself in prison. She tells of "Eva Braun," Hitler's long-time mistress; the occult, devil worshipers ... all of them.

She mentions Jews, millions put to death in concentration

camps. On and on she continues; while Ailene sits taking it all in…fighting back an urge to vomit.

A twenty-minute break, and she's back moving forward.

She tells of the American occupation by the "101st Airborne" at the end of WW11. She tells of priceless relics falling into hands of the victors. On and on … hours upon hours describing history till, halting a moment, regaining her breath again.

"Long moments of silence and she's back at it again; continuing on and on … lecturing, praying, beginning again.

"You'll be dressed as waiters in black trousers, white shirts, black bow-ties. From the Inn … Hans will come … escorting you and others to an elevator at the base of the mountain."

"From the mountain base … you will proceed further to the highest point upon "Kalkstein Mountain" … gazing down upon the one and only, "Eagle's Nest!"

"Questions …?"

"But the "Eagles Nest," … tell us some more about the "Eagles Nest," Ailene shouts.

"There's nothing like it the world over. It's made of solid marble stone, carved into a play-house at the top of the mountain. It's a magnificent work of art; a history that only the devil himself could imagine"

Suddenly, she stops, looking sadly … beginning again.

"But the most spacious of all is the large ballroom, leading out onto a large overhead balcony. There upon the balcony… the evilest plans ever were set in place killing millions; witchcraft, all of it never ending."

"Long nights of debauchery, sexual depravity; a play-pen for Hitler and his cult of devil worshipers, conceived by the devil himself," she says, teary eyed, staring down and away … praying.

"Questions?" She asks waiting, seeing Mike's head bowing low, never questioning, never speaking.

"Nearing the ball-room you'll be met by Jonathon, one of our own. He's knowledgeable of the territory; a take-charge person. He will direct a procession of twenty or thirty waiters and waitresses throughout the parade; ending up before the altar of ..."

"The altar of whom, Golden?" Mike asks, suspiciously ...

Golden looks up at him differently, afraid to say the words, but does ... "The altar of Satan ... Mike!"

"But how do we recognize Jonathon from others, Golden?" Mike asks.

Her face brightens, showing her pleasure, "Just look for the biggest, the sweetest, the most handsome waiter ever; that will be Jonathon!"

"He will place you behind a cart at the end of a line of waiters and waitresses dressed the same. And you Ailene, will be at the head of the cart ... Mike trailing at the rear behind you. The two of you will remain this way ... till you reach your destination."

"And my destination is where?" Mike asks, confused again.

"It's wherever the *Satanic Bible* is placed. It will be spread open, lying upon an altar honoring the devil as the one and only God ever. Every eye will be fixed upon it from the moment it's placed before you, Mike."

"The top of your cart will be neatly displayed with wine, liquors, drinks of every brand. Under the cart's cover will be hidden our "Holy Bible" ... the same Bible used for the swearing in of "President Ronald Ragan" in Washington years ago. Now ... the both of you look at me and tell me you're with me!"

Again, they're shocked, wondering why the doubt.

Ailene can't wait, grasping her hand, moving up in her face

shouting, "But Golden darling, we are with you! We love the Lord as you do, Golden!".

Her eyes brighten, looking upon Ailene smiling ... "Sometime before midnight you will deliver the cart with our "Holy Bible" hidden on the second shelf below."

"Surrounding you celebrants will gather in the main ballroom. Look them over carefully, but never worry. When you see figures dressed in black robes standing one upon one at the wall ... disregard them: they're Satan's warriors ready to do battle. But more important is ...

"What is more important, Golden?" Mike asks quickly ...

"It's far more important, Mike. I leave you this from Him up above ... "keep your eyes upon the cross: The Lord our God will always be with you, no matter what!" She says, spreading her arms, upward smiling.

"But, the cross, Golden ... what happens if they see the cross?" Ailene shouts.

Golden begins to smile, standing, facing Ailene, "But they will not see the cross, Ailene, they're blinded by those standing before them!"

"You mean-----

"Yes, my dear ... light before darkness, remember this always!"

"But then what ... Golden?"

"Look up and pray your heart out, Ailene. Pray, pray and keep on praying you're up to the task ahead of you."

"But Golden ... tell me what then, Golden?"

She gathers her folders clasping Ailene's hand pointing upward. "But never forget this Ailene ...

"Forget what, Golden?

"He will never leave you or forsake you no matter where, no matter when Ailene ... He will always be at your side ... waiting!"

CHAPTER 24

Halloween

Whereas you know not what shall be on the morrow ...

James 4: 14

It's here! The night of all nights—Halloween. Plans are laid, time grows short. Ailene and Mike stand outside the Inn gazing up to the mystery place ... Kalkstein mountain-top, home of the "Eagles Nest."

They struggle to visualize the past; what the "Eagles Nest" had been during Hitler's reign of terror against Jews. Nervousness, filled with apprehension runs rampant in their minds. It's six hours till take-off and Mike can't bear the thought of failure. Victory is the way... the only way with Mike as always; failure never an option.

His eyes close, trying to visualize the '101st Airborne' making this same journey at the end of WW11; a winding road upward to the "Eagle's Nest." He remembers Nate's message and will never forget … "watch a television mini-series … *A Band of Brothers, Mike.*"

Now he's part of it, in a different way; a holy, but deadly way. It's a battle deadlier than anything "Hitler" could offer; a place in hell… filled with devil's advocates.

Heavy blowing rain falls outside the Inn flooding ditches and gullies, as the two stands beneath an over-head shelter. Off in the distance they see a large wooded forest at the base of the huge stone-mountain. And from far off in the forest … they hear the unmistakable howling of blood-thirsty-banshees, signaling the coming of death. It's something Mike swears he heard as a child: just before someone in the neighborhood was about to leave this world forever!

Farther off in the distance, they hear helicopters landing, taking off one after another, bringing dignitaries from far-away places. The atmosphere surrounding the Inn has suddenly changed; it's an eerie----dreary evening--- chilling to the bone, as some used to say.

Ailene looks upward seeing nothing but darkness; suddenly grabbing Mike's hand… heading back inside the Inn.

Inside they stand in the lobby gazing upon a never-ending line of chauffeur-driven limos, winding their way upward toward the one and only "Eagle's Nest."

Ahead of them they can imagine a prize of all prizes, a glance at the first and only appearance of the one and only, "Satanic Bible."

Down the road families gather outside watching an endless line of traffic, with no idea why this Halloween is the greatest than all ever.

Ailene holds Mike's hand tightly, looking up at him differently, worried, "I'll be so happy when this night is over Mike, seems as if even the weather is against us."

Mike looks up at her surprised. "This isn't going to be easy for sure my darling … it might get a little rough before this episode is over."

She squeezes his hand looking up to him, "You're right, but don't forget who guides us …

"You mean---

"Yes Mike, I do mean Him! The one who calms the sea, parts the waters; He's with us always Mike," she reminds him, holding the cross … squeezing it tightly.

Mike turns looking again, surprised. "You're amazing Ailene, you're absolutely amazing! I've met some tough ones, but never one like you; afraid of nothing, but willing to die trying."

Minutes later they return to their rooms hoping for some rest-time, but it's impossible. A lot of tossing, turning, thinking, regretting, wishing and repenting; all of it, engulfing their next couple of hours, till the phone rings…hearing an unknown voice.

"Be in the lobby prepared to leave with the rest of the waiters and waitresses in ten minutes. Say nothing to anyone except Jonathon … the handsome one!"

Bang! The phone goes dead, and Mike is prepared to move out. Outside in the hallway, they hear people moving toward the lobby: where a large bus sits in front of the doorway ready to deliver them to the scene of action… the one and only "Eagles Nest."

Boarding is accomplished in minutes. And soon, they're sitting in the middle of a crowded bus with people unknown; seeing a gentleman across the aisle nodding back at them grinning … Hans is here, no doubt about it.

It's party-time! The party of all parties; Halloween of all Halloweens.

Ailene nudges Mike's side, getting attention, "You seem pleased ... but why, Mike?"

"I'm very pleased Ailene. I'm thinking of a song I heard just before I left home. It doesn't go away, I'm loving it."

"Tell me about it, Mike," she whispers.

"It's one of the old never to be forgotten kind of songs; one that never goes away, you remember forever!'

"But the name of the song Mike ...

"What a Friend We Have in Jesus." There's something about it that comforts me when I need it the most, darling."

She snuggles close to him-- squeezing his hand, looking up into tired blood-shot eyes. ... "This might shock you, but I'm beginning to change my opinion of you; maybe just a little, Mike!"

"But why darling?" He whispers, looking around seeing who might be listening.

"Well-- I've discovered something new about you---finally!"

"it's about time you do sweetheart... tell me about it."

"Oh ... maybe you're not really such a bad guy after all Mike. I don't know why, but you're getting to me good: really good might be a better way to say it...thinking back again!"

Mike begins to grin ... moving his head upon her shoulder, moving closer.

Rain pounds hard upon the bus-top, as it makes its' way among a heavy flow of traffic, heading toward the mountain top.

Up---up and up they move over the curvy road: till finally the elevator sits waiting before them. A quick hasty move and they're zooming skyward toward the "Eagles Nest"; where they're ushered down to the waiter's quarters, near the main dining room.

Ten or twelve persons greet them eagerly, but one stands above all: Jonathon the. handsome one, a perfect example of man-hood at its' best. He's a Scandinavian born off-spring; about six feet two or three, blue eyes, long blond hair, instantly noticeable!

He greets them with a hand-shake, causing Mike to look up at him again, shaking his head, unbelievable.

"Follow me closely, the both of you. We need to talk about what's ahead of us," he says, moving out before them.

Moments later they're standing in a secluded area with Jonathon in charge ready to move on.

"You've been drilled on this before, but we'll go over it again. This is a onetime only job, never to be repeated. We have two and a half hours before the real action begins.'

"Once we reach the destination we're heading for... Mike will be at the very end of a long line of carts. The carts will be loaded with food and drinks headed for the main dining room ... a place where the action begins."

And you Ailene... you will be at the head of the procession guiding the way forward. Take nothing for granted, listen, be suspicious of everything; your lives and the rest of us will depend upon you!"

A short break in the conversation, looking around seeing who might be listening and Jonathon begins again.

"During the move down where the Satanic Bible is to be located, my eyes will never leave you. The Holy Bible you placed your hands upon at the Sampson Building is securely placed at the bottom of your cart, Mike.

"Disregard the revelry, it doesn't matter. It will disturb you, make you sick to even think about. The only thing that really matter is sending the Satanic Bible up in flames ... never to be mentioned again!"

He stops suddenly, gazing over at Mike and Ailene only, "But there's something else important---

"Something else important?" Mike asks quickly.

"Every move must be synchronized to perfection! We're dealing with the best there is; headed by the devil himself. Everything must be flawless ... our lives and millions of other lives depend upon us!"

"I've waited for a moment like this Jonathon ... maybe something I can prove to myself!" Mike mutters, standing next to him, waiting.

Jonathon places his hand upon his shoulder, looking again at him, "You'll do great... I know you will Mike. But I warn you again------

"Warn me about what Jonathon?"

"This is the devil's show! He has planned for this moment since he was kicked out of heaven. There's nothing he won't do to keep you from stopping it, Mike!"

They begin moving forward cautiously, following instructions perfectly. Minutes later they arrive outside the kitchen area: where Mike pulls one of the maps from his pocket checking it over... perfect, down to every nook and cranny.

Crowds of people have gathered in the main dining area. Music fills the air, never-ending speeches; all of it giving praise to Satan forever and ever. Booming out over loud-speakers; they're hearing hysterical moments, cursing the name of Jesus.

Evil runs amuck; reminding them of stories about Hitler and the occult. They need something to console themselves: something to depend upon. They hold the cross praying, silently.

A huge German made clock hangs high against the stone wall showing two hours before midnight; time it's all over!

A signal from Jonathon and the march begins. On and on, proceeding toward the center of the dining room, where people crowd together; waiting for the moment of all moments, a view of the one and only, "Satanic Bible."

Glancing back, Ailene sees Mike trailing at the end of the procession guiding a large metal cart, his face full of confidence. On and on they move, till it's here ... it's finally here before them.

Mike stands at the end of the line thinking, "This has to be my destiny; the place I've waited for, prayed for, never ending; it just has to be!

He stops short thinking ... remembering how it all started; his visit from Friend, his forgiveness, his meeting Ailene. His mission is clear: destroy the one and only Satanic Bible!

A large mural upon the wall depicts Jesus upon his knees pleading forgiveness to Lucifer, the devil. Figures dressed in SS uniforms from WW11 stroll throughout the crowd dragging human looking Jewish mannequins; while the place runs wild onlookers, shouting obscenities: laughing and shouting hysterically.

An unmistakable female ... the image of Hitler's whore lady friend, 'Eva Braun," dances nude at the center of the crowd shouting praise to Satan; his Bible of all Bibles spread out upon a table before her.

Mike fights back his temper, controlling his rage. He remembers what Jonathon warned him about; thinking, looking away.

From the other side of the room he can see a man figure dressed in a "Gestapo" uniform... holding a crucifix high over his head; while shouts of joy fills the air around him. And with a might thrust of his arm, he plunges the crucifix downward into a large picture of a Jewish child, wearing the "Star of David."

It's too much ... Mike can stand it no longer. He walks

to the nearest door leading out to an iron railing over-looking forest below. And off in the distance he hears animals howling, running in all directions. From far over-head birds of prey screech and wail endlessly, searching for food down below.

And off in the distance, he can hear wolves sending their eerie sounds signaling the coming of death. Once again, he grabs the necklace kissing the cross; gathering his thoughts, reviving!

And----- Boom! A jolt from out of nowhere shakes the mountain-top. Revelry stops, as worshipers stand gazing in all directions; while high above the bar... a barometer runs wild: showing disturbance below ... never ending.

Memories of WW11 strike fear into hearts of the white-haired ones; nights of horror, bombs falling from high above, searching for "Hitler"; the mad-man, killer of Jews.

Minutes go by and the shaking ends. Mike makes his way back inside, staring in shock; celebration runs full, resumed in all its' glory and splendor.

High above another clock shows an hour and fifteen minutes till midnight; time all hell will be let lose in all its' fury. Forty or fifty feet away sit the sacred twelve, "Satan's disciples," waiting.

Mike stands, feeling hypnotized ... ready to move forward! His eyes feel glued ... staring upward beginning to wonder; asking himself, 'can this be real Lord, or am I dreaming?"

Looking down below he begins to recognize some of his own; American dignitaries, long time public servants in government.

And...the unthinkable happens! The older gentleman sitting near the head of the table with arms folded showing reverence to Satan: *a past Vice-President of the United States of America; holder of the "Nobel Peace Prize."*

Next to him sits another white-haired elderly looking gentleman ... not long ago, "Secretary-of-State." Next to him sits the world's richest atheistic billionaire; waiting to see his master. And ...a breath-taking glimpse of the one and only," Club of Rome members" ... all disciples of Satan, waiting to serve him.

The clock shows ten minutes till eleven, and Mike moves the cart in a slow rhythmic walk trailing at the rear. Time moves fast, and soon he's standing before the magnificent piece of art seeing the altar of their most high ... Satan!

Upon the altar lies the "Satanic Bible," spread-open at the center. It's large ... a show-piece for a thousand drunken, sadistic revelers, shouting obscenities against Jesus.

Mike's eyes strain to look, viewing letters in red, written in blood; while far out against the wall, human-looking figures dressed in black, stand motionless, guarding their masters ... seated before them, waiting.

At the head of the table a figure stands ready to proclaim Satan's Bible to the world, while a bugle sounds far off to the rear...all eyes turn waiting!

And from out of nowhere ... stand four others, dressed in Nazi uniforms from WW11. It's quiet----deadly quiet: while onlookers watch a huge black masked figure standing before the altar.

Outside becomes alive! Guard dogs strain at their leashes; running barking, howling, in circles. Inside naked females run shouting and screaming, in and out around the altar of Satan.

And from far off in the distance ... again there's an unmistakable sound of blood-thirsty Banshee wailing the night away: it's Halloween at its' highest, reigning in the full power of the devil!

Moments of all moments ... it's finally here! Ailene signals

Mike time to begin. She raises her arm high up over her head ... and with a quick stabbing motion her thumb points downward.

Mike stands high over their most precious of all possessions ... the "Satanic Bible." He reaches downward pulling the "Bible of God Almighty" close to him ... kissing the cover.

He raises it high above his head before a stunned audience shouting as never before ..." Jehovah our God ... the one and only God: He lives today, tomorrow, throughout eternity!"

A mighty thrust of his arm sending his Bible into the heart of the Satanic Bible; a huge puff of smoke rising upward before him ... and the Bible of Satan is no more!

CHAPTER 25

Why, Oh Why—Lord

"For I can do all things through Christ which strengthened me.

Philippians 4: 13

His moment of glory is over as quickly as it began. From across the room there's a change of the guard. The once-dark figures lined against the wall have disappeared; replaced by angels of the Lord. The stand boldly in their place's, dressed in long white shining garments.

All hell should be breaking loose, but it isn't. There's a gathering of the faithful, a loud resounding cheer, and the unexpected happens; Halloween continues, moving ahead in all its glory!

Both move quickly away from the rowdy cursing celebrants. They move fast--- picking up speed, and now they're running full out.

"Are you ok Ailene?" Mike shouts at the top of his voice.

"Just keep running, this isn't a time to socialize. Time, we need to get away from this hell-hole before it really gets rough," Ailene says, shoving the cart hard and away, bounding out into a crowd of worshipers.

One more glance back toward the crowd ... and Mike stops seeing; "The Twelve Disciples of Satan," sitting near the altar.

And it's party-time all over! The Halloween of all Halloweens at the top of "Kirstein Mountain" beginning again!

They walk fast, sometime running toward the entrance ... till Mike grabs Ailene's hand, turning her around, shouting, "Stop Ailene ... stop, I can't go further!"

"Now what's bothering you, Mike?"

"This place is out of control ... it's getting more serious by the moment."

"That's for sure, but what are you going to about it ... tell me!"

He reaches into his jacket pulling out the Bible of God, placing into her hands shouting, "Keep the Bible with you and protect it darling, it's precious. And... always remember this... I can handle it!"

She doesn't wait, shouting back, "You can handle it, Mikey Boy ... is that what you said?"

He moves back away from her surprised, "Sure I can honey, we're getting out of this place. We're heading for the departure point: from there we're on our way home again darling!"

"Now hold on a minute Sonny Boy ... here's the way it is! We have only fifty minutes at most to make it down the hill."

"I know darling------

Again, she's back in his face exploding, "Now one more time Sonny Boy ... time you get something straight ...

"Yes darling ...

"I'm not your honey, your darling, whatever; need no advice from you...that's for sure Sonny Boy! I've been around, done it all … seen it all; know the score better than you ever will!" She's shouting up in his face.

Mike moves quickly, backing away from her speechless. He wants to speak, but can't … finally, a moment of calmness.

"Are you finished sweetheart?" He asks meekly.

"You'll know when I'm finished! Don't just stand here looking at me with your mouth open, we're moving on, Sonny Boy!" She's shouting, at her best."

Mike stands listening speechless, till---she begins again.

"We're heading out of this hell-hole before something else goes wrong: up to this point we're doing pretty good… maybe a push-over after thinking about it!"

"A push-over, he mumbles to himself…wondering why the sudden change.

Again, they begin running, slipping, falling on frozen ground; stopping briefly, checking locations: on and on again, till Mike stops, grabbing her arm shouting, "Where's the Bible Ailene where is it?"

Her anger erupts again, exploding, "It's where it belongs you idiot, it's here in my satchel!"

"Good! Hold onto it… protect it honey!"

"Now you just hold it a moment Sonny Boy … I've had enough of your giving orders. It's time you wake up and get your act together or---

"Or what sweetheart?"

"I'll leave your sorry-butt out here alone praying for angels to come and get you! And there's something else you better learn Sonny Boy …"

"learn about what…?"

"It's about time you get something straight … I'm not your sweet heart, your honey; never will be in a life time! And something else … never in your miserable life need you worry about me … that' for sure Mikey Boy!"

And suddenly, quietness reigns throughout! Long un-interrupted silence … till Mike moves toward her, taking her hand, looking up at her… tears in his eyes showing.

"Sorry Ailene, maybe I had you wrong. But, I've other things on my mind: important things I've never told you about!"

Her anger begins to subside, "Maybe I'll never know your problems Mike, but let's move on before we miss the chopper."

But Mike doesn't respond. He only looks down at the cold frozen earth thinking …

"Now what's wrong with you Mike; you're beginning to act hesitant; like you're not ready to leave this God-forbidden-place,"?

Mike only turns his head looking back toward the "Eagles Nest" wondering, what's happening now at that place of hell and misery… never replying.

On and on they move slowly downward, holding hands, stumbling, getting up again; till from out of nowhere someone is shouting loud and clear, "Over here, over here, Mike--Ailene-- over here!"

They move even closer, finally standing before the handsome one, Jonathon!

He's breathless----trying to speak but can't. He reaches out pulling them close to him; his big brawny arms wrapped around them.

Mike looks him over … surprised seeing him here; wondering why Jonathon is here unexpectedly. Was it planned or mentioned before…or has something gone wrong … he begins to wonder.

Ailene doesn't wait, shoving Mike away taking over.

"But, why are you here Jonathon, you weren't supposed to see us again----

"Plans have changed Ailene. I'm going with you all the way all the way to Berlin!"

"But why the switch Jonathon: something wrong back at the base ... someone in trouble?" she asks quickly.

He looks over at Mike hesitant to answer ... but does,

"Someone called Nate phoned the base where I was stationed. He was like an old grizzly bear, kind of rough----you know the type of guy I'm talking about."

"Nate! Did you say Nate?" Mike asks, grabbing his hand, staring up at him ... waiting.

"That's right Mike ... the guy's name was Nate." From the tone of his voice I didn't wait; this guy was serious as gets. Before I could say a word, he was giving orders to me like a wild-man."

"Giving orders about what Jonathon?" Mike asks, innocent like.

"Nate said, "Now listen carefully Jonathon, this is Nate speaking. I'm ordering you to stay with Mike Cutler till the mission is over; talk to you later Jonathon ... just do it!"

"And then what Jonathon?" Mike asks.

"The phone went dead, leaving me wondering; the voice... the way he said it ...

"Yes Jonathan---now the rest of it!"

"I'm sorry to say this but... I've known Nate from way-back; when Nate gets angry nobody between here and hell can stop him, Mike!"

"Is that all, Jonathon?" Mike asks innocently, lowly.

"That was it! I like you a lot, but I didn't wanta argue with Nate ... nobody does, Mike!"

Mike turns away glancing back toward the "Eagle's Nest"; again, he's wondering what's happening after the blast rocking the mountain top.

Jonathon pulls the two bedside him taking their hand, looking up at them, "I'll lead you down the mountain side and we'll be back at the base in no-time: get yourself together and we'll back home in no time!" He says, trying to assure them.

Suddenly … "Boom!" Boom! rattles throughout the mountain top again!

Rock and debris rumble down the mountain side like lava spilling from a volcano. Screaming, shouting, fills the cold night air around the mountain top … finally silent all over.

Ailene lies on cold barren shattered rock searching for Mike or Jonathon, but Mike's plans have changed. He's on his back, flat on the ground, looking out into a different direction; wondering what's left back at the "Eagles Nest."

He pounds upon the ground with his fist, still wondering … 'what's left at that horrible place that I've yet to see!'

It's decision time! Mike grabs his gear running back toward the "Eagles Nest."

Moments later he's at the entrance door, gazing upon the foundation left hanging; while Jonathon and Ailene move slowly downward over frozen rock and stone thinking of Mike: wondering why he's heading back to the "Eagle's Nest", a place filled with nothing but evil?"

They stop, moving together; Jonathon looking up into her blue eyes seeing tears streaming downward. He looks up her, a smile on his face barely muttering, "It's him… Mike… isn't it Ailene!"

A long pause and, "You know it is Jonathon: you know how crazy he is, but I still love him."

"I've never doubted it Ailene, but what can we do about it?"

She turns looking up at him differently, not the same Ailene he saw a minute ago; she's angry and it's showing.

"I'll tell you what I'm going to do about it Jonathan… just stand aside and listen!"

"I knew this would happen Mike. Nate pegged you right clear up to the finish-line. Just play your games all you want to: when you're finished, come back to Momma, I'll be waiting for you," Sonny Boy" she's shouting at the top of her voice.

Off in the distance Mike is about to enter the "Eagles Nest" once again. He stops, looking up into the darkness, shouting, "Sorry darling! Sorry Jonathon! This is something I've been waiting for a life time: unfinished business between my Lord and I only! It has to be, but if it isn't, please forgive me … the both of you!"

Cautiously, Mike moves forward inside the "Eagles Nest." He stops, kneeling upon his knees looking upward toward heaven shouting, "Oh Lord! Oh Lord! … Please here my prayer. The mystery of my life; the search for peace I've still yet to find. It can't be over Lord … it can't be! Please show me the other half my Lord … the half I've yet to see. Please Lord … help me!"

Farther away Jonathon moves close to Ailene hoping to move on, but again another wave of anger over-runs her senses.

"Have you completely lost your mind Mike? It's time to go home---leave this God forsaken place now and forever," she's shouting, sending echoes bouncing off the mountain side.

Mike stands numb from the cold, searching for words … peaceful words; words to soothe her anger.

"Please don't be angry darling! But I'm here in this God forsaken place because of God's will: it must be … no other reason sweetheart. I was hell-bent with no way out, but now … I'm free at last, darling!"

Her heart begins to melt, anger turns to forgiveness.

"But, if you must continue do it well Mike, do it for

His sake …the one looking over you. I'll be waiting for you sweetheart," she's yelling, as her voice drifts away into the cold night air.

"But, it's not over darling! I need another look into where I might have been … except for the "Grace of God… showing His pity upon me!" He shouts, stepping further, out into the unknown …

He tugs at the door and finally it opens … seeing someone standing before him; his Guardian Angel Friend smiling … looking down upon him!

Mike doesn't wait, reaching out to him, hoping to touch him: while Friend moves away from Mike, barely saying, "This isn't the time or place, don't touch me, Mike!"

"But why Friend, why can't I touch you?"

"I have a message for you, a wonderful exciting message!

"For me …

"For you only Mike."

"Tell me the message … please Friend, tell me!"

"Jesus, Our Lord and Savior will never leave you or forsake you Mike!" Friend says, standing before him trance-like… eyes sparkling as diamonds.

Mike stands upright thinking, comforted. He moves toward the front, where devil worshiping ran wild only minutes ago; turning back searching for Friend … no Friend waiting.

He's alone, running wildly toward the dining room where music fills the air, festivities running the highest!

He stops at the edge of the balcony over-looking the ballroom looking down; seeing nothing but human degradation at its' highest! Damage is everywhere; but the show goes on with revelry at the highest.

But how can this be … he asks himself again and again, but never an answer.

At the center of the large room, a well-known Hollywood starlet stands naked, while music plays to a crowd of devil worshipers. Slowly she moves her naked body before the "Twelve Disciples, of Satan" ... sending the audience into a wild sadistic frenzy ... lust without shame all over!

She increases her movement working her body into wild gyrations of passion, as "Disciples of Satan," move closer and closer, beginning the same.

Selecting the moment to please them ... she moves atop the large marble table shouting obscenities; while the former *American Secretary of State* ... pokes at her breast, bringing the crowd into a demonic frenzy!

Music stops with a "bang" ... quietness reigns throughout!

Slowly she walks to the center of the room, where a painted figure depicted as the *"Son of Man"* lies prone on the floor, nailed upon a wooden cross naked.

Cheers ring out unrestrained ... blasphemy against Jesus; all of it ... reigning in the night of Halloween!

She moves slowly, straddling the image of Jesus ... and it's an orgy throughout; an orgy that only the devil himself could have planned ...un-describable!

Her legs spread wide over the image of Jesus hanging from the cross, while she urinates over his body; looking back at onlookers shouting their pleasure.

Mike can take it no more. He's uncontrollable, shouting to a crowd of devil worshipers, "Stop it! Stop it! ... you worshipers of the devil... stop it!"

But his shouts go unnoticed, as ones down below remain staring upon what's going on before them. It's time to move on, get out of this place of hell and debauchery.

Mike struggles to contain himself but fails. His first thought is ... kill or be killed; kill them all and then some.

Spill their blood, feed their guts to animals below waiting. He takes another look, nothing but sin at its' fullest... beyond human imagination!

He must get away from this place of horror and debauchery. He takes off ... running wildly toward the entrance. Outside he stops to vomit... thinking about it.

A glance around at the scenery before him, and he's off again running over broken rock, his heart racing; till suddenly he comes to a halt--- breathless, gazing upward toward heaven, spreading his arms yelling all out ... "But why, oh why Lord ... why is this happening to me Lord?"

CHAPTER 26

To Hell and Back

For if ye forgive men their trespasses, your Heavenly Father will also forgive you.

Matthew 6: 14

His nightmare comes to an end. He stops, looking out at the scenery around, regaining his breath; taking off running wildly into the cold night air. He's running uncontrollable, screaming, shouting hatred toward the celebrants, never looking back; but again ... the unthinkable happens!

Ba-Boom! Ba-Boom! The mountain top rocks like thunder from above! It's another huge underground blast, exploding like a thousand bombs. Kalkstein mountain shakes; rocking the mountain-side greater than before.

Mike lies flattened out on the ground, lost ... groping for something to put his hands around; anything, something to cling to, for only a moment.

Minutes pass like hours. Finally, he's able to stand, looking out into a sea of darkness, feeling alive again.

He turns looking back to where just minutes ago satanic revelry reigned in all its' glory, praising the devil, but now it's different, changed completely! He looks back seeing smoke billowing upward, spewing gases from a bottomless pit.

His legs are numb, no place to rest. He's thinking of Jonathon and Ailene out somewhere searching for him in nothing but darkness. He's in trouble and knows it!

He gazes upward toward heaven holding the cross kissing it softly; his heart calms, beating normal.

His thoughts change again. He's wondering what the once great celebration at the "Eagles Nest" must be like now. The very thought of it hits hard; an unquenchable desire to go back to the place, a horrible place; a place of hell on earth ... a place of torment.

Gazing far out into the night his eyes search the mountain side getting his bearing. One more glimpse of the "Eagle's Nest," becomes his only thought; a glimpse into hell ... viewing the moaning, the groaning.

Enough is enough, he can stand it no more. It's an obsession without end, something only he and God will understand.

Suddenly he's thinking, 'there's only one way to end this torment forever and ever; one more chance to look down into hell: all of it waiting for him here on this barren, stinking, frozen, mountain top.

He thinks back, remembering what he was told before leaving ... 'pray, pray and keep on praying.' He falls to the ground, pounding his fist upon the cold barren earth: looking upward toward heaven, shouting, "Please Lord, one more look ... please!"

Far out to the left, Ailene and Jonathon shout his name without stopping, while Mike musters his strength, crawling on frozen ground toward the sound of voices shouting.

"Mike darling, where are you---where are you darling? Answer me--please darling … please,"

Slowly, he rises from the ground standing, shouting all out, "Over here sweetheart…keep coming and I'll be looking you in the face!"

Ailene and Jonathon walk hand in hand, groping through the cold bitter darkness, when not far away an outline of a figure stands waiting with his arms held out.

Ailene stands rigid, staring upon Mike, panicking; breaking away from Jonathon running recklessly toward him… smothering him with kisses.

Moments of silence, arms holding bodies together as one. And suddenly a yell from afar breaks the sound of the mountain; Jonathon is looking up at them ragged and dirty.

He doesn't wait, engulfing them … his big brawny arms hugging them as family.

But again, it happens! Ailene's anger explodes full out, shouting, "You're a blasted idiot Mike. What were you thinking, running back to the "Eagle's Nest"; it's over Mike!"

Jonathon moves to interfere, but it's useless. She shoves him away angered … beginning again,

"Nate had you pegged right! He pegged you right the second time I met you. You're never gonna quit; same old Mikey Boy forever … that's you Mike," she's yelling up in his face, turning away angry.

Mike doesn't wait, moving against her, pulling her closer, "Are you finished, darling; if you are, I'd like to reply," he says, humbly … waiting.

Jonathon moves between the two without speaking; they're one, huddled together feeling the cold, looking upon someone different.

But, Jonathon's mood is worrisome; his defiance is noticeable.

"Listen to me Mike, time you pay attention. You've been there, did your job… it's over Mike. Now it's time we leave this God forbidden place… no more options, Mike!"

Nothing but quietness all over. They're speechless, standing before him waiting …

"Our situation is serious Mike! Looking at the situation from here we've no idea what's left of the "Eagles Nest": what's down below has to be the same, but only a guess what might have happened!"

"What are you thinking, Jonathon?"

"This I know for sure; the last blast was no earthquake! It was different, completely different. It was power within power, and then some!"

"But what else could it be Jonathon?"

"There's only one thing it could be Mike: it had to be an ammo-dump left from WW11 …something powerful, beyond imagination. Now do you understand Mike?"

Mike looks up at him, as tears begins to show, "I do understand the seriousness Jonathon. But sometime impossible things occur; things like maybe the one and only chance of a lifetime kind of things."

"Maybe it's a time when you can't think of your own life, but maybe something personal. Maybe it's even sacred; between a person like me and … 'Him" … Jonathon. That's how it is with me and Him, Jonathon … today, tomorrow, forever Jonathon!"

Jonathon pulls him close, stopping him, "Maybe it could be that way, but why here, why now Mike; you've been there… it's over!"

Mike looks downward, hand upon his brow thinking; while the urge to return burns inside of him, unstoppable!

"But please listen to me, Jonathon. It's all about what life means to a crazy guy like me. It's something sacred, between God and I alone: it's something you could never understand my friend. You know what I'm talking about; it's what really counts in life when our days on earth are over, or about to be over, Jonathon!"

An eerie feeling engulfs the three-standing high upon the cold barren mountain top; while silence reigns throughout. It's a feeling like the night air surrounding them … an unexplainable feeling."

Ailene and Jonathon hold hands, gazing upon each other, trying to comprehend his meaning; words that Mike alone can explain.

He talks about something past, with only God and him a part of. It makes them wonder; 'where why and when it all happened,' But there's something else; why so everlasting important … why something to worry about … why, something to search for; it has to be something that only God and Mike alone know about!"

Mike is at his end! He's watching and hoping they might understand, but within his heart and soul: he knows he alone knows the story of Friend, himself, his mission.

He thinks back, remembering words from Friend, "You were Chosen Mike … chosen and anointed on an altar of God. Placing the golden chain around your neck means something most sacred: it's like something touched by God, nothing is more important!"

Far off in the distance they hear choppers leaving the nearby airstrip, flying away one after another; while out in the distance, again animals wail, people cry never ending; some shouting, cursing the day they were born… others screaming, shouting in pain pleading.

CHAPTER 27

Place of Torment

And he cried out and said, Father Abraham, have mercy upon me. And send Lazarus that he may dip the tip of his finger in water, and cool my tongue, for I am in torment in this flame.

Luke 16: 24

Jonathon breaks the silence moving up against Mike... "This is a moment I've dreaded Mike, but now it's time for action!"

"What does action mean, Jonathon?"

"It means there's only way or another getting out of here alive Mike."

"And my choice is what?"

"It's very simple Mike; we either move down from this mountain top now ... or stay and die later! Make your choice, Mike!"

Mike stands, gazing upon the two standing before him;

studying his words, knowing they're true. But once again something becomes more important-----

He needs something else, something that needs to be explained between him and his creator. But, all that runs across his mind is one-last-glimpse of the "Eagle's Nest"; his last chance to solve his long mystery, 'why him ... the worst of the worst was selected for "Operation UN-Holy Ground."

He places his hand upon their shoulder; his voice becomes different, peaceful, filled with humility. "Please, the both of you, I beg of you to listen. Try to understand the pain I'm in making my final decision!"

"We do understand Mike. My only question to you is... why the big change of plans here on a mountain top at the very last moment; have you lost your faith ... Is that it Mike?" Jonathon asks, looking up at him, waiting.

He wipes tears from his eyes as many times before. He pauses looking out into the cold dark night, smelling fire and brimstone: the kind of place the Holy Bible describes as hell for believers in Satan.

Hs thoughts drift back to a time before the Lord spoke to him through Friend; but now hear on a mountain top far away from home ... he's ready to make his decision.

"No Jonathon, it's the opposite! My faith alone tells me there's something out there in this sea of darkness waiting for me. But always remember ... no matter how disgusting or bad I might be... I'll always love you Ailene: the same for you Jonathon!"

Ailene moves close against him, her body shivering in the cold night air, "We know that Mike ... the feeling is mutual. But tell me again your reason to find the answer; it's important... most important to me!"

"It is important Alene. But God alone knows how I've

suffered from hatred within. But now, as I'm standing here upon this mountain top thousands of miles from home, I'm still searching for the answer of my life...why I'm here!"

Ailene moves closer to Mike, "But do really think you will find the answer here Mike?"

"I do darling. There has to be someone in this sea of darkness waiting for me ... there has to be!"

"Is this you're final decision, Mike?" Jonathan asks, standing next to him, waiting ...

"It is ... it has to be Jonathon. I'm going back for one more look. There's something that must be answered, no matter how hard I try to fight it. And something else, my friend------

"Tell me something else Mike ...

"Only this Jonathon ... don't ever think about stopping me," he says, causing Jonathon to look again at Mike ...

Ailene stands close to him, wanting to be angry, but can't. She holds his hand, moving against him, looking up at him.

"I'll be waiting darling, waiting and praying you'll come back with me in your arms again," she barely mutters, as tears begin to fall from her pretty blue eyes never stopping.

Tearfully, Mike looks up placing his hand in her hand, hugging her, speaking lowly, "I'll return darling. But if not, leave me here on this mountain top... the place I've always searched for. This is my Shangri-La, the place I've always dreamed about. I'll be in the hands of the Lord, safe and secure for ever and ever... sweetheart!"

Again, silence reigns over and throughout the mountain top. Peace! Wonderful peace! Their hearts become one ... engulfing their worry. Mike joins his hand with theirs, bringing them together for one last moment. He looks up toward heaven; pulling away bounding out into a sea of darkness; heading toward the "Eagles Nest" ... his destiny waiting!"

But, Ailene's thoughts are different. She can only stand looking out into the cold night air wondering about the time they first met; his dreams of-Shangri-La, somewhere high over the mountain tops. She wonders if he could be right: his long sought-after place, the place he told her about?".

Jonathon doesn't wait, pushing Ailene to the side shouting, "But you're a fool Mike, it's not worth it. Listen to me; come back, please ... please come back... Ailene and I need you ... God needs you Mike!"

Mike stops abruptly. It's pitch-dark, hard to breathe as he looks back where they last stood close to him; muttering words to himself, "Someday maybe they'll understand ... it's something between ... "Him and I only!"

He moves inside the "Eagles Nest" where only minutes ago revelry and celebration ran rampant; now hundreds shouting blasphemy toward his Savior. He moves slowly, picking his way forward, searching for what's left of the once-large glamorous mountain of stone... when suddenly the scene is visible, different completely!

Onward he moves, heading to where he watched celebrants chanting their insults toward his Savior, as one of the lowest of the lowest ever! Closer and closer till, finally he's looking down upon the scene where revelry ran highest; but now it's different, It's unbelievably different!

He hears people groaning and moaning far down below, as he moves even closer and closer: stopping at the edge of the massive structure... getting his breath, waiting.

His heart pounds as never before, while he's gazing down into a dark- bottomless-pit: a pit filled with nothing but human anguish, horror unbelievable!

Eyes ... human eyes, thousands of eyes gazing upward through a sea of darkness; moving in circles, gazing upward toward heaven. He hears their moaning, their groaning, begging forgiveness, but useless. He wants to move away but can't: it's too horrible to gaze upon, too horrible to even think about!

Looking down into the bottomless pit, he begins to pray some words he's often thought about … "But why Lord; why am I here on this barren mountain top: looking down into this bottom-les pit seeing thousands of eyes, staring up at me… as if I'm guilty of something?"

Suddenly … Friend, his Guardian Angel is standing above him, looking down upon him, smiling,

"And the answer to your question you've always searched for is … yes Mike, it would be you along with them in the pit below you!"

"But, Friend … I don't----

"Stop and listen Mike!"

"Listen to what Friend?"

"listen to your prayer you just made to our Lord in heaven … it's been answered Mike!"

"You mean …

"Yes Mike! Now say the prayer He taught you; the prayer when you were only a child. Say the Lord's prayer, Mike*!*"

"Our Father which art in heaven, Hallowed be Thy name. Thy kingdom come Thy will be done, in earth, as it is in heaven. Give us this day our daily bread------

Quickly, Friend stops him going further, reaching out covering his mouth with his hand, looking up at him.

"It's time for you to think Mike! Read the next part; the part you've been searching for, but never an answer.

"How can I ever forget; it never stops haunting me. I'll shout it to you Friend … *"And forgive us our debts, as we forgive our debtors."*

But say the rest of the words Mike ... the words you once swore you would never say!"

"I do forgive them Friend! I forgive all of them as God forgives me... forever and forever, throughout eternity!" He's shouting, staring up to heaven; while Friend is watching ... his eyes sparkling as diamonds.

And suddenly, the necklace around his neck begins to move in circles, while Mike lies upon the cold ground feeling different: loved again, a sense of 'holiness. He thinks of words Friend once told him: *The Lord's love looks over His Chosen."*

He rises to stand but can't ... legs numb all over. He hears the pleading, the crying, begging forgiveness: beginning to wonder if maybe they view heaven, seeing Jesus sitting next to his Father.

He's humbled, but happy again! He opens his arms looking up toward heaven shouting full out, *"I thank you, Jesus. Oh, how I thank you my great and wonderful Savior!*

"This could have been me, but you sent your messenger to save someone like me; a sinner, the worst of the worst ... now free at last ... forever and forever!"

He rises from the cold ground, gazing out where once a mountain top filled with evil reigned throughout the cold dark night.

He turns, gazing out into empty space gathering his thoughts; it's frightening to even think about. He has viewed the bowels of hell and found the answer to his long-sought after question: but only buy the Grace of God... he has survived a place in hell, reserved a place in heaven!

CHAPTER 28

Decision Time

Therefore, being justified by faith, we have peace with God through our Lord Jesus Christ:

Romans 5:1

Jonathon and Ailene stand shivering in the cold night air atop of what's left of the once-great mountain top. It's decision time and they're trying to hold on desperately. Wait for Mike or depart immediately becomes the question: it's a matter of life or death between the two of them. Jonathon is worried … and it's showing.

Jonathon stands looking down toward the cold barren ground thinking what to do next.

He looks up at Ailene, "I can't leave him Ailene. I just can't! I couldn't live with myself, leaving him here alone on this barren mountain top. Let's stay a while longer; he's worth it no matter how bad the situation is or becomes … I just can't do it!"

Standing beside him cold and tired, she looks up at him,

"You're a wonderful guy Jonathon ... a life saver for all of us. I was hoping and praying you would come to this decision. I agree with you Jonathon; the guy is worth it: no matter how his crazy mind seems to work overtime!"

"I know how Mike gets a little out of control sometime without reason, but maybe, there's things we know nothing about him."

"You know something Ailene ...

"Know what Jonathon?"

"I believe you're actually falling for the guy!"

She wants to shout back at him ... No! No! a thousand times No! But she can't ... it's impossible.

"Of course, I'm in love with him; tell him I said this ... I'll be kicking your butt all the way back to Berlin."

Jonathon flashes his light down to his watch, showing ten minutes past mid-night; while far out in the distance someone is yelling at the top of his voice: Ailene ... Ailene ... Jonathon, where are you?"

Ailene doesn't wait, taking off shouting back ... "Mike darling! Mike Darling! Thank God you're safe

A moment later she's hugging and kissing him ... till again things begin to change; her warm, loving attitude ... no more, changing dramatically, she's like the old Ailene, tough as nails; back at the Star newspaper spouting orders.

"You insane good for nothing stupid Irish idiot, what has happened to you Mike! Have you lost your mind again?" She's yelling up in his face...

But, as quickly as she began berating him; suddenly she stops, gazing up into his tired, weary looking eyes ... waiting--

He pulls her tightly against him, her body shaking from the cold. His lips touch hers, resistance ceases. Anger turns to desire, love turns to passion ... they're together again.

He holds her close whispering words of tenderness, while tears move slowly down her beautiful loving face.

Jonathon moves beside them, "Our time has come and gone upon this what this used to be a mountain; the battle is over, soon to be forgotten!"

"What's next on our agenda?" Mike asks, standing beside him, grinning.

"The best question ever, glad you asked. It's time for us to bundle up and get ready to move out; that's our agenda Mike!"

"And how's our chances going home, Jonathon?"

"Well ... maybe with a little bit of luck from above, the weather might change a bit: but our big problem is hope and pray Golden doesn't take off without us Mike."

Mike isn't worried whatever! He places his hand upon Jonathon's shoulder, "But, Jonathon look up and see what I saw just a few moments ago."

"What did you see Mike?"

"I saw what heaven looks like Jonathon. I saw what hell looks like; we're going home Jonathon; the Lord our Savior is with us always!"

Jonathon turns, looking out into the darkness wondering, "but why so sure, why so pleased, he's asking himself; is this the same guy Nate worries about?"

The journey is rough from the start. A heavy splattering rain falls causing treacherous footing. Every curve, every stone and tree has been moved. On and on, never stopping till ... the unbelievable happens!

An amazingly beautiful moon shines over the mountainside displaying everything below. They're thrilled, moving full-steam ahead; finally stopping, gazing upon solid ground ... different from only moments ago.

Far off in the distance they hear the undeniable sound

of chopper-blades warming up for take-off: while Jonathon doesn't hesitate, heading for the chopper full out.

His arms stretch out waving wildly, as he's stumbling again and again; getting up beginning again. On and on he moves toward the sound of motors; seeing Golden, sitting inside the chopper waiting.

Chopper blades cease their swirling, while Jonathon stops, looking around, finding his bearing. His eyes strain, viewing dead and injured scattered over and throughout the base of the mountain. He looks upward viewing birds of prey circling, sensing the scent of blood: while far down below he sees animals devouring human remains. It reminds him of something he read in scripture, a place yet to be; but not far away ..." **A place called ...** *Armageddon!"*

> *"Thou shalt fall upon the mountains of Israel, thou, and all thy bands, and the people that is with thee: I will give thee to the ravenous birds of every sort, and to the beasts of the field to be devoured."*
>
> *Ezekiel 39: 4*

Jonathon breaths easy for first time, regaining his senses; seeing two figures emerging out from nowhere, ragged and dirty. His arms raise upward beginning to shout.

"Mike! Ailene! Keep coming this way...I'm waiting for you."

A moment later they're standing as one...their arms extending out and around each other

Golden can stand the excitement no longer. She moves down from the chopper running toward the three of them, gathering them beside her. Her voice is broken ... her words unmistakable.

"I was about to leave…time had run out, but something happened …

"Tell me what happened Golden!" Ailene shouts excited.

"A voice from someone out of nowhere spoke to me saying, "Wait Golden … Wait!"

"Yes Golden … yes … Ailene shouts…excited.

"I knew without doubt from where it came from, Ailene!"

"You mean …

Golden places her hand upon her lips stopping her, "It had to be Him only Ailene!"

Pleasure is everywhere … worry is over! It's time to move away from this nightmare of hell.

Golden turns glancing back from her pilot's seat seeing Mike sitting peaceful: his arms stretched out engulfing Ailene beside him.

Chopper blades roar; a whiff in the air, and they're off into the wind heading home again.

They're tired, exhausted, while Mike sits silent, gazing up toward heaven; remembering how it all began.

He thinks of Nam, the church that turned him away; the hatred he bore for them: It's over---finally it's over! Peace, wonderful peace, love as never before; a love for their God … forever and ever runs through him.

His thoughts ramble again and again; thinking of a song his grand-mother would sing just before bed-time … ***one of the old ones he will never forget.***"*Jesus loves me yes I know, for the Bible tells me so, yes Jesus loves me … yes Jesus loves me …*'

His head lowers thinking back … wanting to cry but doesn't. It's over and he's happy again, ready to move forward.

Gazing upward toward heaven he holds the necklace kissing the cross. His head bows low commencing a prayer …

Arthur "Mac" McCaffry

"Thank you, Lord, … thank you Friend; it's over … finally it's over! I look up into your heavens, gaze upon your mighty wonders; knowing I'm free at last, by your grace only … my Lord … my Savior!"

CHAPTER 29

Looking Ahead

"Therefore, be ye also ready; for the in such an hour as ye think not the Son of Man cometh."

Matthew 24: 44

Election Day in America has come and gone. Weeks have passed, and Mike hasn't heard from Doug or Martha. He's enjoying the company of Ailene; love is in the air.

He lays sprawled out on the couch at home drifting off to a well needed sleep. The phone rings in the middle of the night... it's Doug...speaking in a voice he's never heard before...excited from the beginning...

"It's great to talk to you Uncle Mike, I've some things to inform you about, but little time to do it."

"I've been worried about you Doug ... been wondering what's going on with you and Martha."

"There's a lot going on Mike. Things are moving fast all over; people who never worried before are suddenly becoming awake to what's happening in this old world!"

"I'm glad you called, but I'm far and away ahead of you." a sleepy voice mumbles.

"Good for you Uncle Mike. I have some information you might be interested knowing about, but it's only between the two of us."

"I understand ... but when are you going to be leaving Doug?"

"I'm not sure ... but I'm heading for the Middle-East definitely. The place is on fire; burning from one end to the other. First it was Egypt, Libya and Somalia: now it's all over Syria, Iraq, Lebanon, Jordon, the United Arab Emeries! It's spreading like wild-fire... there's nobody to stop it Uncle Mike!"

"Makes you think about the Bible, doesn't it, Doug."

"You mean wars and rumors of wars?"

"I do for sure, I've been waiting for this. I'll quote it to you, Uncle Mike."

"For nation shall rise against nation, and kingdom against kingdom: and there shall be earthquakes in diverse places, and there shall be famines and troubles; these are the beginning of sorrows.

Mark 13: 8

"I've seen it coming Doug. The sad part is... Christians are in the middle of it, hunted like animals. Seems like everyone's holding their breath waiting for something big to happen ... always praying it doesn't happen!"

"I don't know the answer Mike... nobody knows the answer. Countries we've never worried about are changing sides, and there's no way to stop it... But the scary part is ...

"The scary part is what Doug?"

"It's all part of biblical prophecy; something everyone should worry the most about. It's not in the news … it's all in "God's Holy Bible Mike!"

"It is in the Bible…but what else is going on in this new kind of world of ours?"

"I've been assigned as an aide to retired General Nathaniel P Roberts, a former member of the 101st Airborne … U. S. Army. He's in charge of our "five people think tank commission" … along with others from different countries, different cultures. From what I've heard about Roberts: it could end up a little messy before we get started!"

Mike rises from his pillow fully awakened, wondering if it will ever stop; Doug's new boss is none other than Nate … his worst nemesis ever.

"What do you know about Roberts Doug?" He asks, innocently.

"I haven't met him, but I understand he's one of those guys who tells it like it is. My part is complicated … maybe a little more than complicated."

"Tell me about it."

"Some people describe our mission as the mission of all missions. We want to set the stage for peace talks; like Jews and Arabs living side beside in and around Jerusalem!"

"But where at around Jerusalem?"

"Historical places; places like … *The Dome of the Rock, The Temple Mount … The Wailing Wall…* holy places from way back."

"Tell me some more Doug … you're about to get interesting!"

"The Dome of the Rock is a holy place to Muslims: It's where they believe the "Prophet Muhammad," ascended to heaven on a rainy night; about the time Jesus went to heaven to be with his Father!"

"And… the Jews; tell me about the Jews, Doug!"

"They have a religious history just as good; a history that goes back to the days of "King David." It's all about the *Holy of Holies:* Jerusalem's biggest trouble spot, been going on forever!"

"But the time element Doug, when is all of this about to take place?"

"It's unsure, but I'll be leaving soon."

"And Martha, Doug …

"She's staying in Washington as usual."

But she's qualified … why not her?"

"Oh yes…she's qualified, but she's more valuable for us knowing what's going on here at home. There could be another reason she wasn't included …

"Another reason …?"

"Think again Mike… you know she's outspoken, always ready to give her opinion freely. But again … it could be due to the fact she's an aide to Roberts: they deplore the guy! He wouldn't be overseeing of our group unless Military Intelligence insisted upon it. But there's one thing for sure Uncle Mike …

"Sure, about what?"

"The administration isn't happy about it; that's the only way I know how to say it."

"But I don't understand…why not Doug?"

"There's only one way I say it, Mike: Roberts keeps them guessing!"

"What else is happening?"

"There's suspicion about everyone. Suddenly the State Department has adopted a kinder attitude toward Muslims."

"That's different … we've been friends of Israel forever. I'm beginning to worry which side were on."

"It's really hard to explain Mike, but the only straight-out way to say it is the way a Jewish friend of mine told me …

"What was that Doug?"

"He looked up at me with tears in his eyes and said… America is no longer America!"

"He really said that---

"He sure did, and it almost made me cry hearing it. But that wasn't all he said. He shocked me again!"

"Tell me about it Doug."

"He said, "Americans are changing partners in the middle of the dance, leaving their best partner ever!"

Wow! And what was your thoughts when he said it Doug?"

"I couldn't hold back … I cried without stopping Uncle Mike!"

"That's a good way to put it, he's probably right. Tell me some more … I'm loving it!"

A long pause and, "Maybe it's time we talk about something we're sure of … something we don't have to think twice about."

"You're talking Bible … right Doug"

"All the way, I'll quote it to you."

And I will bless them that bless thee, and curse him that curseth thee,"

Genesis 12: 3

"Makes you feel sorry for America if we desert them, doesn't it, Doug."

"It sure does Uncle Mike. It makes you wonder if that's the reason our country isn't mentioned in the Bible!"

"They're His Chosen Ones and it's never going to change. But, what's in your mind for a solution to this never-ending problem Doug?"

Again, he hesitates. "I'm not sure if there is a solution. The biggest hurdle is trying to find a way to keep the Jews and Palestinians from killing each other!"

"It's biblical history Doug! Its' been that way since Abraham, the father of Ishmael and Isaac: one son went one way, the other son went another way!"

"It has to be the reason Mike. I've studied the subject over and over, and I'm still hoping something can be worked out to end it. Maybe an agreement; something like the one presented to the world by President Bush, Prime Minister Rabin and PLO Chairman Arafat back in 1993."

"The Oslo Accord... I presume you're referring to Doug."

"Yes Mike. You remember how they gathered outside the "White House" ... shaking hands celebrating ... forever."

"I'll never forget it. I thought it was a bad idea then, and I still do. It was a lot of work for nothing!"

Doug pauses, "But some are thinking maybe something more enticing could be offered; something special, like the Oslo 11 Accord in 1995 with a different leader, a different director!"

"Enforced by---

"Maybe the European Union: someone powerful. I'm thinking someone with clout, a political leader, a religious leader; coming onto the scene from out of no-where!"

"You mean someone charming, playing dumb; deceiving the "Very Elect" as the Bible calls it?"

"Perhaps Mike, but only god knows, that's for sure!"

"But partitioning Jerusalem is something Jews would never go for Doug!"

"The world is aware of it. But this is a new world; not the kind of world we once knew. Something has happened to our way of life ... hard to put your finger on it!"

"No doubt about it Doug; wish I was wrong, but I'm not!"

"But there's something different this time Mike; scary to even think about."

"Tell me about it."

"The previous American president tried it; the one before him tried it. But for some unknown reason … I've a feeling this just might end up being a treaty both Jews and Palestinians might go for!"

"Maybe something like a seven-year treaty between Arabs and Jews living side by side in Jerusalem?"

"As we said before Mike … God only knows the end of this!"

"Tell me some more Doug. My bell is ringing; don't wanta stop!"

"I'll do my best. The "Oslo Accord" fell apart when the participants began throwing rocks at each other. Today, with some persuasion from the right people … who knows what might happen. It might end up changing the course of history!"

"I believe you're right Doug. If someone could come up with a treaty between Jews and Arabs living side by side in Jerusalem it would be the greatest treaty ever!"

"No doubt about it Mike."

"But maybe, there's something else; something else we need to think about-----

"Think about what?"

"Think about the orchestrator of the treaty Doug: he would be the greatest peacemaker ever in history."

"He would be someone people would follow to hell and back; maybe someone like a God … or someone pretending to be God!"

"Especially if they go back to existing boundaries before the "Six- Day-War" … back in 1967, Uncle Mike."

Mike's head is swirling, trying to keep up, still going on and on …

"Hang with me, you're talking some serious stuff Doug. You're talking about Israel putting their worst enemies in their own backyard!"

"I am Mike. But I can't forget what "The Book of Revelation" tells us about a seven-year treaty being agreed upon just before the Lord's return; you know what I'm talking about … sure you do Mike!"

"I do understand what you're referring to, and a lot of other people are thinking the same, Doug."

"But calm yourself Mike. Only a magician could sell the Israelis something as dangerous as we're talking about."

Mike gets his breath, rubbing his forehead, "But … there are other things for Jews to worry about Doug; things that make you think twice about."

"Tell me what you're thinking about."

"Israel is a very small nation … eight million citizens at best. They're surrounded by enemies on every side. Now think about this Doug; imagine what we would be doing if we were Israelis … the same situation facing us.""

"Drop dead brother, forget about it: that would be us Uncle Mike!"

Mike gazes up at the clock showing past mid-night. He's tired … growing impatient.

"Tell me some good news for a change Doug, there has to be something we can cheer about."

"Maybe there is. I'll tell you something about the Israeli leader."

"Tell me about him Doug"

"He's tough to deal with. He's smart as they come, knows what he's doing. He represents the "Likud party." But most important … he has a lot of respect from some of our own here in America."

"Our own …and what does that mean Doug?"

"It means people like you and I Mike: Evangelicals, God fearing people, hard to convince people!"

Mike comes alive shouting, "Don't say the word Doug, has to be none other than "Jacob Behrman!"

"He's the man Uncle Mike!"

"And what's his feeling about all this?"

"We haven't talked privately, but he takes orders like everyone else does. President Forestall gives the orders, we carry them out; it's just that simple."

Mike pauses, "But, where do you begin this journey for peace … or is it a secret, Doug?"

"It's no secret. The first part of the journey is scheduled to leave New York heading for Rome. We need the blessing of the new Pope … "Peter the 11…at the Vatican."

"Rome's moving up; a hot spot since Peter took over. But after Rome … then what Doug?"

"Who knows where?"

"Makes you wonder … doesn't it?"

"It does. But we're heading for the Middle-East for sure. I know we had our sight on Dubai being the next place after Rome, but things are happening fast all over the area, causing some to think differently. But Bali; you can be sure of!"

"Why all Muslim countries Doug?"

"That's where most of the trouble is. It's a dog-eat-dog situation: to hell with the rest of the world to put it plainly!"

"I'll be praying for you…that you can be sure of Doug."

"And I'll be needing it. The world is in trouble like we've never seen before, gloom and doom everywhere!"

"I'll give you something to think about Doug ... think about this--------

Watch ye therefore: for ye know not when the master cometh, at even, or midnight, or cock crowing, or in the morning.

Mark 13: 35

"You're right again Uncle Mike. Jesus gave us signs of His coming over 2000 years ago and still people can't see it."

"What are you trying to tell me Doug?"

"We're coming down to the final count-down! The things we talk about are coming true. Nations surrounding us are choosing sides and the clock is ticking; it's time we pray and get ready Uncle Mike!" Doug is beginning to shout.

"I've been thinking the same, but afraid to say it. But, what do you hear about Europe?"

"It's the same all over. People are frightened; grabbing their money, searching for a place to hide it!"

"They have good reason to run scared Doug, there's no place to hide their money; confidence in banks and government is shattered!"

Again, Doug hesitates ... "But there's other problems Mike ... problems with-in!"

"What are you talking about now, Doug?"

"Think back to a guy named "Judas" ... the guy that kissed our Lord, sitting beside him at the table eating and drinking."

"I know what you're thinking but tell me the rest of it."

"Some of our own remind me of him Uncle Mike! I can't talk about the subject at present, but I wanted you to know the facts before I leave!"

"And ...

"It's getting crazy! I'm talking real down and dirty crazy; the kind you never see coming … till it hits you!"

"But, there must be a solution Doug… there just has to be!"

Again, he takes his time …searching for an answer, till, "There's only one solution when you think about it. It's always something always out their waiting!"

"Like what Doug?"

He stops, getting his breath, "When I was a *kid* going to church, people got down on their knees at an altar of God praying forgiveness. They called it repentance! When they finished praying asking forgiveness … they would stand straight up; gazing around staring at their friends smiling… feeling better!"

"But a friend of mine told me another way Doug."

"Now, it's your turn to straighten this old world out, Uncle Mike; tell me about it!"

"I'll be glad to. This guy I knew never took things lightly. He said things, bluntly … right to the point; didn't worry whoever it was. He was my Uncle Joe … I would call him."

"Keep going Mike."

"He said to me over and over … "You have a choice in life lad, but always do what God tells you to do."

"And …

"It made me think … I'll never forget his answer, Doug!"

"Yes Mike. …

"He would look up at me with his big old Irish grin and say, "There's only one way to put it Mikey Boy, its' repent or perish; the king is coming … time to get ready!"

"Thanks for the warning Uncle Mike, you told me the same when I was seven. Call Martha if you wish----at home of course!"

CHAPTER 30

Help Us Lord---Help US

Eye hath not seen, nor ear heard, neither have entered the heart of man, the things which God has prepared for them that love him.

1ˢᵗ Corinthians 2: 9

Doug and Roberts stand waiting to board the plane inside "Kennedy International Airport." It has been interviewing after interviewing always ending with a question: 'can peace become reality in Jerusalem, dating back to Abraham?'

Thousands hold signs, wishing hope in what has been described as, "The Impossible Dream." Boarding begins, and they're ushered inside with other staff members seated beside them.

Another twenty minutes, and the huge A380 Airbus rumbles off the air strip amid roaring applause: destination, *'The Eternal city of Rome'* ... *home of the Vatican!*

Inside the giant plane is a crew of twelve, along with a twenty-member think-tank-commission selected by newly elected American President, "James Forrestal, political leader … the best of them."

Think-tank members are persons with impeccable records, dealing with diplomats throughout the world, but never important as this; peace between Jews and Palestinians in the holy city of Jerusalem.

American delegates are headed by Nathanial P Roberts, a disclosed past member of Military Intelligence: now serving as a retired statesman with impeccable credentials. He's assisted by his aide Doug Cutler, another with ties to the "Intelligence Department." Doug is known to be a person with a bright future … energetic as they come.

Everything moves like clockwork, and soon they're seated ready to move forward. Doug sits next to Roberts as the plane settles down to a speed of 623 m. p. h.

Across the aisle sit three other members of the delegation: Ann Rabin, a prominent lawyer, Susan Brantley, a well-known medical advisor to members of Congress. And yet another someone to make the trip interesting … Howard De Plume; a bright young man well-known for handling world financial problems.

Robert's selection of Doug for the journey remains to be known, but already … critics are hearing the name "Friend" … always praising Doug's ability to lead when things look hopeless.

It's time to relax and Roberts gazes down below, looking into a sea of white clouds. He feels like someone lost in a dream world where war and hatred no longer exist.

His mind reflects to a different time, a different life. He wonders why he finds himself about to enter an era never known. Most of his career has been in the "Far East," serving in the army he loves so well. But now, he's headed to something on the other side of the world as an "American Statesman," ready to tackle the biggest problem ever: Jews and Arabs living alongside in the holy city of Jerusalem.

Roberts wants to relax, think of tomorrow, draw from the past; knowing this might be the end of his adventuress career.

He moves closer to Doug tapping his shoulder, "Take a look at the older guy reading the book Doug. Remember the face and don't forget it," he whispers.

Doug glances over, turning back to Roberts whispering, "Someone important, sir?"

"He's very important. He's Israeli, 'Joshua Steinberg.' I last saw him at the Israeli Embassy in Washington. He never draws attention, but he knows what's going on everywhere; some call him a genius."

Doug glances over at Joshua again, turning back to Roberts, "Can we trust him sir?"

"We can Doug, a hundred times more than others. In case he contacts you let me know immediately. He's a member of the "Likud Party," ... a friend of Prime Minister Behrman."

"I'll do it sir"

"Inform the others Doug, we're a team and it pays to have back-up. But now, it's time you take a break and get some shut-eye. I'll do the same later," Roberts whispers, turning away satisfied.

It's not long till Doug drifts away in deep sleep, but for Roberts, his thoughts run different. He's busy reminiscing his past, maybe his future. He's wondering what life will be like settling down at his ranch in Montana; if this could be the last trip of his journey.

He gazes down below, his thoughts shifting back to childhood. He remembers how his mother came to him at school during WW11 at the ripe old age of seven.

He remembers how she gave him the news with tears

streaming down her face, emitting words of sorrow; frightening words he didn't want to hear, '*It's up to you and me son ... your daddy isn't coming home ... he was killed at a place called Normandy!*'

He sighs long and hard, continuing in a dream world; remembering how she accepted the news as part of life military life, God and country first, now and forever.

But now, he sits with Doug flying high above an ocean of water asking himself the age-old question: '*was* it all worth my father's life; that dreadful, horrible day, at a place mom called Normandy?'

From across the aisle news-people move closer taking pictures, gathering information.

His mind wonders again, remembering how he stood by as a young boy holding his mother's hand on a cold winter day at "Arlington National Cemetery." Soldiers, sailors, and marines stood at attention near his father's casket, giving him a feeling of family; one of them, the proud, the faithful, Americans."

He remembers the sound of taps being played as they lowered his father's casket into a grave at the ripe old age of twenty-nine. He remembers tears flowing down his mother's face in a never-ending stream.

He remembers the American flag being handed to his mother, and how she protected something most precious; holding it tightly against her, listening to her heart pounding in reverence.

He remembers going to the 'White House,' ... where his mother accepted the "Medal of Honor" ... for his father's action displayed on the field of battle.

He remembers his mother's words like only yesterday ... "It's called patriotism Nathanial, and nothing except serving God is greater." Again, he wonders if his father's life was worth the price he paid, fifty years later in a world of turmoil and trouble.

Several delegates have traveled this road seeking peace before; here today, back again still dreaming.

Soon, there's a mingling of personalities and cultures, all hoping and dreaming the same; something Doug calls ... "The Impossible Dream," ... love and peace the world over."

Time passes quickly. Details, people moving back and forth ... becoming acquainted.

A short stop in London and soon, wheels hit the ground landing in Rome.

From the cabin door a flight attendant stands ready to give an announcement.

"Give your attention, please! I wish to express the crew's sincere wishes for you to have a safe and successful mission. Our hopes and prayers go with you."

She stops, getting her breath, continuing. "I'm pleased to announce a crowd of thousands are here to greet you; wish you well on your journey for peace. Limos stand waiting just outside the concourse, ready to deliver you to greatest city ever ... "Vatican City!"

A few standing applauses greeting her announcement, and she's ready, beginning again.

"But there's more awaiting you at the Vatican. After you're blessing by Pope Peter 11, you will be ushered to the library ... the most prestigious library ever." She says, getting her breathe, looking out over the crowd, beginning again.

At the library you will be given the privilege of viewing manuscripts written thousands of years ago, some written by prophets of old; all written in the Bible. This a privilege granted by His Holiness, Peter 11 ... enjoy this moment and time ... everyone!"

It's noontime at Vatican City. A city with a history going back thousands of years. Back to the time of once glorious Roman Empire.

Thousands stand waiting for the appearance of their new heroes: ones headed to the Middle East searching for peace in Jerusalem.

Pope Peter 11 and an entourage of Cardinals, Bishops, and Priest sit waiting to greet them.

The sun shines brightly upon a crowd of the faithful, while the delegation is moving before the Pope waiting ... and suddenly it happens!

Peter 11 raises his hands high up and over their heads blessing them; while the crowd of the faithful stand sweltering in the midday sun ... clasping their rosaries, praying.

They move to the library walking behind an army of well-wishers, police by the hundreds; camera men and reporters trailing.

Roberts and Doug stand off to the side looking for manuscripts from the Bible; when suddenly Roberts takes his hand pulling him away, standing before him ... speechless!

"What's wrong sir, you look like you've just seen a ghost," Doug whispers.

"You're right Doug ... I have seen a ghost! The guy I just saw walking by heading for the door is someone I know as Anthony De Marco. A couple of years ago some friends and I were chasing this guy all over the planet."

"Chasing him for what?"

"He was laundering money for the Iranians here at the Vatican Bank, during sanctions imposed upon them by our country, and the rest of the world in 2007 and 2008.

"Tell the rest of it, there has to be more."

"There is more Doug...he sold the oil on the black market,

handing the currency over to De Marco. He would move the money to different currencies; handing it back to the Iranians keeping them going. The guy's a genius Doug: he was running the place making millions, and we couldn't touch him!"

Doug grabs his hand stopping him. "You couldn't touch him, is that what you said ...?"

"That's what I said Doug.'

"But I don't get it, Mr. Roberts. Tell me why you couldn't touch him ... doesn't make sense!"

"Plain and simple lad. De Marco was top-dog at the Vatican City Bank, on holy ground ... untouchable!"

"But the Iranians---

"Oh yes ... the Iranians! They loved him like a brother: he saved them from going under. They're brothers for sure, but only they know about It!"

"This is crazy! What's the guy doing here parading around like he owns the place?"

"Why not? He doesn't need to worry; he's been exonerated from everything ... given a pass to go anywhere. The best way to say it is----

"Don't stop sir...tell me the rest of it!"

"It's hard for me to say this Doug, but we can't touch him no matter what he does. The guy has connections all over the world, But the hell of it is nobody knows where he came from!"

"But, Mr. Roberts ...

"Roberts takes hold of his hand stopping him, barely whispering, "Let's say no more about this Doug, it's dangerous. De Marco is a guy to be reckoned with, and you better be sure you know how to do it."

"I'm glad you warned me Mr. Roberts. I was about to go crazy even thinking about it."

Roberts moves closer, barely whispering, "Move back over

to the manuscripts and act normal: act as if we're like the rest of the crowd. We can't just stand here gawking at the guy!"

"I understand, believe me, I do."

Librarians stand beside them explaining books and whatever; two hours later, they've only looked upon a couple of the priceless manuscripts... still wondering about De Marco, his business.

Dining at a nearby restaurant is pleasant, but not what Roberts planned for. He motions Doug to follow outside, take a walk, see the sight around "St. Peters Square."

They begin walking slowly, over and around the square, till Roberts pulls him over to the side, ready for business.

"I haven't the slightest idea what were into Doug. We've only began, and I feel something different ... something unnatural. When I see someone like De Marco hanging around, my blood runs cold thinking about it."

"Tell me about it."

"It frightens me to even think about Doug, but there has to be a leader among this crowd!"

"But, from what I've been thinking, maybe it's better that way, till it's time for you to take over." he says grinning.

"That'll be the day! I can already see I'm not loved by the ones sitting behind me. They only look at me when they have to, Doug!"

"But, you do have all the newspaper people watching you. They're about to go crazy waiting for something to happen with you in the middle of it. I can see it in their eye's sir."

"let's get serious Doug. When I see someone like De Marco appearing from out of nowhere it's scary, believe me, it's scary!"

Doug gazes far out to the side seeing Joshua sitting alone, reading his Bible: causing him to wonder 'what's going on with Joshua the Jew ...always reading his Bible?

"This may sound like treason, but my honest belief is …

"Is what lad?

He gets his breath, exhaling deeply, "I believe we're being betrayed within our own government Mr. Roberts!"

Roberts hesitates, looking him over again. "That's a pretty heavy statement lad: maybe it's time you let it all hang out!"

Doug's head drops even lower, looking up at Roberts, miserable. He's thinking, 'never ever before something like this with a guy like Roberts.'

"I don't what has happened to America. It's beginning to look like a completely different nation that our parents fought and died for. It's beginning to look like a nation wondering out in a wilderness searching, but never finding what they're searching for, sir."

"Keep going Doug, I'm listening!"

"I've finally convinced myself there's people within own government deceiving us! Never ever, in my life time would I say such words, but facts don't lie Mr. Roberts!" He says, getting his breath, waiting.

"Something else you would like to say Doug?" Roberts barely whispers, looking around … seeing who might be listening.

"Only this sir, Martha agrees with me. She's in the middle of this mess every day. She hears conversations from our very highest … our very lowest: knowing they're lying every breathe they take!"

Roberts lowers his head, turning away and back again. "You gotta a lot of nerve telling me this Doug, but the sad part is … I actually believe you!"

"I'm glad you believe me, I was beginning to think I might have to convince you Mr. Roberts."

Roberts places his hand upon his shoulder surprising him.

"I believe you because there is a problem we need to deal with. Facts are facts! Now, tell me the problem."

"I suppose when I first became suspicious of what was going on, I just didn't know where to turn ... except to you Mr. Roberts."

Roberts pauses, "I've suspected a lot of people close to me the same. I've learned some things ... things making me miserable to even think about Doug."

"like what, Mr. Roberts?"

"Our every move has been monitored since we began this trip to nowhere. And the bad part of is it's being done by our own people; the ones we never think about!"

Doug looks up to him again, barely muttering, "I've never thought differently. But is there hope, maybe a way out of this, sir?"

"There's only one thing we can do Doug ... we go on offense. Never in history has a war been won playing nothing but defense."

Doug looks down, and back up at him.

"Something bothering you Doug?" Roberts asks.

"Maybe ... but I don't know where to begin ..."

"Try me lad ... we'll worry about it later."

"I don't know what has happened to America. It's like we're a different nation--a nation without a goal; it frightens me to even think about!"

A long pause and ... "I've never thought differently, Doug... were on the same track."

Silence! Nothing but silence, till ... Roberts looks back at him seeing the strain he's in, "Need help trying to figure out what's going on, Doug?"

"Nothing I can't handle Mr. Roberts ... but I could use some assurance...something I can depend upon."

"A smile begins to show upon Roberts face, "But there's always something we can depend upon Doug. Walk with me where nobody can listen. When I give you my nod, we'll repeat the "Twenty-Third Psalm."

"You mean about right now …?"

"Why not now? This is as good a place as any. It makes me feel like David with a sling-shot facing Goliath."

They head toward an open area in the concourse reciting the words …

The Lord is my shepherd; I shall not want. He maketh me to lie down in green pastures; he leadeth me beside the still waters. He restoreth my soul: he leadeth me in the path of righteousness for his name's sake. Yea, though I walk through the valley of the shadow of death, I will fear no evil: for thou art with me; thy rod and thy staff they comfort me. Thou preparest a table before me in the presence of mine enemies: thou anointest my head with oil; my cup runneth over. Surely goodness and mercy shall follow me all the days of my life: and I will dwell in the house of the Lord forever.

It's finished, and Roberts places his hand upon Doug's shoulder looking up to him asking, "Did it help you, Doug?"

"It did, sir … it really did! "David" was always at his best … when talking to the Lord high up above him!"

CHAPTER 31

A Stranger from Nowhere

He shall magnify himself in his heart, and by peace he shall destroy many.

Danial 8: 25

Daylight comes, and everyone is loaded aboard the giant airbus, ready to visit the great city of Dubai ... a city a part of the United Arab Emirates.

There's a loud sound of motors revving up, and they're on their way across an ocean of water toward, a land of nothing but sand; where once Nomadic tribesmen traveled on camels, searching for food, water and shelter.

A film displays the wonders of this great city, while a group of hopeful delegates from all over; sit marveling in awe; its beauty, its wealth unbelievable!

The film shows a city with condos rising, up into the heavens, while Doug and Roberts sit among them; remembering something they heard in a church a long time ago; a song called... "*Shifting Sand*."

They begin to wonder ... 'can this be heaven in all its' glory ... or maybe something here on earth, a short time only.

At the front of the plane, a tall dark-haired gentleman emerges from the cabin dressed in a dark blue suit standing before them.

His long dark hair and piercing eyes causes Roberts to freeze; seeing Anthony De Marco, the man he searched the world over for!

Doug doesn't wait, pulling Roberts closer, "That's Anthony De Marco; the guy you told me about at the Vatican sir!"

"You're right Doug, but this isn't the place or time, we'll talk about it later."

De Marco stands gazing out over his audience smiling.

"Dear members of this delegation, I wish to introduce myself to you. My name is Anthony De Marco. And I've been delegated to take charge of this delegation of peace-makers. I will place my papers before you on this table and you may examine them thoroughly."

"I'm sure many of you may not have heard my name before, but those at the "Vatican Bank" know me well. I served as President of the bank for ten years ... along with Cardinal Angelo Martinez ... a friend of Pope Peter 11."

"I'm a very common person as most of you. I'm sure most of you are aware things have changed throughout the world and we are going to do our best to solve the problems. We have little time to waste; failing our mission of peace is unthinkable!"

"I've met with world leaders throughout and there's one common subject we always agreed upon; peace between Jews and Palestinians is the biggest problem the world must face ever."

Roberts stands looking out over the crowd of delegates seeing nothing but smiles, except the Americans looking

downward; Joshua reading his Bible, shaking his head …
wondering.

Susan Brantley, a member of the American delegation
raises her hand ready to speak …

"Yes, Mrs. Brantley …

"Sir, I'm sure we all agree in our effort for peace but tell us
some more about your background before the Vatican Bank!"

"Your question is well taken Ms. Brantley. I've served
people the world over. People throughout the *Middle East* knew
me well. Many benefitted from my position as *President of the
Vatican Bank.*"

. "I made them players in the oil industry… when the rest
of the world looked down upon them suspiciously. I fed them,
I clothed them … today they still love me!"

Thirty minutes into the trip and it's the same; question after
question to De Marco, pleasing those sitting before him; but
not the Americans and Joshua the Jew … still sitting reading
his Bible.

On and on it goes till, De Marco raises his hands looking
out before them announcing, "Sorry my friends, but I must
leave you: the crew in the cockpit has summoned me to get
with them Immediately!"

Roberts doesn't wait, going to the front gaining their
attention without asking.

"Fellow delegates …I've news for you, theirs's something
you must be informed about Mr. De Marco before we move
forward!"

Quickly one of the delegates rises from his seat looking
up to Roberts, "Mr. Roberts if it's important concerning this
mission we're about to begin then tell us about it!"

Roberts looks out over his audience trying to find the words till, "My fellow delegates, this is hard to say but I have no idea what's going on with this guy Anthony De Marco!"

"I've been this route before with Mr. De Marco. He's a guy who plants his feet one place and gone tomorrow."

"Back in 2007 and 2008 during sanctions imposed upon Iran for going ahead with their project developing a nuclear bomb: myself and two others attached to CIA: searched the world over and never found him. This is one dangerous guy to put your future in his hands.!"

From the back of the American delegation, Howard De Plume comes walking forward facing Roberts

"I believe it's about time we take a break Mr. Roberts."

"You're right Howard. Go out among the other delegates and tell them it's break-time for thirty minutes…we will come back later."

Roberts gazes out over the crowd seeing other delegates moving about, except Joshua the Jew, sitting alone reading his Bible.

Thirty minutes later, break time is over and everyone seated. From the cabin door emerges De Marco and the pilot standing beside him. De Marco's head lowers, gazing downward and back up to the pilot.

"Come closer Captain, I might need you," De Marco says, reaching for his hand bringing him closer.

"Need me for what Mr. De Marco?" He asks, surprised.

"I think it would be more appropriate if you give our delegates the sad news Captain," he says, handing him papers … moving beside him.

Moving further to the front the Captain stands tall, gazing out over his audience.

"My name is Roger Craig. I have an announcement to make that isn't easy to say, but I must-------

His words take hold immediately ... silence all over!

"At about seven a. m. this morning, an earthquake approximately 8.5 magnitude struck all along the Pacific coastline causing terrible loss of life and damage!"

"The center of the earthquake was in the San Francisco area along what is known as the "Hayward Fault Line." There's another fault line within the same area known as the" San Andreas Fault Line. The San Andreas is the fault line that destroyed the city of San Francisco about a hundred years ago; it too, could explode most anytime!"

"There is a communication problem throughout the entire area of the west coast and it's causing a problem. There-fore it's necessary for me to ask for your phones, till we reach out destination."

Shock sets in quickly. Hands begin rising. From the center of the crowd Howard De Plume stands interrupting,

"What about tsunamis Captain?" Someone from the back shouts, quickly.

"There is always a possibility tsunami could be created rolling out across the Pacific Ocean; maybe spreading all the way to Japan or Hawaii! Traffic throughout the entire area is shutdown except for emergency crews and medical persons."

Looking out over his audience, the Captain sees nothing but a stunned looking audience waiting ... till the American delegate Ann Rabin rises, raising her hand ... looking up to him.

"My husband works in this area you just described Captain. I would like to check upon his whereabouts ... see If he's been injured or needs some help. What is there I must do Captain?"

Suddenly it's silence all over, till the Captain shakes his head looking down upon her," I give to you my deepest condolence,

Mrs. Rabin ... but at this moment I know nothing you can do Mrs. Rabin," he says, humbly.

"But, how can we carry on with this trip to Dubai... knowing there's trouble at home Captain?"

"Ms. Rabin! Ms. Rabin! The trip to Dubai has just been cancelled; we're on our way back to Rome!"

Looking out and over his crowd of stunned onlookers ... Captain Craig and De Marco join hands, heading back to the cockpit leaving their audience wondering.

CHAPTER 32

Welcome Aboard Marla

He tends his flock like a shepherd; He gathers the lambs in his arms and carries them close to his heart.

Isaiah 40: 11

A night of rest in Rome, and early the next morning they're on their way to Bali Indonesia, the journey to Dubai cancelled. The new destination…Bali Indonesia.

Roberts moves close to Doug, whispering, "It's about time I brief on something Doug."

Doug turns looking up to him, "I've been waiting for this … tell me about it Mr. Roberts."

"Settle back and make yourself comfortable, and I'll brief you on some things to look out for in Bali."

"Great, I've been waiting for this."

"Once we arrive in Bali things will pick up for sure. Our hero, De Marco knows the place better than anyone: the guy was born in Bali, Doug!"

"Did I hear you say he was born in Bali, or am I dreaming…?"

"You're not dreaming lad. The guy has been all over the world, but only a few know where he came from. I found out the hard way: I told you about it in Rome!"

"You did, but I didn't know he was coming with us that's for sure."

"Just settle back and I'll I brief you on a couple of other things…things to look out for in Bali."

"Tell me whatever you want Mr. Roberts … I'm beginning to feel I might need it."

"Once we arrive in Bali things will pick up. It's a highly populated city with about three million people … ninety nine percent Muslim. And for you… a Christian, it wouldn't be healthy to be out and around the city at any time!"

"I know what you're talking about…keep going!"

"Keep your eyes open and take in the scenery; anything else…could get you in trouble trouble like you've dreamed about!"

A bulletin moves across the screen reading, "Ms. Marla De Marco has been added to our staff, and she will be your stewardess throughout our trip!'"

Quickly, people take notice, glancing up where De Marco sits … viewing a nothing but perfect looking blond headed beauty seated beside him.

Chairman De Marco moves to the front of the plane joined by *Club of Rome members* A couple of pats on the back … and his fist pounds hard upon the table…drawing attention.

"By now, I hope you're all aware Bali is our destination before heading back to New York. After arriving in New York, I will submit a recommendation before the U.N. General Assembly for a treaty to be signed for a period of seven years.

"It will be a treaty solving a problem the world has searched for forever: Jews and Palestinians living in the great city of Jerusalem near the 'Dome of the Rock!"

A quick glance out and over his audience waiting ... beginning again.

"Marla will place documents before you to read and ask questions."

Susan Brantley rises from her seat immediately, "Is this something new, I've never heard of a treaty drawn up by you Mr. De Marco!" She asks, looking up at De Marco...waiting.

A look of surprise and, "No it isn't new Ms. Brantley. Your president, the Pope and other members of the U.N. are aware of it completely!"

Roberts punches Doug in the side grinning, "Thank God for one of ours Doug; she didn't let it pass unnoticed."

"My only desire is to bring peace in a place the world has given up trying to find an answer for, Mrs. Brantley. This is a treaty the U. N. will except gladly!"

Again Mrs. Brantley stands before him interrupting,

"Tell us your secret Mr. De Marco: the whole world is waiting for something like this," she says, staring up at him, defiantly."

"I've stated this before Mrs. Brantley. This treaty I have proposed is different. Jews and Palestinians will live in Jerusalem as brothers and sisters for the first time ever!"

"Then what Mr. De Marco?" She asks boldly, her eyes never blinking.

"It will be peace forever... throughout eternity Mrs. Brantley!" he shouts, causing his audience to come alive. looking up ... waiting.

A look of disgust is beginning to show upon Mrs. Brantley's face; she doesn't wait, returning to her seat... still not satisfied.

De Marco doesn't wait, motioning his friends from *The Club of Rome* come forward and stand beside him.

"And now... I wish to introduce to you my most trusted friends ever: my brothers who stood beside me while the rest of world looked down upon me. They alone stood beside me when I needed them most. They were like a brother to me, while I was planning this treaty for peace!"

Doug can stand it no longer ... whispering to Roberts beside him, "Is he ever going to stop Mr. Roberts ... or do you want me to go up and shut him up for good, sir?"

"This isn't the time Doug, this isn't the place. Let him keep on speaking till he hangs himself!" Roberts whispers, grinning.

Marla comes forward moving from delegate to delegate placing documents, when she comes to Roberts... a single paper falls to the floor unnoticed.

She bends, reaching down picking it up slipping documents in front of him ... waiting.

Roberts glances over the first document showing, *"All Praise Be unto Allah!"* His anger erupts immediately, ripping documents to shreds.

He doesn't wait, confronting De Marco shouting, "Mr. Chairman! I have an objection!"

"State your objection...we have a busy schedule ahead; make your objection brief and to the point, Mr. Roberts!"

"I'm about to do just that Mr. De Marco. As representative of the United States of America I'll state my position plain and clear Mr. De Marco! You and I both know your proposal is nothing but a charade. Your true purpose is to destroy the nation of Israel! I hope you understand my position clear and to the point, Mr. De Marco!"

De Marco stops, looking down upon him, fighting his

desire to contain himself: finally shouting up in his face…
"Proceed as you wish Mr. Roberts!!"

"Do not consider the United States one of your protégés
Mr. De Marco. I know you're a friend of our President, but it
doesn't make you a friend of the American people!" Roberts is
shouting back at him.

De Marco's fist close, clenching his gavel! His eyes show
rage, his breathing, noticeable … still holding back.

Roberts doesn't wait, looking up to him, "We began this
trip with the understanding our purpose was to solve problems
between Jews and Palestinians, but you have turned it into a
political issue, Mr. De Marco!".

Many times, I've had to bottle my emotions listening; while
you heap praise upon yourself and your Club of Rome brothers.
But it's not working, Mr. De Marco: maybe it's working on your
Muslim friends, but never working upon Christian Americans!"

De Marco interrupts, pounding his gavel … facing him,
smiling.

"I assume you're not happy, is that your problem Mr.
Roberts?" He asks, politely.

"Your assumption is correct Mr. De Marco: I'm mad as hell
might be a better way to describe it. Now, with your permission
I'll continue."

"The floor belongs to you Mr. Roberts!"

"Now, as far as the United States of America is concerned …
your days as chairman of this trip to nowhere is over Mr. De
Marco! America will not give in to your wishes now or ever!"

A lot of staring, murmuring throughout; while at the center
of the crowd Roberts remains silent…gazing upon De Marco,
waiting.

De Marco explodes shouting, "I believe it's time you go
back to go back to your seat and take your place with other

delegates, we're accomplishing nothing. Any further conflict we may have from you I'll summon your President and let him take care of your desires and wishes."

Roberts remains calm, seating himself, while Doug and other American delegates sit collecting their thoughts; still wondering, pretending it never happened.

De Marco stands tall, looking out over his audience differently. He's the old De Marco, smooth talking, peaceful looking person.

"You have made yourself clear Mr. Roberts. You have given us a display of American diplomacy at its best. But I'm a man of peace: a man willing to negotiate with anyone who is searching for peace…as I am!"

Again, it's nothing but silence, while at the back of the gathering, Joshua the Jew, still sits reading his Bible … listening.

"Once again, your attitude displays why the United States can't conduct world affairs the way there it's supposed to be handled. You simply don't understand the way we negotiate problems today, Mr. Roberts!"

"This is a different world than it was yesterday Mr. Roberts; time you begin to recognize it!" He shouts back at him, his fist pounding the table.

"May I have a minute to answer your criticism of the government I represent Mr. De Marco?" Roberts asks calmly.

"You have a minute Mr. Roberts … proceed."

"Who has given you the power to assume the chairman's seat for this venture of peace as you describe it … I'm fully aware, *His Holiness* approves you … but not the American people, I represent Mr. De Marco!"

De Marco begins to smile, looking up to Roberts, and back to the audience, shouting, "Is there anyone among you wishing to object to my leadership during his journey?"

A moment of silence ...looking around seeing nothing; while Roberts stands gazing out over delegates stunned... accepting the verdict.

De Marco doesn't wait, looking up to Roberts smiling.

"Explain this Mr. Roberts! Look at your own government delegates sitting near to you; no opposition to my plan except the so-called, *Evangelical Christians*. They're like you, Mr. Roberts ... they're laughable. It's about time you and the rest of your flock wake up and accept it!"

Roberts turns, observing his audience ... lowering his head, sitting.

"My American friend, little do you know whom you have offended this day. Once this Jewish situation is over, things will change as never before," De Marco shouts, slamming his gavel hard upon the table, returning to the cab, joining the Captain and pilot.

"Finally, we see his other side, the side we've been waiting to see Mr. Roberts. Does it cause you to fear him sir?" Doug whispers.

Roberts begins to chuckle, "I was born without fear Doug. You should have been in Nam with your Uncle Mike and I back in the sixties and seventies... ask him the question lad!"

"I doubt if he would answer. The word Nam irritates him; something I don't need right now Mr. Roberts!"

"I understand lad."

"One more question Mr. Roberts ...

"Yes, Doug ... .

"Why does De Marco put you down before other delegates; the guy seems to enjoy making you sound ridiculous!"

"It's obvious lad. He knows I've got something he will never have and can't touch. It causes him sleepless nights ... frightens him more than all else put together!"

"You're losing me Mr. Roberts."

"Think again Doug. We Christians have never doubted Jesus is the Son of God; it's something he can't live with… but he'll die trying!"

"But I'm lost again----why only us?"

"It's simple Doug! De Marco wants to be God; Christians, stand in his way!"

CHAPTER 33

Strangers in Paradise

And they four had one likeness: and their appearance and their work were as if a wheel within the middle of a wheel.

Ezekiel 1:16

Marla walks slowly down the aisle collecting phones. Coming to Doug, she bends low picking up his phone; while Roberts' watches tear-drops falling from her deep blue eyes.

"Find out why the tears Doug, there has to be a reason." Roberts whispers ... as Marla remains bending low, while, picking up phones,

"But, why do you cry Marla?" Doug whispers?"

Her head drops further ... barely mumbling, "Take this she whispers slipping him a note moving on; while De Marco's eyes remain glued to Roberts.

Twenty minutes pass, and De Marco again stands at the

front addressing his audience, "My dearest friends … there's good news for everyone, especially the American delegates!"

"President Forestall has instructed his military and other government agencies to rush all necessary aid to people who have suffered due to the earthquake. I feel for them…my heart bleeds for them!"

Roberts whispers to Doug. "I'll bet his heart bleeds: the problem is he doesn't have a heart! But … when I look at the expression on these people's faces, its' unbelievable; they actually love the guy!"

Doug heads for the rest-room, pulling the note from his pocket, beginning to read.

Dear American friends.

My message is short, but urgent. I was born in Los Gatos, California. At the age of two I was kidnapped near my home and taken to England. Today I'm twenty-three years of age, and life has been a living-hell. While in England I was with Arabic-speaking people till the age of six. Later I was sent to Dubai as a servant to a very wealthy Saudi Sheik, 'Omar Khatami.' He's a friend of De Marco … has women from different parts of the world serving his needs; believes, it's his given right by "Allah" to use them as slaves. Many come from Russia, Indonesia, France, England, Italy … all over. Most live without hope … doing anything to please him. I ask Russian girls if they want to go home, and they answer the same … 'why would anyone wish going back to Russia to live in poverty; it's better here … even if it kills me!' But I'm different. I'm still an American!" I want to return home to California and see my mother. I've prayed to God without end, but still no answer. But, if you are the answer to my prayers, help me … please help me."

Your fellow American ... Marla.

Doug reads the note over and over, and when he's finished, he shreds the note to pieces.

"How's everything going Doug?" Roberts asks, nonchalantly.

"We'll soon be getting company sir."

Suddenly ... the plane begins to role from side to side, storage bins unload luggage down upon passengers seated below. Panic takes over, shouting, screaming throughout: while passengers scramble searching for oxygen-mask!

Moments later the plane begins to level... under control again. And from the cockpit the door slams open; passengers seeing the co-pilot standing alone ... crying as a baby.

De Marco doesn't wait, rushing over to the pilot... throwing his arms around him shouting, "What happened pilot—tell me about it!""

A pitiful look upward facing De Marco, and the pilot is under control again. "I was flying the plane when it happened sir----- Captain Craig was sitting over at my side, taking a break."

"None of that stuff...just quit your crying and tell me what happened!"

"The pilot stiffens, staring up at him ..." It's the ones you told me about; the ones I can't ever see because of their brightness, Mr. De Marco!"

"Hold your mouth and be careful what you say, you coward! You mean it was--- one of them----

"It was sir. It was one of those you call *Cherubim.*"

De Marco's face turns pale, his body goes limp, finally, gaining control himself, shouting, "Get back to your senses man... tell me the rest of it!"

"Doug looks toward the front where other delegates sit

motionless; while Roberts moves against him whispering, "Look over to the other delegates Doug: look at the fear upon their face hearing the word *Cherubim!*"

"Pull yourself together and tell me what happened you idiot!"

But the pilot can only shake his head looking up to him ... unable to speak.

De Marco doesn't wait, pulling him against him, "Did you notice the Jew, the Americans---what were they doing when this happened pilot?" He barely whispers

Finally, a pitiful voice can barely utter, "When I first came out from the cab...I looked over to the side: the Jewish guy, was reading his Bible... the Americans seemed to be enjoying the moment; I couldn't believe it sir!"

"And the rest of the delegates—

"They were sitting in their seats... looking over at the Americans, speechless, sir."

Again, his anger runs out of control, "I see you looking at the Americans do it again, your head will be hanging from the nearest tree when we arrive in Bali. Now do you understand pilot?"

"I do understand, sir."

"Continue on and tell me the rest of it pilot."

"I was flying 700 m p h at 60,000 feet; when out from nowhere objects appeared like streaks of lightning... blinding me. They came without warning. They had four eyes, six wings, the color of beryl: it was like nothing I've ever seen before sir!"

"Speak lower you imbecile, can't you see people listening?"

"Sorry sir, it was like nothing before...I'm still can't get over it. It happened so fast; there was nothing I could do, sir."

"Tell me the rest of it, you idiot!"

"Everyone was frightened sir. I've never seen such unearthly creatures. Their lights were as bright as the sun … pulling up next to me. They were flying a straight path----passing by again and again. Their speed was unbelievable … impossible sir!"

"Tell me the rest of it, you idiot! Hurry man … hurry!"

"Vibrations took over … the plane began shaking: I didn't know what to do…I felt helpless---

"How many were they pilot?"

"I don't know sir. There could have been hundreds, all looking the same. I was frightened, my crew was frightened: it wasn't our imagination, sir."

"But a description, any kind of description … tell me pilot!"

"This is hard to explain Mr. De Marco, but I noticed something I'll never forget----

"What was it man? Let it out It before I grab you and shake it out of you!" De Marco is shouting: while around him an audience of delegates sit frozen.

"Well sir, I saw what looked like a bright shining cross; the kind the Christians wear around their neck…you know sir, something they're kind of proud of."

De Marco's face turns ghostly; his hands shake… his body trembles. He remembers something he heard from past; a place called *Calvary!*

Silence rules the air till, "Is that all: is that all you have to offer pilot?"

"Not all Mr. De Marco. Inside the cross I saw something different. I saw what looked like a wheel within a wheel…all colored like beryl…

"What else…

"I'll never forget…I can't forget! It was like blood pouring downward from a cross: I couldn't look at it any longer Mr. De Marco. Suddenly I felt different. I had a feeling of guilt, like I've never had before. I don't know how to describe it sir."

"Then what pilot?"

"When I looked again... the cross and the wheel were gone...where I don't know, sir."

"Shut your mouth and say no more pilot! Say the words to anyone else; you're a dead man for sure!"

"But sir---what did the cross... the blood, what did that mean?" He asks, his voice quivering.

A moment of silence all over till, "It means the cross and the blood, you idiot! It's all about a worthless Jew called Jesus: *the holy one sent by his father to die upon a cross... at a place called Calvary-----*

But why did you stop sir?"

"Shut your mouth you idiot! I don't wanta talk about it!"

"But why ... tell me why sir!'

"It's the prophecy told by Ezekiel ...another worthless Jew! The thing you call a cross and a wheel, is nothing but a myth: those fanatical Christians sitting out before us smiling, worship the person that died upon it, you idiot!"

"Now what must I do Mr. De Marco?"

"Go back to the cab and call my friends at *Mauna Kea Observatory* immediately, they'll know what's going on for sure!"

Roberts looks over at Doug, nudging his shoulder ... "A penny for your thoughts Doug."

Doug looks back at him grinning. "You know my thoughts better than I do Roberts. De Marco knows Ezekiel's dream better than anyone ... except his master!"

"You're right again Doug, but this time a cross has been added. I've been waiting for something like this all my life. It makes me want to stand up and sing to the world ...

"What would you be singing sir?"

"There's only one way to say it Doug ... a song I once heard ...

"And the song, sir!"

"*How Great Thou Art!* It soothes my mind; it soothes my conscious … whenever I need it."

Minutes go by, and the pilot appears facing De Marco shaking his head, looking up to him, "This is crazy, it's absolutely crazy, Mr. De Marco!"

"Tell me about it…but speak lowly; the Christians are listening!"

"Mauna Kea observatory saw nothing. They searched the heavens over; except for hundreds of shooting stars heading downward toward the volcano above the observatory!"

De Marco lowers his head, his body lifeless, "Enough of this foolish nonsense; no more of this kind of news … understand, pilot?"

"I do sir. No more of this kind of news--- even if it kills me."

"For once your right pilot, your head is at stake! Now get back where you belong, and never again will you utter the words … *Cross or Calvary!*"

"Never again will I mention the word Cross or Calvary, I swear to you sir."

It's not long, till wheels strike the surface in Bali, causing a screeching sound, finally stopping.

Doug moves close to the window viewing a never-ending sea of people waiting; ready to welcome home their greatest hero ever. … De Marco.

An attendant leads the way to the exit with De Marco beside him… looking out upon hundreds.

De Marco doesn't wait…standing before them, raising his arms shouting, "What a beautiful and wonderful day this is being home with friends from my past," he shouts as he watches the crowd waving their hands and shouting his name forever.

"Doug whispers to Roberts, "Evidently these people love the guy Mr. Roberts...it makes me wonder ...

"Wonder about what?"

"Why they love the guy so much; Bali Indonesia ... of all places!"

"Evidently, they do love him Doug. Maybe this is where he got his charm."

"Whatever you're thinking...I'm thinking the same Mr. Roberts"

Marla stands close by returning phones. She hands Doug his phone with a note attached...reading, "Talk to you later Doug!"

He slips the note in his pocket moving away unnoticed: thinking maybe it's time we find something more about this lovely person serving De Marco, wanting to go home to America!

CHAPTER 34

Celebration

"The Lord knoweth who are his.

2ⁿᵈ Timothy 2: 19

Back home in America Mike and Brad leave *Indianapolis International Airport* headed for New York a week ahead of the church delegation. There's places to see, people to talk with, praying together.

Passengers have settled down to rest and Mike is feeling happy again. He sits next to Brad gazing out the window, while his thoughts creep back to the past--- three years ago; before his new life began.

He remembers his attitude ---filled with anger, but now he's a free man with love for the church, and what it means to him. Peace---wonderful peace he has finally found. Now ... it's time to discuss some things with Brad,

"I've been doing some reminiscing Brad, and for the first time in many years I feel good about myself. I guess you might say, I've made a change in my life...right partner?"

Brad lays his book down, moving closer, "You did make a change Mike. It was nothing but a miracle from God that sent you to us. But there's something else you probably never knew about-----

"I never knew about what, Brad?"

"We were about to go under Mike: financial problems plagued the church to no end. People were dissatisfied the way things were going: they needed something to perk them up. Mike!"

"But, I don't understand!"

"When you became a part of us, people began to see what God did for you. They knew your wife and loved her … she was one of them, Mike."

Mike can only look at Brad… thinking back.

"I don't know how to say this Brad, but Joyce was one of the faithful… she loved the place."

"But it wasn't only you that benefitted from coming back to church Mike."

"What are you trying to tell me?"

"Remember the small group of people at church … the ones who sat before you the day you gave your testimony------

"I'll never forget. I told the audience before me … "I'm the worst of the worst…the least of the least… and I was Brad!"

"But hears the good news Mike: the ones sitting before you listening went out and told their friends about it. People we hadn't seen for months came back to church again."

The Sundays we had before you came, only a few, today three hundred people. It was your testimony that made them wake up; they were just like you Mike!"

Mike looks over to Brad searching for some words, but impossible. A tear begins drifting downward.

"It could be Brad. I was at my lowest, but He wasn't finished with me. Sometime … even today, it's hard for me to believe I was sent to Berchtesgaden."

"It's a mystery for sure …except for the Lord up above us Mike."

"I'll never forget a remark Ethel once said to me … when I first came back to church …

"Tell me about it."

"She looked up at me with that certain little twinkle in her eyes and said, "Quit your worrying Mike …just trust in the Lord and he will provide for you."

"You're a very lucky guy to have met someone like Ethel, Mike."

"I'm aware of it. She doesn't hedge talking about things she stands for: she's a right to the point kind of person if there ever was one. I truly believe God planned her that way, so she could straiten out a guy like me. I feel the same way about you Brad."

Brad places his hand upon his shoulder looking up to him, "I'll always be here for you Mike. Our relationship has been wonderful; one on one from the beginning."

"But, there's other things I'd like to talk about Brad…

Brad looks up at him smiling, "We've understood each other from the very beginning, but if you're going to tell me about your past … forget it, brother!"

Mike sits silent, his eyes gaze downward searching for words. He wants to explain something troubling him forever.

"But you don't understand Brad, believe me you don't. It's not only the thirty wasted years, there's more!"

"Like what Mike?"

"My debt is paid in full … my heart, my soul, is at peace. But, still I've yearning for something greater; maybe something I could do for another!"

"Now slow down a moment Mike, take your time and tell me about It."

"But this is different--honest it is Brad!"

"Why different?"

"I've no idea what this burning desire inside me might be, but it never leaves me: it just doesn't go away Brad!"

Brad looks up at him again, wondering ... studying his thoughts, his mind.

A smile begins to show upon his face like none ever. He's beginning to realize this is something different; something between Mike and God alone to decide.

"I hear you, but this is strictly between you and God only Mike. The only advice I can give you is ...

"Is what Brad ...

Brad takes his hand, looking into his eyes... "God bless you my friend; do or go wherever He leads you: I'll be here praying for you!"

His face brightens, a smile returns immediately.

"I knew you would come up with some pleasant words... thank you Brad. But whatever may come or wherever I might go: I'm bound to find a way to help another ... as God helped me!"

"I hope you know something I don't Mike. Are you saying you're not satisfied after your trip to *Berchtesgaden*?"

Mike hesitates, finally beginning, "I realize I might sound a little irrational Brad, but there's things we have never talked about."

"Like what Mike?" You did it all and nobody could have done better!"

"Not all Brad. After my trip to the *Eagles Nest* I felt sure that was the end of my troubles. But today... for some unknown reason it isn't: there's more Brad----there has to be more.!"

"Like what---

"I want to go back to another time: back to the time I loved Him with all my heart, and all my soul. I want to go back before my problem with the church, before I felt the hatred I had for them,"

"But It's over. I've told you this repeatedly, it's time to move on and forget about it!"

"I wish I could, but it's something I can't get rid of Brad! I'll never forget my dedication at the altar as a child: it was exactly the way Friend told me about."

"But, if you haven't figured it out by now, I've got good news for you!"

"What's that, partner?"

Brad begins to chuckle, moving up in his face grinning, "No matter when, no matter where ... Friend will always be with you Mike!"

"I understand what you mean ... only a guy like you could say it any better,"

"But always remember this Mike."

"Yes Brad ...

"Whatever He might have in store for you will happen; no matter where, no matter when ... it will happen Mike!"

"You really believe it don't you Brad."

"I do believe it. Remember how it was before your mission to *Berchtesgaden*. You surprised us all, but the world still doesn't know the story. When it's all finished and over... it's only what God knows that really counts in life!"

Mike is surprised! His words are welcoming; especially words like, "*what God knows that really count in life!*"

"Thanks ... now I'll tell you the rest of my story."

"I'm waiting Mike."

"This is hard for me to explain, truly it is. But for some

unknown reason I feel my time on earth is short. But it doesn't bother me Brad."

I remember how I lay wounded in a rice paddy in Nam still wanting to kick butts; but couldn't rise to do it. But I'm different today; my wounds are healed; my sins are forgiven … that's all that matters, Brad!"

Brad tries to understand but useless. He's thinking, "maybe … just maybe the Lord isn't finished with Mike."

They sit quietly concentrating till, Mike breaks the silence

"'I remember Ethel telling me how life is so short; like a vapor disappearing high up into the sky. She was right Brad, it's that way for us all of us: here today … gone tomorrow!"

"You mean----

"Yes, my friend. But for the first time in my life I've no fear of tomorrow. He will be waiting to greet me… along with Ethel and a thousand more like her!"

"You're different Mike … completely different!"

"I've a lot to be thankful for Brad. I've met you, Ethel, Ailene, Doug, and Martha: I'm the luckiest guy in the world my friend."

"But why do you talk this way; this isn't you at all Mike. It's over and forgotten; it's time we change the subject and forget about it."

"But I can't forget Brad … everything is beautiful… I've no regrets … no sorrows."

"I'm envious of you in a loving sort of way. …

"You're envious of me … that's a new one for sure, something I'll remember forever… and then some," Mike says, shaking his head … wondering.

A couple hours later they stand registering at the hotel in New York looking forward to nothing but a week of pleasure; before Martha will arrive to meet the love of her life … Doug.

CHAPTER 35

A New Player

And God shall wipe away all tears from their eyes; and there shall be no more death; neither sorrow,

Revelation 21: 4

It's Sunday morning in Bali, and Doug sits alone in his hotel room watching news from America concerning the great earthquake.

San Francisco lies in ruins, looting runs wild; while citizens live in fear without food and water.

Mountainous tidal waves have destroyed everything in its path, running from San Francisco down to Los Angeles.

Hollywood remains active and moving, while casualties run high throughout the area. National Guard units are called in from other parts of the United States: while military bases prepare for the worst. Martial Law is put into action throughout the area, while churches remain filled to the brim!

A news bulletin flashes across the television screen

announcing the United Nations Assembly in New York has been cancelled; a later meeting will be held in Rome, near the Vatican.

Doug sits at his bedside ready to call Martha, and there's a slight knock on the door. He peers through the peep-hole… seeing Marla standing alone, wiping tears from her eyes.

He opens the door, takes her hand seating her at the nearest table … waiting.

A couple of moments later she's looking up to him barely muttering, "The phone. it's bugged Doug!"

He looks back at her grinning, "Don't worry about it, Marla …took care of it when we arrived here. Now tell me what your problem is before someone comes looking for you."

She looks up at him with tears still showing, "I need your help Doug. I need it more than you can ever imagine," she tries to explain, tears still falling.

A long pause and Doug takes her hand, looking up into her eyes, "Tell me what's going on and maybe I'll help you: tell me a lie and you're out of here immediately!"

His words cause her to take her breath …barely muttering, "I'm desperate with no-where to turn Doug. My friends are all departed or dead. You and Roberts are the only ones left I can turn to…your part of me Doug!"

"What do mean saying we're part of you, Marla?"

"I sent you my note---you know the story. I know what's going on between you and Roberts!"

"What does that mean?"

"It means I'm aware you're opposed to De Marco the same as I am. We're partners …both us with the same problem… De Marco! I deplore the guy! I need to get away from him once and forever, Doug!" She says, looking up at him, pleading.

Doug takes his time, trying to figure out a way to reply, still thinking it over.

"It's nice to know some good news for a change Marla, most everyone else adores him!"

"I despise him more than you and Roberts despise him, but there's nothing else I can do. You and Roberts are my only hope: this the only way I know how to say it Doug!"

"Tell me some more Marla."

"Your friendship means everything. It brings me hope when I thought there was no hope. You're my last and only chance to get away from him Doug... there's no other place I can hide," she whispers softly.

He stands close to her, thinking about the many times Roberts has warned him about a situation as this: no matter how innocent it may seem.

He remembers the time he warned him of dirty-tricks, set-ups looking innocent... always ending in tragedy.

But now he's thinking again; Marla could become a player... someone they can depend upon.

She moves against him, barely whispering, "Please listen to me Doug ... I'm an American as much as the both of you; but I can't disguise my feelings about De Marco any longer."

"He's nothing but a beast without a heart; not the one he pretends to be. I need to get away from him...or I'll kill myself and get it over with Doug!"

"Do you realize what you're saying?"

"Every word of it ...there must be an end in my miserable life sometime, Doug!"

"But think about the position I'm in Marla: you with me alone in my room at this time of the evening!"

She looks up at Doug, lowering head...nothing.

"This is crazy, unbelievable Marla! How do I know you're not one of De Marco's plants?"!"

"What I tell you is true; hard to believe, but true. I swear it from the bottom of my heart as a Christian …as much Christian as you are Doug!"

Doug is speechless…saying nothing, waiting.

"I'm fully aware my being here is dangerous, but I've no other choice; it's do this… or do the unthinkable!"

"Keep going Marla…

"My entire life has been lived with this kind of existence; a life of shame and misery from the beginning!"

"Don't stop Marla…

"There's no other way out of this situation for Marla: it's you and Roberts or nothing Doug! She says, dropping her head down upon his shoulder, waiting.

A long moment of thought, another moment of pity, "But explain to me again … why now, Marla?"

Her head lowers, finally able to speak, "This is my last chance to get away from De Marco. He treats me as a slave… I'm afraid to cross him."

"I'm beginning to understand!"

"I plead with you and Roberts to help me from the bottom of my heart … return me to the country and family I love… please help me…Doug…please do----

"But Marla… can you possibly understand the situation Roberts and I will be in if it all goes wrong?"

"I'm aware of everything Doug; believe me I am. I've been with people like De Marco my entire life. But when there's no other way out … nowhere to turn: I'll do anything to get away from him. It's either help from you and Roberts…or I'm dead!"

"But understand something else Marla …

"Yes, Doug …

"Roberts is the man! To decide this. He alone makes the decisions. He's rough, he's tough … there's none better. I'm his aide and I do what he tells me to do; that's how it is Marla… that's the way it has to be!"

"Then what's my chance of going further, tell me Doug ….

"If he believes your story we're in all the way. But if you're setting us up for something different … you're dead as hell… and so are we, Marla."

A long moment of silence…a couple of tears falling downward from Marla's big blue eyes, and, "That's the only way I know how to say it; do you fully understand my position Marla," he asks, frightening her.

Her body quivers, her voice is broken, "But I do understand Doug. I've played this game all my life, but never with friends like you and Roberts. I read something long ago that touched me deeply … today it's all I can think about."

"Fill me in…tell me about what touched you deeply. Marla."

She hesitates, thinking back, "It was a history book I found someplace. I read about a person named Patrick Henry …

"Tell me the words you will never forget Marla …

She looks again at him pitiful like, *"Give me liberty---or give me death … that's me; that's the only way I know how to say it, Doug!"*

Doug looks up at her smiling, "I heard the same in grade school and loved it too, Marla, but first, I must ask you a question …

Her head lowers, looking back up at him, "Help your-self, asks me whatever Doug."

"What does De Marco say about Roberts and me in private?"

"I've heard him tell others you're in Military. Intelligence! De Marco doesn't like you Mike, but he hates Roberts more.

He tells everyone he despises Roberts as a man to look out for... wishes he could shut his mouth forever!"

Doug sighs ... a smile for a change. "That's what I've wanted to hear... Roberts will love it. Now maybe we can do business!"

"But understand this, Doug ...

"Yes Marla ...

"I don't care if you're KGB, CIA, or Military Intelligence: I just need to get home. I need to live again as God planned me to live... not a slave to guy like De Marco!"

"You will get home if Roberts agrees. Just pray that everything you told me is correct. But there's something for you to look forward to ...

"Look forward to what-----

"You'll be checked and double-checked before Roberts makes a decision. That's the way he does business Marla ... all or nothing with Roberts!"

"I understand...believe I do. I know the risks he's taking, but I'll be doing the same. everything I told you was true ... but never forget this ...

"Now what...

"It's far worse than you could ever imagine... everything about him is rotten!"

"Nothing about De Marco surprises me... Roberts knows about him from way back."

"But wait till you hear some of the tapes I have in their entirety...this is all I ask of you, Doug."

"But I warn you again Marla ...

"Warn me about what?"

"You better be telling the truth, if not...you're in a heap of trouble; trouble like you've never seen before!"

Quietly, he moves from the room heading for Robert's

quarters, two doors down the hallway. He knocks repeatedly, but never an answer. Finally, he stops … returning to Marla.

"Roberts isn't available at the present, Marla … would you like to continue our conversation or wait for him later?"

"Let's get it over with Doug. Some of the things you need to know are too important."

"Then, let's get started Marla, time's wasting."

"Last evening, I was sitting in the lounge next to De Marco's meeting room and the door wasn't fully closed. People were going in and out like a bunch of tourist. But for some reason nobody paid attention to me."

"The only reason I could imagine was… they were not paying attention to me. I'm sure it was because what was going on inside the room, listening to De Marco!"

"Keep going.…"

"Later, I noticed the situation had changed!"

"Changed …and how was it changed, Marla?"

"Numerous persons entered his office, but none were coming out; naturally … I was curious!"

"How many were they, a rough guess…

She pauses--thinking, "I'm not sure, maybe up to a hundred or so, it was hard to keep track: they were coming and going all evening long."

"You're sure about this…

"Positive…I heard every word they spoke, and they weren't aware of it. I speak five different languages and know most of them by face. I met many of them while serving the Sheik … before he sent me to De Marco."

Doug grasps her hand stopping her. "Are you telling me you heard their entire conversation… and you're willing to tell the same to Roberts?"

"I am willing to tell the same to Roberts: that's why I'm

here pleading with you to help me. I took pictures, cell phones, recorded conversations: I have it all here with me now; that's why I'm worried Doug!"

"Worried about what, Marla?"

She stops ... looking at him differently. "If they have the slightest thought of what I'm into---I don't even wanta' think about it. Some of these people are ISIS; the most vicious animals ever. Killing and torture means nothing to them ... it's more like a pleasure, Doug!"

Doug moves closer ... "Are you telling me you've seen De Marco, or his people along with ISIS ... killing people?"

"Sure, I have! I've seen him kill people many times! I'll never forget the last one---a young British soldier serving in Iraq. De Marco stabbed him with what looked like a writing pen; in minutes the young soldier lay on the floor dead."

Doug bristles, holding back, till "But, why an ordinary soldier ... doesn't make sense Marla?"

"He refused doing what De Marco wanted him to do ... it's just that simple Doug!"

Doug slows his questions ... looking again at Marla.

"What was he asking from the soldier, Marla?"

"Same as usual, he wanted him to sign a statement--a false statement; saying he killed women and children for pleasure. But that's only part of it ...

"Keep going ...

Marla looks up at Doug, with tears beginning to show... "I was forced to watch as they cut his tongue out... feeding to some dogs...waiting!"

Doug can only stare at her ... looking at her pitiful like, "Sorry I had to ask, but it's things I gotta be sure of when Roberts hears about it," Doug says, apologizing.

She looks across the table, fighting back tears, "Don't ever ask me to say this again Doug. I won't do it ... I can't do it!"

"But, have you thought about the other side of this situation: what they might do if everything doesn't work out the way we want it to go, Marla?"

"I have thought about it. But I'll never go with De Marco again, no matter what it comes to Doug!"

He waits ... pausing again. "And, the other people, the visitors De Marco brought with him ... do we know them Marla?"

"Sure, you do! De Marco had them waiting in Rome with him.... none of your delegates: they were the ones who joined you later...the "Club of Rome people. They were the Millionaires, Billionaires... his best friends ever!"

"Give me some names..."

"I know a lot of them They're the most dangerous people on the face of the earth.

"They come from Russia, Iran, China, the Muslim Brotherhood, Libya, Lebanon ... all over, Doug! There are four or five new ones from Myanmar, but those I didn't know. They flew into Bali this week, while others were here getting acquainted here in Bali!"

"And ISIS ...

"Oh yes ISIS ... they're right in the middle of it, frightens me to think about! If they find out what I'm holding ... the end of the both of us, Doug!"

"Take it slow and easy before going further Marla, I don't wanta miss anything... Roberts will love it!"

"I understand ... believe me I do! But one more time Doug, something for sure...

"For sure...

"You and Roberts are my last resort; my only ticket out of

this place of hell and murder. I'll do anything but let them kill me. But If worse comes to worse … then that's something I'll have to do!"

"But don't forget this Marla …

"Forget what?"

"Roberts can be the most pleasant guy you ever met, but if he even suspects you're lying: you'll wish you were never born Marla!"

"Don't try to frighten me Doug, it doesn't work. I've wished I was never born a thousand times over. Many times, I was used by some fat miserable looking pig from a place l like to call hell. I tried the suicide route, but thanks only to God … it didn't work for me," she says … looking up at him with tears beginning to show again.

"Suicide route …

She turns her head displaying marks around her neck … "A rope--how else Doug!"

"I'm sorry Marla… I shouldn't have asked!"

"I told you I'm desperate. I've told you how De Marco killed the young soldier; but there's other things I'll never forget!"

"Like what?"

"I was in Saudi Arabia with De Marco. He and some of his friends were reading an American newspaper article explaining how terrorist in the United States were read their rights under the Constitution."

"And what did they think about it Marla?"

She holds her breath a moment and… "They were laughing so hard it made me laugh along with them; it's the truth Doug … I swear it!"

"What were you thinking?"

"I was thinking what the whole world thinks Doug; American's are fools when it comes to justice! In America they read them their rights and let the lawyers take over: in the Arab world they stone them to death and let the dogs take over! It's a different kind of justice Doug ... it's the Muslim way of dealing with justice!"

But the cell-phone, the pictures, the recorder ... all of it; do you have them with you?"

"I do have them with me, glad to get rid of them." Marla says, reaching into her purse ... handing them over to Doug.

"You've been through a lot, a lot more than the average person. But understand the seriousness of the situation, Marla?"

"I understand everything ... tell me what's next."

Doug sits across from her wondering ... how to say it, till ... "This could end up being something more important than you ever dreamed about Marla ... are you ready for it?"

She brushes back her hair, staring at him. "I've had enough of this Doug ... I can't go on. You have all the evidence before you: now it's time to speak from my heart!"

"Yes Marla-----

"I want you to promise me one thing for sure Doug---

Doug hesitates ... looking again, feeling her pain ... "If your story is true and Roberts goes along with it ... consider it done Marla!"

"One more question...

"Yes Martha ...

"When we arrive at New York, will you help me get away from De Marco?"

"Sure, we will. Roberts will see you're well taken care of and a place to live the rest of your life. How does that make you feel, Marla?"

"It's all I've dreamed about from the moment I was kidnapped. I want to feel like an American, enjoy freedom as God wanted me to have freedom: not the kind of freedom granted for sexual favors to the world's worst ever!"

"You have my word. I'll get with Roberts immediately ... but theirs other things to do--------

"What other things Doug?"

"We need a plan to move what you gave me, and Roberts isn't aware of our discussion!"

"Now what are you trying to tell me?"

"Roberts is the boss and he will make the plan how to handle this. If he decides to go along with what we've been talking about: get ready to move out Marla. I'll talk to you later!"

She looks up to him smiling, "Later ... but when is later?"

"Whenever or whatever Roberts decides to do. It's all in his hands from now on Marla. He will know the time and place when the action takes place!"

"Then what?"

"You'll be going home to be with your family again... how does that make you feel Marla?"

"It would be like heaven on earth. But there's something else ... something for you to know Doug----

"Tell me what I need to know, Marla."

"Always remember no matter whatever might happen ... I'll die happy knowing we tried!" She says, turning her head to the side, hoping he can't see a couple of tears falling.

"But nothing is going to happen Marla. Roberts is the best... his record is perfect. I hope I haven't missed something, but that's up to Roberts to decide. Do I make myself clear Marla?"

"Very clear. I'm beginning to feel like I'm being born again--- a life beginning over: a life I've dreamed about, but never had before."

"It could be Marla ... we Christians do it all the time."

She hugs him warmly, looking up to him, "I believe the same as you, Doug ...I really do."

"Why so sure Marla?"

"Someone called a Missionary stopped to help me when I was at my lowest. She told me about Jesus ... and from that day forward I believed in Him only, Doug!"

He leads her toward the door, whispering, "But there's something else you must know before you leave...

"What's that, Doug?"

"Roberts could make a change in plans at the very last moment. Be ready for anything, and don't be surprised whatever might happen: he's the best there is for a job like this and everyone knows it, Marla."

A soft kiss on his cheek and she leave the room smiling ... never looking back... satisfied.

CHAPTER 36

Changing Plans

Verily, verily, I say unto you, he that believeth on me, hath everlasting life.

St. John 6; 47

Doug sits alone pondering how to present the information to his boss. He hopes he approves his action with Marla without his presence;

He quits pondering … heading for Robert's room once again. He knocks lightly on the door and Roberts appears dressed in a long black robe, inviting him inside.

Doug doesn't wait, pointing toward the phone whispering, "The room is bugged, Mr. Roberts."

"Forget it lad: took care of the problem the moment we arrived."

A couple of moments to get his breath and, "I've something to show you Mr. Roberts … it's dynamite!"

"Sit down beside me and tell me about it lad … we'll see if it's dynamite."

"Marla came to my room unexpected only a few minutes ago. I tried to find you… but you weren't available."

And-------

She was crying her heart out… I felt sorry for her. She showed me some things that will shock you!"

"And … what did you do about it … tell me about it Doug!"

"I did what you would have done under the circumstances Mr. Roberts. I took the liberty of giving her some of my ideas, and what could be lying ahead of her and the rest of us."

"And then what?"

"I made it clear to her you would be the one to make the final decision before going further, Mr. Roberts."

"That's the way I want it to be. We're a team and I'm the leader; show me what you have planned out for her."

Mike doesn't wait… displaying everything upon a table.

Pictures show Europeans, Arabs, Chinese and Russian diplomats huddled together with a couple from the *Muslim Brotherhood*. They're pointing to maps showing American military being blown to pieces by road-side bombs in Afghanistan.

Halfway into the showing Roberts grabs his hand stopping him.

"Stop where you are Doug, I can't believe what I'm seeing; look who stands next to De Marco."

"You're referring to whom sir?"

"None other than the past president of Iran! He's the same guy who stood in the United Nations Assembly in *New York* blasting our country before the world."

"He's the same liar that told the world the holocaus*t* never took place in Europe during WW11. He's the same devil who wants to wipe Israel off the map. But the most amazing thing is … I'm beginning to believe he doesn't really care for us Americans!"

"You're right, it is him sir. I don't know why, but I never recognized him when Marla showed it to me."

"Take a look who stands next to the Chinese delegate. None other than Brutus Zurko, one of the old Communist pals of Brasov. Standing next to him is their Foreign Minister, Victor Mein off … past president of the Communist Party!"

"This is hard to believe Doug. But look at the guy standing next to the door near the Chinese delegate."

"Wow! It's none other than, "George Whipple," a former member of Congress. I'd recognize him anywhere. He was supposed to be one of the "think-tank" members selected by some of our own: but for some unknown reason he was replaced at the last moment."

Roberts begins to grin. "Now, we know why lad: he was more valuable here in the states furnishing information back to our enemies," he adds, wiping his brow thinking about it.

Doug ponders on and on without speaking … till, he looks up moving across from Roberts.

"I don't know why, but I'm beginning to believe they're gathered here to unite forces with De Marco sir. It's becoming scary … makes me believe something big is in the air…or these guys wouldn't be here."

"You're right Doug. They're preparing for something big, no doubt about it. Are you ready for it lad?"

"Ready as I'll ever be. But do you think we'll get a chance to show this stuff to the right people, before they try to stop us Mr. Roberts?" he asks, holding his breath waiting.

"There's no limit to what they'll do to stop us Doug. From this moment forward keep your eyes and ears open. Remember everything I'm telling you; its important more than ever in a place like this lad."

"How important?"

"It's important enough to keep you alive before this incident is over. We're about to do business with the best of them: the kind that would slit your throat for a nickel and laugh about it later, lad!"

"You really believe it's going to happen... don't you Mr. Roberts."

"Sure, I believe it...and so should you. Everything in this game is serious. life means nothing to these guys Doug. They actually believe if they give their life for Allah: they'll end up in heaven with a bunch of virgins waiting for them!"

Doug looks up at Roberts shocked; surprised again ... apologizing.

"I wanted to be sure sir. What's our next move?"

"I might sound a little blunt at times, but when you described the things we hold as dynamite; you described it lightly! Right, now... most book-makers would probably say odds are about ten to one against us making it back home again. This is going to be a tough job to pull off lad; but we'll do it ... our way only Doug!"

"And our way only is what... Mr. Roberts?"

"We live with it. We play the game the way we like it; not the way they like it! This is our game and we hold the aces. We play by our rules, not their rules ... understand lad?"

Doug begins to smile, "As you would say, *'Sure I do----clear as hell, Mr. Roberts!'* But there's something else I need to tell you about ...

"Tell me about what?"

"I'm not a kid any more, Mr. Roberts! I'm a man as much as you are. I stand ready to go to battle with the best of them sir!"

Roberts stops ... looking up at him; reminds him of himself thirty years ago and then some.

"I'm happy you said it that way, Doug. The only reason I asked was to make you realize what we're into; who stands with us ... who stands against us!"

Roberts stops ...looking away, thinking again ...

"Something wrong sir?"

"There's a lot wrong! I'm searching my brain trying to find out the ones against us. Tell me something Doug ...

"Tell you what Mr. Roberts?"

"Tell me what Marla thinks about all this happening in her own back-yard!"

"She thinks the same as I do. She's ready to do anything to protect the information, and she isn't afraid to do it. She has a lot of guts...she's ready to go to war with the best of them sir!"

"Great...she's different for sure! I want you to remember something Doug; something important to think about before this mission is over."

"Like what...?"

"Right now, my mind is running like a locomotive without an engineer. But before we reach Kennedy... I'll have a plan ready for you to go over with Marla; in the mean-time don't ask me about it!"

"I'll be waiting Mr. Roberts."

"Whatever I decide to do between here and Kennedy we'll do it my way. I'll make the plan ... I'll study the strategy ... understand lad?"

"I expected no less ... told Marla the same, Mr. Roberts."

"That's good... really good. But sometime before we reach New York I want you to get with Marla and go over everything again. Whatever you want to tell her beside the plan is your privilege; make her feel like she's one of us for a change."

"That's what she wants Mr. Roberts."

Roberts stops, thinking… "If anyone ever deserves a break in life … Marla does for sure Doug!"

"She does Mr. Roberts She told me things about the scum she had to serve under; made me want to vomit my head off. She's one of us, a Christian, sir!"

"What makes you believe she's a Christian, Doug?"

"She told me so. She told me about a missionary who helped her; told her about Jesus and she believed. She's a Christian if I ever saw one Mr. Roberts!"

"But now… time we get ready for some more of this crap; we're going "big-time Doug!"

"Big time … that's a new one. Tell me about it, Mr. Roberts …

Roberts looks up at him grinning, "It means all the way, no holds barred… it's them or us Doug!"

Doug begins to grin, a smile appears …

"Why the sudden smile on your face, Doug---

"I've nothing to worry about … I'm covered by the blood of Jesus. I took care of that about twenty years ago in my Uncle Mike's backyard: while my aunt Joyce was praying for me!"

Roberts face begins to show differently, he's looking downward thinking------

"Something's wrong… isn't it Mr. Roberts?"

"It sure as hell is Doug. I just realized we've been had big time. Now, it's time we play the game the way they do …

"What are you talking about?"

"I'm talking about playing down and dirty; that's what I'm talking about lad!"

"But I don't understand … we have the proof here with us; surely you don't worry about its' authenticity ……

"Not in the least. It's dynamite as you called it; now, we're about to prove it, Doug!"

"Then why the worried look?"

"It's all about this trip to no-where: it has been nothing but a sham from the beginning!"

"A sham! Now what are you trying to tell me, sir?"

"Only this my boy ... De Marco is using this trip to nowhere as a front for his real purpose. He's here to gather his armies together for the big one coming later. This is the time, and this is the place; the forming of the greatest army ever: a two-million- man army ready to go to war at the Euphrates River!!"

"Battle of what-----

"But, I still don't understand ...

"It's simple lad. Think about what the Bible tells us about a seven-year treaty between Jews and Palestinians living in Jerusalem: just before the battle of all battles... Armageddon!"

"You're getting to me real good Mr. Roberts ... are you thinking the same as I am?"

"Of course, I am! This has gotta be him! He has appeared from out of nowhere: we've been had by the biggest scam artist ever Doug!"

"I believe you're right, sir."

"But think about this...

"This what... Mr. Roberts?"

"Something from the Bible ... something to make you think about ... I'll quote it to you."

> **"Whereas ye know ye not what shall be on the morrow. For what is your life? It is even a vapor, that appeareth for a little time and then vanisheth away.**
>
> **James 4: 14**

"It's great Mr. Roberts but think about the good side of life!"

"Tell me about it!"

"Something I'll never forget. 'If your right with Him … it's forever and forever walking down streets shining as gold!'"

"Glad you said it that way Doug, I'm feeling better now."

There's still no sign of De Marco or his friends in public area. Many of his friends are seen leaving from the back entrance heading for the airport, while Doug and Roberts act unconcerned; watching people move in and out of De Marco's headquarters, smiling.

Mike is lonely. He wants to call Martha from someplace safe. He heads out toward the ocean with only the sound of waves splashing up against the sand.

"Hello my darling… I just had to call and tell you some things."

"Tell me what sweetheart?"

"I miss you terribly. I'm lonely, wanta be with you and hold you in my arms again… like I always did."

Her heart begins to pound, "But when will you be coming home darling?"

"Pretty soon, I hope…maybe only a couple more days. Hang with me and don't worry about me. My biggest problem is how much I miss you, sweetheart!"

"You're on my mind always …and always will be Doug."

"It's the same with me sweetheart. I've been doing some thinking lately … all about the two of us!"

"Thinking about what Doug?"

"I've been thinking about how time is so precious… how important it is!"

"I'm doing the same. Have you found a solution?"

"Well ... I was thinking when this is over we might take another vacation: a long vacation; one without end!"

Tell me some more about this vacation, sweetheart...it's getting interesting."

'I'm beginning to think this isn't the kind of life we planned darling. It's a long story for sure: something we need to talk about when I get home again."

"We will talk about it, darling. I've dreamed of you every night, think about you constantly. Some of my friends tell me I'm becoming hard to get along with ... funny, isn't it!"

"It's the same here in Bali...I'm not the most pleasant person around ... Roberts is even worse. I'm afraid to talk on my cell-phone... watch everything I say or do. This is one dangerous place to be hanging out in for sure!"

"When will you be coming home sweetheart?"

"I'll be in New York Tuesday for sure. Meet me inside the airport near the concourse, be careful who is standing around you. There'll be a huge crowd, so be there early, honey."

"I'll be there before anyone...you know I will. I've talked to Mike on the phone... he and Brad are in New York now, waiting for you to arrive. I'll be leaving tomorrow with the rest of our group from church---ok with you, darling?"

"Sure, it is. I'm anxious to see all of them: a lot to tell Mike about what I was thinking about him the other day!"

"Thinking about Mike ... why darling?"

"From out from nowhere ... a song he and a friend used to sing came to my mind."

"Tell me the name of the song and I'll sing it for you sometime."

"I'll never forget ... *Everything is Beautiful!* It reminded me of you sweetheart!"

"You say the nicest things darling. I suppose you know

by now how bad the earthquake has affected America: how people gather outside churches hoping to get inside and ask forgiveness."

"It's been that way since Adam and Eve in the garden honey!"

"It's worse than *"Nine-Eleven,"* Doug. People appear on television crying, begging for help ... but there's no help to give them."

"Get used to it sweetheart. When people have it all they follow the flow: in trouble they head for the church begging the Lord to forgive them. It's been that since Jesus walked in the streets of Jerusalem! That's what it's about sweetheart!"

But now It's time to move on---see you soon, my darling!"

CHAPTER 37

A Time to Heal

I have made a covenant with my chosen; I have sworn unto David my servant.

Psalm 89: 3

Roberts is beginning to feel the strain he's under. He's tired, weary ... walking toward small palm trees a short distance from his quarters. He sits glancing out across the scenery; seeing his friend Joshua Bernstein, a member of the Israeli delegation sitting close by.

He watches him pick up his brief-case approaching him, seating himself looking worried.

"I've been taking a stroll to nowhere Mr. Roberts, do you mind if I join you?" He asks, casually.

"Please do Joshua. I've been hoping to meet with you ... there's unfinished business we need to talk about."

"There has to be Mr. Roberts."

"It's important we talk low without drawing attention, there's cameras and listening devices everywhere Joshua."

"I'm sure there is ... you begin, and I'll listen Mr. Roberts."

Roberts looks up at him grinning, "But for the moment, just refer to me as Roberts ... it sounds better."

"I was thinking the same, and from this moment forward refer to me as Josh!"

"Before we move forward I must have your complete confidence. I want to know if I can trust you ... good or bad Josh."

His eyes light up, a smile appears, "I give you my word in the name of Jehovah ... I'll never lie to you, always be truthful Roberts."

"Jehovah is good enough. We're off on the same track at this point. Now let's get started ... tell me what's bothering you."

A deep worried look, desperation showing at its' highest, and ... "I don't know if I'm doing the right thing or not disclosing this information to you, Roberts, but I've no other choice."

"Keep going Josh ...

"Night after night I lie awake imagining the most horrible things ever; my heart grows weaker and weaker ... I don't know who to turn to Roberts!"

"I know your feelings; hasn't been easy for Doug and me either."

His head drops, looking down to the ground barely muttering, "In all the trouble I've ever known, I've never felt so desperate as I am now. I try to understand what's going on in this crazy world of ours, but I can't find an answer no-where, Roberts!"

"Let it out all out Josh."

"I've searched the world over ... climbed every mountain; as some I've heard say ...

"I'm waiting ... Josh."

A long moment of thought ... looking again at Roberts and, "I've finally conclude you and your group of Americans, are the only friends Israel has left in the world, but ...

"But what Josh ..."

Josh takes his time, moving closer, "I've just learned persons in our government want to go along with De Marco ... sign the peace treaty immediately!"

Roberts turns, looking away, "And what's your opinion ... give it to me straight out!"

"I want nothing to do with it ... it's nothing but treason: that's the only way I know how to say it, Roberts!"

"Tell me about the other people in your party Josh ... what's their feeling about these issues?"

"They feel the same, but afraid to say it."

"You're sure about this, Josh!"

"I'm saying it! There's a problem of trust all over the world and everyone knows it. But if this could keep us from going to war I'll do it. I sit and ask myself for how long this kind world is going to last...but never an answer, Roberts!"

"Tell me the reason Josh?"

Again, his head bows, barely muttering, "It's him ... De Marco ... the one everyone is talking about."

He has only been on the scene only a short time, but now millions follow him. It's scary as it gets Roberts; keeps me awake night after night!"

"Keep going... I'm listening ...

"I think back to child-hood ... remembering something foretold in the scriptures. I read it again and again; it causes my body to shiver thinking about it, Roberts!"

Roberts' moves closer ... "Tell me some more, Josh."

"I'm not sure how all this is going to end; nobody knows Roberts!" He says, moving closer to Roberts.

"I'm loving it … keep going Josh."

"Perhaps I shouldn't say this Roberts, but I must speak truthfully. There's times I worry where your President and others in government fit in the picture; whether they're trustful or not!"

Roberts turns, placing his hand upon his shoulder, "I can't blame you; I've done the same a hundred times over. But I remind you again this conversation between the two of us never was, never happened Josh."

Josh holds out his hand joining his, looking up to Roberts, "It was never discussed … never happened my friend," he says, squeezing his hand forever.

"But you can rest assured of something important …"

"Assured of what Roberts?"

"Doug and I are only two in millions, but we stand with you; today … tomorrow … forever, Josh!"

"Tell me your reason Roberts, something to make me feel good."

"Jesus … the Son of God was a Jew, but he died for all others; millions of Gentiles like Doug and I Josh!"

His eyes light up … a smile appears, "I'll sleep well tonight Roberts, I needed to hear those words. But again, I need your confidence; there's something else important …"

Roberts turns his head away---"But maybe if it's that important … you shouldn't tell me Josh."

"We're friends Roberts; I've got to trust someone Roberts."

"But think it over again my friend, perhaps I shouldn't know."

Sweat appears upon his face … "I'm talking as serious as it gets, I'm talking about peace for the world over. We're living in a world completely different: nothing is sacred in the world we live in today Roberts!"

Roberts stands upright, looking over the scenery and back to Josh, "You have my trust from this day forward … get with it my friend!"

"I've been informed this very day … if the treaty isn't approved our forces will take all necessary action needed to stop Iran from completing their nuclear bomb. Our agents are positive the bomb will be deliverable in two months; there's no hope left, Roberts!"

"Are you sure about this Josh?" He asks, whispering.

"It comes from the top. We have no choice but to fight back. Put yourself in our place, but don't say it: the fall-out from this could prove disastrous the world over!"

"I believe you're right, but where does De Marco fit in? He has promised his protection, but do you trust him Josh?"

"We trust him only so-far Roberts; after that we check him again. He tells us his *"Seven Year Treaty"* has a covenant as good as the one God gave Abraham."

"What do your people say about it?"

"God, we trust … De Marco we worry about … that's the only way how to say it Roberts!"

"You have reason to worry Josh, but the outcome … the most important part; what's the outcome going to be?"

"I don't know my friend … I truly don't know. Therefore… I'm asking you Roberts. I want your opinion … someone I can trust!"

"This is far beyond me Josh. But there's a way out of this mess for sure …

Josh looks up at him hesitating," Out with-it…tell me the way out of this mess!"

"Pray man! Pray with all your heart, your soul … your mind … everything you can think about Josh!"

Josh looks up at Roberts stunned again. He's wondering why he didn't think of it before. He turns his head away chuckling.

"Now what's so funny Josh?"

"Only this Roberts … you, a gentile telling a Jew like me to pray; our people were born to pray. But somewhere along the way we've forgotten how to pray. Thanks to you my friend: maybe someday we'll understand one another and pray as one, Roberts!"

Roberts looks up at him grinning, "Happens to the best of us my friend; prayer works when everything around us fails. The one looking over us now… never fails Josh!"

"But, we really don't have much choice Roberts."

"Sure, you do. Everyone gets a second chance sometime in their life. Let's walk to the Palm tree, come back and try to clear our mind for a change."

Josh looks up at him suspiciously. He turns looking at the Palm tree shaking his head; *thinking what's next with this gentile friends of mine!"*

Ten minutes go by and they return sitting upon the bench. Roberts finally breaking the silence.

"I believe the walk did some good Josh. It made me think different."

"What does different mean Roberts?"

"I've concluded De Marco holds the aces. He's the shrewdest I've ever met, and I've faced the best of them Josh! But I keep asking myself the same question over and over------

"What question?"

"Why are your people going along with this guy; there has to be a reason!"

Josh takes his time, moving closer to Roberts, barely whispering, "De Marco has promised to build us a temple next to the *Holy Mount* … a place for us to worship as we once before did Roberts! It's something our people have dreamed about forever!"

Roberts looks up to him barely whispering, "It's something sacred to Jews … isn't it Josh …

"It means everything to our people; something we've always prayed for, but never happening my friend!"

Roberts looks again at Josh … shocked again. The very mention of a Jewish temple built near the sight of the *Temple Mount*; something to think about from the Bible…he's thinking.

"Hold it a moment…did I hear you say he has promised you a Temple near the Temple Mount in Jerusalem, or am I dreaming Josh?"

"You're not dreaming Roberts … I did say it! It's something sacred to my people, as it is to the Palestinians. Since the beginning of time we both have had the same love for Jerusalem!"

"You have a problem my friend. something you need to think about!"

"Now, what are you telling me?"

Roberts looks up in his face grinning, "It will not be you and your people in the temple Josh!"

"Then who will it be in the temple?"

"Nobody but the one we've been talking about Josh … De Marco!"

"But, I don't understand---

Again, Roberts places his hands upon his shoulder, "It's all about him, Josh; not your people. Jerusalem is where he wants to end up as God: the whole world worshipping him … not our God for sure Josh!"

"But why do you say this Roberts-----

"Read the Holy Bible Josh … read "The Book of Revelation."

"The book of Revelation you say----Roberts?"

"That's right my friend. According to John's writing he ends up in Jerusalem at the temple pretending to be God; It's all in the Bible Josh!"

Josh lowers his head looking up to him, "You're sure of this Roberts?"

"No doubt about it Josh!"

"But why would God permit this Roberts?" He can barely mutter.

Roberts sits wondering how to say something he hates to say, but does, "The Bible tells us God has blinded your people because of your unfaithfulness: it's time you open your eyes, look up and pray your heart out my friend!"

Josh looks up at Roberts still wondering, "And then what?" He's barely able to ask.

"Only one thing you can do Josh; do what the rest of us do!"

"What's that Roberts?"

"Get down upon your knees, pray your heart out and asks forgiveness Josh!"

"But are you sure about this Roberts?"

"I'm sure. Read the "New Testament", read all about the antichrist, unfaithfulness, deceit; all of it coming before the return of our Lord Jesus!"

"But Roberts, if I try telling those words to my brothers … they'll laugh at me for sure. They don't understand things like you and I do Roberts," he tries, to explain.

"I'm glad you mentioned your brothers Josh … It brings up another question."

"Today is your day … out with It, Roberts!"

"It's hard to say this, but it's time we understand each other before continuing further, my friend!"

Josh's head drops even further … his face turns pale.

"You can't hurt my feelings … I'm accustomed to live in doubt; go ahead and let it all out Roberts!"

"I've always wondered why Jews in America criticize Christians for everything they should be doing. Throughout the Middle East they call your people *The Little Satan; Christians … The Big Satan!* You've heard it a thousand times undoubtedly Josh!"

"But you're wrong Roberts!"

"Why am I wrong … explain it to me?"

"I've heard it ten thousand times and then some Roberts!"

"But, there's some good news for sure Josh …

"Tell me about it Roberts, I need some good news for a change."

"Christians always have and always will support your people Josh. We know you're "His Chosen Ones" … are you following me Josh?"

"I'm ahead of you. I thank my Christian brothers wherever or whoever they might be; they mean a lot to me, Roberts!"

"I'm glad you call us brothers Josh, but there's something else … something that never goes away with me …

Josh takes his time thinking… "Like what Roberts?"

"Your fellow Jews here in America; their disregard for their mother-country Israel!"

"You get right to the point, don't care who it hurts … right Roberts?"

"I was born that way. I'm not one to beat around the bush just to make you happy: I get to the point no matter who it hurts!"

"Are you finished Roberts?"

"I'm only beginning. I watch wealthy Jewish millionaires strolling down *Wall Street* with no regard for the poor … the needy … the helpless."

"I see them politically support the ones who hate them

most: the ones your people called, Pharisees in the Bible. It's hard to say this Josh, but it's true … you know it's true Josh!"

"You're right about many of us, but I'm at the end of my rope… no place to turn. I try to explain this to my brothers, but they never listen, Roberts!"

"But there is a way to change things Josh. I've a message for you; a wonderful message … something different!"

"A Message--something different you say …

Roberts places his hand upon his shoulder, smiling, "Jesus, the Son of God … He loves you Josh. He paid the price for your sins and my sins at a place called, Calvary. We're brothers and sisters to the bitter end, no matter what lies ahead!" Roberts says, turning his head away, waiting.

Tears drip downward on a tired worried face looking up to Roberts.

"But what must I do? I'm ashamed, don't know how or where to begin. Help me Roberts," he's pleading …

"Josh my friend, it's time you look up and do what we all must do …

"What's that?"

"If you truly believe within your heart and soul Jesus is the Son of God …, tell me so Josh!"

"I do believe with all my heart and soul Jesus is the Son of God Roberts!" He's beginning to shout.

"That's all it takes, your faith, your belief in Him… Josh: it will take you to heaven my brother!"

"But Jesus, our Savior … when is he coming back Roberts … when?"

"The day or the hour I don't know, but He's coming back again for sure. He's just around the corner … a friend of mine once said to me!" Roberts replies, placing his arms around him, hugging him as a long-lost brother.

CHAPTER 38

A Time to Pray

*For through him we both have access by one Spirit
unto the Father ......*

Ephesians 2: 18

A short break in the discussion and they're gazing around the area observing what surrounds them. Suspicion grows ... seeing strangers huddling together, causing them to wonder.

"What else do you know of De Marco Josh?" Roberts asks.

"I know one thing for sure...it frightens me to even think about it, Roberts."

"Tell me about it."

"I know the world supports him, while we stand with our back to the wall; all our supposed friends running like a bunch of scared rabbits!"

Roberts only sits thinking ... while Josh looks out and around beginning again.

"I ask myself repeatedly, what can seven million people do against millions upon millions ...

"But why are you stopping Josh?"

"The very thought of it causes my sweat turn to blood Roberts!"

"But there's always a way out of this mess, Josh!"

Josh looks up at him puzzled once again. "Explain it to me Roberts. I've wracked my brain searching for an answer."

Roberts doesn't wait, moving closer, "But your searching in the wrong place my friend, the answer you seek isn't here: it's high up above waiting for you!" Roberts says, pointing his finger upward.

A moment to think about his words and, "I'm ready to try anything Roberts … tell me about it," he barely whispers, gazing around, seeing who might be listening."

"You've forgotten your past Josh; open your eyes and think back to the *Six Day War!*"

"But why Roberts?"

"You ask me why … the answer is simple Josh! it's because your people have never learned that God is watching your every move … standing beside you waiting. It's the way your people think Josh: always leaving "Him" out of your plans for the future."

Josh sits contemplating his meaning … never speaking.

"I look at you and I'm pleased, but when I see how your people shun what God has given you; it's hard for me to understand the reason for it. You've gotta be the most hard-headed people in the universe without saying Josh!" Roberts says, turning his head away, waiting.

Josh lowers his head dumbfounded again; while Roberts fights back his inward thoughts … continuing.

"Think about His covenant with your people … it's unbreakable. I know your history better than you know it Josh!"

Josh looks up at him … barely uttering, "But world political pressure---you just don't understand Roberts!"

Roberts can't wait … stopping him quickly.

"I know the position your people are in but agreeing with De Marco isn't the answer Josh!"

"I doubt if you'll ever know how I feel; you're not a Jew Roberts. Some want to strike first and worry about it later, but I'm not part of it at the present!"

"Then, why the big hurry, my friend?"

He moves even closer, next to him barely whispering, "De Marco has set back his appearance at the U.N. due to problems in America … that's why Roberts!"

"But what does that have to do with it Josh?"

"It adds to his preparedness time… making it even more dangerous Roberts!"

"And then what …

"In the event his plan is approved at the U.N. … he'll come looking for us with blood in his eyes; prepared to destroy us Roberts!"

"He has the muscle to put us down forever; now that the rest of the world is following him. There's nothing we can we do about it Roberts!"

Roberts can't wait, moving even closer, "Your right Josh. Look around and see how people adore him when he's present; he's their God. It's about time you wake up and smell the roses; either that … or you're nothing but history my friend!"

"I've no other words to express my feelings Roberts, time is running out; we're at the end of our rope!"

Roberts looks again at Josh, wondering if he will ever understand his message.

"I hear what you're saying Josh, but still you're not getting my message. In our Holy Bible we were warned of him thousands of years ago by one of your own ... a prophet called John."

"He referred to two of them; one as the antichrist ... a world political leader. He referred to the other as the false-prophet, a religious leader: both appearing at the end-time. They're here today among us Josh, but people don't recognize it!" Roberts says lowly, turning away seeing who might be listening.

"Are you sure about this Roberts?"

"I'm sure of it Josh! The signs given to us in the Bible happen every day, but people don't see it. I've wanted to tell you this before but knew you wouldn't accept it. I've studied the Bible my life over, and concluded...

Josh reacts quickly, placing his hand against his mouth, asking, "And your conclusion is what Mr. Roberts ...?"

Roberts can't wait, blurting out, "Now that you're a Christian, it's time you understand the Bible our way ... the Christian way Josh!"

"The Christian way ... Mr. Roberts!"

"The Messiah you've been waiting for has been here. He was crucified upon a cross ... descended into the center of the earth ... and in three days He rose again and ascended to heaven!"

Josh takes his hand stopping him, looking up to Roberts, barely asking, "But now ... where's our Messiah today Roberts?"

"Today ... Jesus our Savior sits next to his father in heaven, waiting to come back again: taking you to heaven to be with Him forever and forever Josh!" He says, beginning to shout.

"But the ones who aren't ready to meet him ... the ones we've been talking about Roberts---

"They're in trouble ... trouble like nothing ever before; hate to even think about it Josh!"

Josh smiles for the first time, looking up to him, "But I do believe Jesus is the Son of God Roberts!" He says, coming alive.

"But, you can rest assured of something certain Josh ...

"Something certain ... Roberts?"

"Oh yes ... very certain my friend. Your people will understand someday, but only God knows the hour and the day his son will be coming back to earth again!"

"But, I still don't get it Mr. Roberts ...

"Now listen closely. ... I'll tell you again Josh. Before the end of the tribulation period your people will know Him and recognize Him as the one they've been waiting for!"

Again, he's lost ... asking, "But when is the tribulation period you talk about coming Roberts?"

"Roberts shakes his head disgustedly ... growing weary. One more time----one final time ... listen carefully; are you ready Josh?"

"I'm ready ... I'm waiting Roberts ...

"The tribulation period begins after signing a seven-year treaty between Palestinians and your people: at the middle of the treaty Jewish heads will begin to roll like nothing you've never seen before Josh!"

"Yes! Yes! ... Tell me some more Roberts!" He's beginning to shout, excited.

Roberts pulls him against him, looking deep into his eyes, "Your people will know Jesus is the one you've been waiting for ... your long sought-after Messiah, you've been waiting for Josh!"

A moment of thought, looking up toward heaven and, "Then what Roberts?" A pitiful sounding l voice asks.

"It will be over Josh. Your people will know the one called the antichrist has betrayed you and all who worshiped him!"

A moment of sadness thinking back, and his head drops even lower ... shaken again.

"But how can I warn my people before it's too late?" He asks, grasping his hand, looking up to Roberts, waiting.

"I haven't the answer Josh. Jesus told your people over two thousand years ago and they didn't listen: how can I a Gentile tell them the same today? They wouldn't listen to Jesus when He walked with them, talked with them all the way to the cross!"

Josh shakes his head---wringing his arms, lost again; while Roberts places his hand upon his shoulder comforting him.

"I understand the pressure you're under Josh: all I ask is keep me informed of your whereabouts."

"I'll keep you informed as best I can, but it won't be easy. That's all I can promise you Roberts," he says, grasping his hand, looking up to him with tears in his eyes.

"But there's something else we need to understand before you leave...."

"Hope it's not something you're irked about, Roberts!"

"Nothing irks me now Josh ... you'll know what to do the next time."

Josh begins walking slowly away ... stopping, looking back to Roberts shouting, "But there's always one sure way out of this mess Roberts ...

"What are you talking about Christian?" He shouts back at him ... no longer worried about whose listening.

"Remember the *Six Day War* ...?"

"Remember it as yesterday Josh."

"He was there for us then and he hasn't changed. He will never leave us or forsake us. He gave us a covenant we hold dearly Roberts!"

Roberts wants to send him away feeling good ...

"You're right my friend; you'll win again … no matter what may be waiting for you!" Roberts is yelling at the top of his voice.

Josh keeps walking slowly away, till he turns looking back shouting again, "But Roberts … now that I'm a Christian, I'm depending upon something different!"

"What's that Josh?"

"Faith Roberts …faith! Something the "Apostle Paul wrote about; something I read about in the Bible just yesterday."

"Tell me the words one more time before you leave me, Josh."

Josh stops … removing a Bible from his briefcase, shouting back to Roberts …**For I am persuaded, that neither death, nor life, or angels, nor principalities, nor powers, nor things present, shall be able to separate me from the love of God, which is in Christ Jesus our Lord!"**

Josh gives a farewell wave to Roberts, never looking back; humming a song Roberts taught him the first time they met … *'What a Friend We Have in Jesus.'*

Roberts listens … enjoying the words shouting back, "He is our friend Josh; nice to have a Jew like you remind me about it!"

Josh is gone, while Roberts remains sitting upon the bench reminiscing their meeting. He's finished and begins walking back toward the hotel shaking his head, muttering a prayer, "Oh Lord, my God … I hope he's right: Israel's very existence hangs in the balance leaving them wanting! Help them Lord … be with them Lord, I pray unto you … my father in heaven!"

Back at their quarters in Bali, Doug sits alone gathering his thoughts. He's lonely, wishing Martha was here beside him. Never has he missed someone so greatly.

He begins walking slowly toward the water's edge not far

away; while a beautiful bright red sunset far off against the horizon hovers down to meet every lasting blue water below. His eyes focus up on it, reminding him of God's great power, the great everlasting beauty ... all His creation.

He wonders why he ever became involved so young in life with people so unsure. Again, his mind runs rampant, beginning to wonder if everything will go as planned before reaching, Kennedy. He continues walking, at times stopping to kick the sand watching it scatter in the breeze, falling all over.

He stops at intervals, gazing back toward the hotel being sure he isn't followed; while the sun is about to settle over the beautiful clear blue ocean water ... bringing him a sense of calmness.

On and on he walks till ... appearing from out of nowhere, a beautiful lady with long dark hair flowing half-way down to her waist appears, walking beside him toward a never-ending sunset.

Doug stops ... gazing upon her beauty; perfect, beyond imagination. A short pause, and he's beginning to wonder why she's out here on a sandy beach with him alone."

They reach the water's edge where huge waves rush in from deep blue water, splashing up against sand ... flowing back with the tide.

Doug peeks at her shining blue eyes, while she's standing beside him gazing upward, riveted to the evening sun about to disappear.

He gazes upon her white nylon pants, her red silk blouse ... exposing a golden cross over her heart.

She's petite, perfect bronze skin, teeth white as snow. Her sandals glide across sand like petals from flowers falling upon still water; while he can only imagen... where she might have come from.

Doug pauses again, gathering his thoughts. "I didn't see you coming, beautiful one. Have you come to warn me about dangerous waters?"

She smiles beautifully but doesn't answer. Her eyes remaining glued to the blazing red evening sunset.

Finally, she turns facing him smiling, "I've came to warn you of something only He knows, Doug," she says, softly.

Doug looks at her differently: she knows his name, but they've never met before.

"You know me from where?"

"I know you Doug ... know you well. You prayed to Him asking for help," she reminds him as a longtime friend.

He begins slowly walking toward the water's edge, with her moving beside him; till once again he stops suddenly staring at her, wondering where ... she came from.

"I've a feeling we've met before beautiful one, but can't remember where or when," Doug says, friendly.

But, still she doesn't answer, she's gazing out toward the evening sunset; finally turning, facing Doug.

"I've heard the same many times. Some call me *"Deborah"---others call me, "Sunset at Even-Tide"; a name given to me by the one I serve, Doug!"*

Doug likes the name, wonders about the other.

"But, the one you serve is ...

Deborah looks at him smiling, "I serve the great "I Am" --- our father in heaven Doug!"

Doug is speechless! His arms and legs useless; finally moving close to her looking upon her in awe...waiting!

Suddenly she stops her walking, not wanting to frighten him further. Her eyes glow like fire... pulling him beside her; while Doug can only stand beside her, gazing upon her wondering, "how can this be, how do you treat an angel a beautiful creature of God?"

She bends low writing letters in the sand, while Doug watches her every move… admiringly.

"You write letters well Deborah," he says, feeling helpless … trying to be pleasant.

She's happy and it's showing. She begins humming a song, bringing her pleasure. She gazes up into Doug's eyes, while the brightness of her face causes him to look away … with deepest regret.

Another beautiful smile and Deborah moves before him speaking softly, "Look into my eyes and don't be frightened, the Lord above is looking down upon us Doug!"

Again, he feels paralyzed, unable to move … helpless to reply.

"Listen to my words Doug; take them seriously! I watched His son as you watch me standing before you. He wrote words in the sand two thousand years ago in the Holy city of Jerusalem: while an angry group of Pharisees stood gazing down upon him.

When He was finished, they looked upon his words, unaware that ---*He, the one standing beside them was the Son of God; the long awaited, Messiah … the one they had been waiting for!*"

Doug's knees bend, beginning to realize; this beautiful one has spoken with his Lord above him. He wants to fall upon his knees and worship her but can't; it's for "Him" only he's thinking.

Long moments of silence and he's able to speak without crying …" You mean …

"Yes Doug …" Him."

Doug bends upon his knees, touching the sand … moving

293

closer; seeing big bold letters written in deep white sand ... *"Danger ahead, Kennedy Airport."*

He rises slowly looking upon Deborah. He feels as if he's in a trance; maybe this is only a dream, but it isn't. He gathers his senses, looking up above seeing only heaven. He begins walking to her, standing at her side, marveling her beauty, her wonders.

"I thank you for bringing the warning, but a question please Deborah."

She turns, looking up him smiling. "And your question is what Doug ..."

"The song ... the one I heard you humming a moment ago; I've heard it before... but can't remember where or when Deborah."

"I heard it only yesterday Doug. It touched me, made me happy. Now I can't keep from humming the words; beautiful, so very beautiful words!"

"Heard the song where Deborah?"

"Oh, yes Doug ... I heard the words from someone you love dearly."

"But, the words ... tell me!"

"On Eagle's Wings," she says, turning back and away, looking out into the sunset ... still smiling; while Doug stands rigid, his mind thinking back to something from past. ... shouting, *"On Eagle's Wings ... no. no. it can't be; that's Uncle Mike's song!"*

He rushes to the water's edge---gazing out toward an ocean of blue; where a glimmering brightness shows Deborah dancing upon ocean waves; heading out into the evening sunset.

Gazing far out as his eyes will take him ... he sees a beautiful rainbow hanging just above the clear blue water.

His heart pounds, as he watches her skipping over waves of

never ending water. Faster she moves, while her figure begins to diminish, smaller and smaller … heading toward the beautiful sunset at the end of the rainbow.

A moment or two later she's only a dot, fading into the far-off distance before her; while Doug stands searching, but useless.

He rises from the sand walking slowly back toward the hotel; thinking of her beauty, her mission and where she might be headed for. He wonders if she's headed for a place called *Paradise, the Garden of Eden, or maybe over the rainbow---- a place his Uncle Mike calls, Shangri-La*

CHAPTER 39

A Stranger in Paradise

The angel of the Lord encamped round about them that fear him, and delivereth them

Psalm 34: 7

"This can't be true, he keeps telling himself. He's wondering what Roberts is going to say. It's hard to believe, but too important to let it pass. He heads back toward the hotel, hoping and praying Roberts accepts his story.

Roberts stands outside the hotel seeing Doug walking toward him. He raises his hand, motioning him to come and join him.

"You look like you've just seen a ghost, something wrong Doug?" He says, jokingly.

"Not a ghost, something better; a real live breathing beautiful angel. I don't know how to tell you this … but it's true Mr. Roberts!"

Roberts looks again at him, wondering, "Get your breath and tell me some more about our angel."

Doug doesn't know where to start. He's thinking, 'how do you tell somebody about an angel, but I'll do it."

"I was walking on the beach heading down to the water's edge when I was approached by the most beautiful person I've ever met. Her name was Deborah…some call her Sunset at Eventide."

Roberts places his hand over Doug's lips stopping him, "Slow down Doug, calm yourself for a moment … tell me about what happened."

"Deborah told me she had a message from the Lord, and it frightened me. She told me God sent her, and I was the one to receive her message."

"Sure, it was an angel---not one on the other side?"

"She was definitely an angel sent by God sir: she had to be … she was perfect in everything!"

"Prepare for it Doug. Do you remember how we discussed the subject before, God's Holy Angels amongst us; they' will always will be amongst lad."

"I do remember, but I never once thought it would happen to me. It's like a dream come true sir."

"But I had a bigger problem after she left."

"Tell me about it."

"Well Mr. Roberts--- I felt maybe you would think I was losing it; you know, imagining things that never happened. I don't know why, but I can't seem to get her out of my mind. Her voice so sweet and tender, her eyes sparkling as diamonds."

"Let's talk about the message Doug. She wouldn't have been there if it wasn't important."

"You're right sir. It all happened so sudden. She appeared from out of nowhere walking beside me: it was shocking how she took over."

"Shocking?"

"It was unbelievable! She did everything so easy. I'll never forget how she took her finger and wrote in the sand. She wrote something the same as Christ did before the Pharisees 2000 years ago!"

"But, tell me what she wrote in the sand Doug. It had to be important or she wouldn't have been there!"

"She wrote, "*danger ahead at Kennedy Airport*" and that was it sir. I was overwhelmed, but I knew she was on my side. Even now it's still hard to believe I've been visited by an angel, but I have sir!" He says, getting his breath again.

"Calm yourself Doug. Get your breath and tell me the kind of trouble she spoke about. Was it something we can handle before leaving this place?"

"That's up for you to decide. But I do believe there's something planned to stop us from making our delivery. There's nothing else it could be Mr. Roberts."

"Roberts pauses, his mind is rambling----

"Are you going to make a change, Mr. Roberts?" Doug asks. waiting …

"No other way out Doug; something has to be done. Let's call it, "*the big switch*" … a switch we make at the last moment!"

"Mind explaining it to me sir?'

"I'll explain it to you for sure Doug. It's about a dream I had last night."

"Good or bad sir?"

"It was bad, really bad. It was a horror story If there ever was one. But the bad part was; it was something I couldn't run away from. But, now I'm beginning to believe it's coming true… that's the sad part of my dream Doug!"

"Are you telling me you can't make a change … is that it?"

"No way in hell will I make a change! But, you're not going to like this one either. I've been doing some research about what's been going on within the department, and it doesn't go away lad!"

"You're losing me...."

"I'm talking about a switch at the last moment to protect us Doug. Last night I dreamed we were being double-crossed by some of our own when we arrive at Kennedy Airport. Now, it's beginning to fit perfect. Deborah's warning told us what to expect when we arrive there."

"But I still don't understand. I thought you knew these guys meeting us at Kennedy."

"I've told you before Doug, things change. There's times it becomes necessary to make a switch at the last moment. You will arrange to be in a position able to pass the tapes to Marla as we make the walk through the concourse.

"But how, Mr. Roberts?"

"You'll write a note to her and tell her to put a satchel over her shoulder with the top part open as she leaves the plane. Tell her you will place a package with our material inside her satchel, as you and I are passing by her."

"Anything else to tell her Mr. Roberts?"

"There is lad. Tell her to tear the note to shreds after reading it; no time for slip ups at the end of our journey to nowhere!"

"I understand Mr. Roberts. All you need to do is give me the word. But your friends at Headquarters ... how are they to know the change?"

"They won't know Doug. I don't want them to know. Telling them without being sure who is with who, would be like playing with a stick of dynamite. Many of my old friends are no longer safe to call friends. I can't be too careful in a time like this Doug!"

Doug looks up at him surprised again.

"But why the distrust ... they still look at you as a friend,

I've watched them laugh and joke about things of the past a hundred times!"

"But not anymore…things have changed! Politics has a way of changing people. I've got to be sure of this one Doug!"

"I understand what your saying, it's something you've preached to me over and over."

"By now word has gotten around at Headquarters what we're coming with. But there's always someone in the crowd with opposite views than ours."

"Is that a problem sir?"

"You can bet it is lad. They're willing to die for their fanatical beliefs no matter who it hurts; that's the way it's done today … not the way we did it yesterday!"

"I'll get with Marla right now and let her know what to expect. Now that you've solved Deborah's message… I'll feel a lot better on the plane heading home."

"That would great, wouldn't it Doug."

"You bet it would Mr. Roberts. It reminds of something Uncle Mike would always say to me."

"What would that be Doug?"

"Everything is Beautiful" … that's the way Uncle Mike would say it sir!"

"Couldn't be better Doug; we're heading home, and nothing could be sweeter."

"Where's home Mr. Roberts?"

"Oh, I suppose it's wherever you find happiness; maybe someplace over the rainbow!"

CHAPTER 40

Looking Ahead

My help cometh from the Lord, which made heaven and earth.

Psalm 121; 20

Early the next morning the Airbus glides off the runway headed for New York, while Delegates sit gazing out into nowhere. Worry is showing. The long tiring trip to solve the problems of the world is about to end.

Roberts places the Bible inside his briefcase ready to talk... "I've made a decision Doug ...

"A decision about what Mr. Roberts?"

"As soon as we take care of business here... I'm throwing in the towel and retire lad!"

Doug places his book down looking up at him grinning. He's wondering if he's in one of his joking moods again.

"You, retire ... that'll be the day Mr. Roberts."

"But, I'm serious Doug. I've been there and done that all over the world; I'm tired ... I wanta go home!"

"I'm beginning to believe you. Bu why so suddenly Mr. Roberts?"

"I'm worn out…I'm tired and I wanta go home. I've had it Doug! After this trip to nowhere I'll be heading home with no regret. I've spent my last thirty years working in Intelligence, one way or another. My wife is gone, and I get lonely… never satisfied."

"Doug moves closer, waiting…

"I should have called it quits when she was killed twenty years ago but didn't … regretted it ever since. Today, when I look at you and Martha, it makes me envious … seeing how happy you are!"

Doug still can't believe what he's hearing. To him there's never an end to someone like the Colonel.

"But, what's on your mind for your future sir … maybe a woman, or a place to settle down and do nothing?" Doug, asks smiling.

Roberts looks at him surprised, wondering if he's reading his mind.

"Who knows what might happen to a guy like me Doug; might still find someone to enjoy life for a couple of more years."

"But, your leisure time, how would you spend it sir?"

Roberts looks at him confused, till … "Years ago I bought a ranch In Montana, but never had time to enjoy its' pleasures. I love good music, you know … the kind that really gets to you when you're feeling tired and lonely: the kind that makes you think and enjoy the pleasures of life."

"But, when I look at you now … I can't help but think of you as an old war-horse, ready to go to war with anyone. But … think about this sir …

"Think about what Doug?"

"It might just might take some time, getting use to just sitting and rocking in the noon day sun all day!"

"But not for me lad, I've seen it all … the good, the bad-- I've nothing to regret. I've planned for this day a very long time … it's finally here Doug!"

"But, who knows … I might wanta come calling on you sometime Mr. Roberts."

"I'll be waiting for you Doug … come ahead. I'll be sitting in an easy chair listening to some of the old-ones; like *Perry Como* … singing one of my favorites."

"What would that be Mr. Roberts?"

"Let the World go Away." And then, I'll listen to Julie Andrews sing, "The Sound of Music" … while I'm sitting in my big old rocking chair … having a glass of wine, smoking a big cigar. And, when I'm finished … I'll quit smoking again … for the ten-thousandth time!"

Now … It's Doug's time to laugh, and he does.

"Well …I've solved the mystery of all mysteries Mr. Roberts … you just let it slip!"

Roberts turns his head away grinning. "What are you talking about Doug?" He asks, sheepishly."

Doug can't hold back, "Oh, yes you do know… Montana is your, "Shangri-La" … or maybe someplace, "Just over the Rainbow" ----the place you've always searched for … but never been able to find, Mr. Roberts!" … Doug says, as his boss turns his head away … beginning to laugh his heart out.

"You got me Doug! You've finally got me. I'll sit in my rocking-chair watching the sun go down over that big red Montana sky. I'll be dreaming of my wife, snuggling up close to me."

Doug's eyes look down upon Roberts … filled with emotion! His mentor talks about things his Uncle Mike talks about, enjoyable things of life; things that make him want to be there with them.

"What was your wife doing at the time of her death sir?"

He doesn't answer quickly as usual; he's looking out the window at a sky full of clouds down below. His head lowers ... teardrops fall upon a newspaper beside him.

"She was killed in an automobile accident. Her name was *Maria;* maybe that's why I have a feeling for Marla. She was beautiful Doug. Every cadet at West Point had their eyes on her from the time they saw her."

"Her father was military all the way ... had it in his blood like I have. But, the thing I didn't know was ... her blood was different than his or mine."

"She had her own ideas about life and success; today I'm beginning to believe she was the smart one..." He says, turning his head, wanting to cry.

"But what led you to Christ Mr. Roberts ... or am I out of line asking the question?"

"It's ok to ask Doug ... I'll tell you my story."

"It was a cold winter night in Chicago, and I was about to hit the hay after a bad day at the airport. *Billy Graham* was on television preaching. He was explaining how life is so short, like a vapor as he put it. I thought about it over and over, and I began to realize it was true."

"I listened to *George Beverly Shay* singing one of my favorites ... *"How Great thou Art"* ... and my heart began to melt as never before. The next thing I knew ... I was on my knees spilling my heart out to Jesus. He touched me ... oh how he touched me... I was never the same thereafter... Doug!"

"But, I see you smiling ... what's the sudden look of pleasure upon your face Mr. Roberts?"

"I'm thinking of De Marco. He's the bright and shining star to most everyone aboard Doug."

"But I don't understand!"

"I'll put it to you as plain as I know how Doug. it's been tough for me to listen to De Marco's lies during this venture for peace ... but maybe it's worth it!"

"Now, what are you trying to tell me?"

Roberts takes his time thinking how to say the words... "Maybe we've just defeated the greatest deceiver of all time; the antichrist! We've been with him almost a month ... and we still have our souls within us."

"Look around you Doug; notice how he has won every single person's soul during this trip; except our delegates Joshua, you and I!"

Doug looks out over the crowd and back to Doug grinning, "You might be right ... never thought of it that way Mr. Roberts."

"But ... that's what it's all about. It's all about souls and more souls ... good against evil. His destiny is set; he's going to burn, burn, burn ... in hell throughout eternity Doug."

Wow, what a speech, sounds like a preacher, Doug is thinking.

"I believe the same Mr. Roberts ... anything else you might want to tell me?"

Roberts begins to smile ... a grin appears that Doug knows well, "He wants to take you and I with him to hell Doug... he's never satisfied!"

"You're right again Mr. Roberts, but I never looked at it that way before."

"I've explained it to you before, maybe in a different way; I'll tell it to you again Doug."

"I'm waiting Mr. Roberts ...

"Without the *Holy Spirit* within us we would be like putty in his hands. He can't touch us… and he knows it. The very minute we first acknowledge Christ as the Son of God; we're new people, born again people!"

During this trip to nowhere I've never felt more secure… never Doug!"

"But why … tell me Mr. Roberts."

Roberts stops…taking his hand, looking up to Doug, "My name is in His book, the greatest book ever. The same book Jesus will open on Judgment Day!"

Doug looks up at him speechless, contemplating the meaning.

"I've learned a lot from you Mr. Roberts. I truly believe this is the most important issue I've come to understand. Never, did I ever understand the power, the fullness of … *The Holy Spirit.*"

"Maybe someday we'll understand things better Doug. But, more than everything … I pray for the ones who haven't accepted Christ as their one and only Savior! Someday very soon, they'll look up and see heavens glory … their saddest day ever!"

"No doubt about it Mr. Roberts."

"But never forget Ethel's quote Doug … the one she tells everybody!"

"You mean …" He's just around the corner?"

"I do for sure lad!"

"Marla walks amongst the passengers glancing over to Doug, raising her thumb upward smiling, but never stopping.

De Marco comes from the cockpit making an announcement, but nothing important. The journey is about to end; some look sad … while the Americans look happy.

The expectation of meeting friends is growing; while

concern for those injured or dead in the quake… grows deeper and deeper.

Marla moves from the cab of the plane standing before the passengers. ready to make an announcement.

"Please listen and give me your attention. Everyone aboard must leave in an orderly fashion, beginning from the front of the cabin. A huge crowd is waiting to greet Mr. De Marco. It's most important you be aware of everything surrounding you. Thank you for your patience."

Roberts is worried and it's showing. He looks over at Doug uttering a deep sigh of relief, gaining his attention

"I'm glad this journey is about to be over Doug, but I'll not feel safe till we hand everything we have over to Headquarters."

"Stop worrying Mr. Roberts. A couple of hours from now, you'll be sitting and rocking in an old rocking chair home again. You'll be safe and secure for the rest of your life."

"Wrong again Doug, this is where it just might become interesting for the both of us: lots of people, lots of noise … the perfect setting for anything to happen. Keep your eyes peeled and miss nothing lad!"

"Tell me what you're talking about Mr. Roberts … I don't get it!"

"For the first time in my life I'm not sure who our friends are. I wonder who to trust no matter who they are. This is serious business…keep your eyes and ears open Doug."

"Everything is going to be just fine, I'll be at your side Mr. Roberts … don't worry about it."

"I know you will Doug … couldn't want anyone better. When we walk down the steps leaving the plane hang with me; nobody gets between us till after we meet Marla … understand Doug?"

"I understand, believe me I do."

"But still; for some reason I've got one bad feeling ...

"like what Mr. Roberts?"

"I'm beginning to worry If some of the ones we talked about not being friends. If they might have found out about the-cell phone and recorder. All hell could break loose if they have Doug!"

"Maybc it's time I give you a quote from the Bible, something I read just yesterday Mr. Roberts. It caused me to do some praying myself last night!"

"Give it to me lad...I need it!"

"I'll quote it to you Mr. Roberts.

> *Whereas ye know ye not shall be on the. morrow. For what is your life? It is even a vapor that appeared for a little time, and then vanisheth away.*
>
> **James 4: 14**

"But there's a better way to look at it Doug ...

"What's that sir?"

We'll be walking down streets of shining as gold ... forever and forever; God's holy angels surrounding us!"

"You got me again ... I feel a lot better Mr. Roberts!"

CHAPTER 41

The Reception

Greater love hath no man than this, that a man lay down his life for friends.

John 15: 13

Wheels screech loudly as of the plane strikes the runway at Kennedy International Airport. The huge plane taxies to a passenger unloading zone, and in a short time people stand at the gate ready to move out. Marla moves near the door holding a loud-speaker, ready to begin unloading.

"Please listen everyone! I want everyone to comply with my instructions during the unloading. As you can see there's a huge crowd of people here to greet Mr. De Marco."

"To make this quick and safe I want all delegates, to leave the plane at the head of the line … except Mr. De Marco of course."

Unloading begins with Doug and Roberts at the head of the procession; while Marla leaves her station walking between the two toward inside the concourse. Her satchel fits snug against her side open at the top; while Doug moves against her, slipping the cell phone and recorder inside the satchel the without notice.

Standing a few yards among the large crowd of people, stand the delegation from "Morris Avenue Baptist Church", gazing out over the crowd of people searching for Doug.

A door swings open and De Marco moves from the plane amid a standing crowd of worshipers, shouting over and over ... "De Marco! ... De Marco!"

Roberts and Doug are still moving ... on and on till, Doug feels a tug at his shoulder, glancing back... seeing Joshua, looking up to him.

"What's going on Joshua ... why are you here... Roberts and I have been worried about you."

"There's a lot going on Doug. Tell Roberts we're on hold till we see what happens when the seven-year peace treaty is in place."

"What else do you want him to know, Joshua?"

"Wish I had time to go over everything Doug, but I don't. Things are happening fast; every time the news comes on it gets more frightening. You don't know who to believe ... you can't trust anyone. The government is filled with traitors in the highest offices, and the world is beginning to realize it!"

"You're right, but what's your biggest worry?"

He shakes head, looking down ... finally looking up at Doug, "My biggest worry is always the same Doug... I worry about what's going to happen in Israel!"

Doug searches his words ... staring up at Joshua, "I can't blame you Joshua, you have a good reason to be worried. I'll tell Roberts your message as soon as I catch up with Marla and him. They went ahead to meet some friends of mine."

Doug turns looking back searching; turning back again … no Joshua!"

Roberts and Marla stop, looking around and Doug appears joining them. They never stop to look elsewhere.

They continue walking toward the airport entrance seeing two well-built men approaching, dressed in black suits, white shirts and blue ties… Roberts recognizing them immediately.

He doesn't wait… holding his hand out smiling … "Hi, boys, be sure and take good care of this young lady … she's one of our own," Roberts says, proudly.

"She will be in good hands for sure, don't worry about it Mr. Roberts," one of them replies, grabbing Marla's hand: taking off heading toward a limo, waiting just outside the concours.

Suddenly, Marla stops walking … looking back shouting, "I love you Mr. Roberts … I love you Doug … you've answered my prayer my Christian friends!"

Doug and Roberts continue walking toward the front entrance when suddenly, two friendly faces appear dressed in black suits, white shirts, and blue ties … standing before Roberts holding their hand out smiling.

Roberts doesn't wait … pulling them closer, looking up at Doug, "Meet a couple of friends of mine Doug … this is Glenn Orwell and Ernie Duncan … friends of mine from way back."

"Great, but why wait so long to tell me sir," Doug asks.

"I didn't want to upset you at the end of our journey Doug. I've been concerned about our safety carrying the kind of cargo we have. But, now seeing these two guys … my worry is over."

"But why over now Mr. Roberts?"

"I've known these two guys for a life-time Doug …we served ten years in the Far East protecting each other."

"How did everything turn out when it was over Mr. Roberts?"

Roberts turns looking back at the two of them grinning, "it wasn't a picnic … was it boys?"

"You can say that again pal; it was never a picnic when the three of us were together!" Orwell says, chuckling.

"You boys got your credentials?" Roberts asks, nonchalantly.

Orwell puts his arm around Roberts, handing him their credentials grinning, "You're a fine one to ask for credentials after what we've been through … you old Dog Face Sky-jumper!"

Doug moves beside them … taking the papers from Roberts glancing over them, looking up at Orwell, "Good as gold, Mr. Orwell!"

Orwell doesn't wait, looking up to Roberts… "You got the cell phone and recorder with you, Roberts?"

"Oh yes… we have them Orwell … but just as a matter of formality … tell me the code word for this operation."

Suddenly Orwell is different! His face turns pale, never speaking; while Roberts stands … waiting.

A long pause and, "I believe maybe we need to step inside the restroom across the way to make the transaction Orwell; we may need some privacy!"

Mike and Martha stand a short distance away with the church group, when suddenly … Martha comes alive, beginning to shout …" Doug darling! Doug Darling! … Don't move away I'm coming to you, sweetheart!"

Mike stands frozen, watching Martha heading for Doug; suddenly, he's taking off running beside her.

Dodging in and out between crowds of people, they find Doug in the middle of it; Martha rushing up, placing her arms around him, smothering him with kisses.

Things are changing fast, while Doug, Roberts, Orwell, Mike and Duncan, huddle close, searching for a code-word; that only Roberts knows doesn't exist.

The once peaceful atmosphere of meeting friends with honor and trust is over; cursing, swearing, and shouting fills the air. Outside the restroom people listen … scattering in fear.

Chaos takes over, while Martha and Doug stand as one; holding their arms around each other in another world … their world only.

Orwell and Duncan become transformed; two different people completely! They're no longer old friends of the past. Attitudes change … fists begin pounding Mike and Roberts.

Mike doesn't wait. He reaches over pushing Doug and Martha away grabbing Orwell around the neck, holding him: shouting back to Martha and Doug: "Get the hell out of here … this is something for Roberts and me only!"

Across the room Roberts struggles with Duncan… still holding on to the brief-case.

All hell is breaking loose, while police stand looking … till someone in crowd, begins to yell, 'guns … guns … they're about to shoot someone!"

Mike, Roberts, Duncan and Orwell stop outside the restroom entrance, when suddenly Orwell pulls a pistol from his side… shoving it hard into Robert's stomach.

Bystanders begin moving away heading to where police stand observing; when someone in the crowd begins to shout "Guns! Guns! He has a gun---

And from the far side of the concourse people come running, shouting to people in panic; while Orwell and Duncan stand looking at each other… desperate.

Duncan grabs Roberts by his arm opening the restroom door, seeing occupants left inside crying hysterically.

Orwell doesn't wait, pointing his gun toward them shouting, "Get out of here immediately, you bunch of parasites… unless you want the same thing these two guys are about to get!"

He places his pistol to Mike's head, shoving him inside … while half-dressed men begin running for the door, leaving.

Time is running out and Orwell knows it. He pushes Mike against the wall, striking him hard; causing him to fall to floor… helpless.

Outside the restroom sirens wail, people run screaming; while Duncan stands over Mike poised like a giant…waiting!"

Roberts' remains calm, gathering his strength … slowly moving closer to Mike.

But Duncan isn't finished with Roberts. He shoves him hard against the wall again, pounding him with his pistol. Blow after blow falls hard upon Roberts head and shoulder … finally dropping to the floor… again, looking over at Mike … his eyes barely open.

Duncan's face shows nothing but rage … grasping Mike by his hair shouting, "Time's running out … give us the tapes and recorder… or get ready to meet your maker. The decision is up to you … boys!"

Roberts can only stare toward Mike's bloody wound still bleeding, while his sense of pride overwhelms everything surrounding.

Mike looks over toward Roberts smiling: he's thinking the same as he did thirty years ago, at a place called Phu Bai…never give up…till it's over!

It makes him grin, being a part of this … maybe his last moment ever. He looks over toward Roberts pointing his thumb upward toward heaven … smiling.

Blood flows from Robert's nostrils, while he's looking back toward Mike barely muttering, "Maybe I don't know how to say this, but it looks like we're right back at Phu Bai with our back to the wall …doesn't it Mike!"

Mike gathers his energy, gritting his teeth, moving closer,

"Well … we sure as hell didn't quit then … too late to think about quitting now Colonel," he can barely, mutter.

Duncan's anger explodes … pulling Mike up from the floor ramming his pistol into his ribs; causing him to hold his breathe, regaining his senses … waiting for more as usual.

Orwell moves quickly toward Roberts, grabbing his arm, shouting up in his face, "Just shut up and say nothing you old good for nothing has-been: you still haven't learned what it's all about. Maybe, it's time for me to show you the hard way Roberts."

Duncan joins the act making the situation worse. He picks Mike up bodily, dropping him to the floor, kicking him again and again.

Again, Orwell moves up in Robert's face exploding, "I'm telling you, for the last time Roberts … give us the tapes here and now … or I'll shove this pistol down your throat and blow your brains all over this place. I'm as serious as it gets Roberts!"

Roberts looks over at Mike lying beside him in pain. "You're right with the Lord aren't you Mike?" He asks, grinning.

"Never better sir. My score is settled: my name is in His book. I'm beginning to feel like words the Apostle Paul once said."

"What words Mike?"

"I'm the least of the least. Pretty soon…maybe Paul and I will sit down together and talk about it, Colonel!"

Roberts looks upward to where Orwell and Duncan stand looking down at him.

"It looks like you two boys have us in a hard-spot. I'm old enough to know when I'm licked: no use to go further," he barely utters.

Orwell stares over to Duncan … the both grinning …" And your choice is what Roberts?" Orwell asks … moving closer.

He motions him come closer beside him, barely whispering, "You surprise me Orwell … you're smarter than I gave you credit for!"

"Now what Roberts…

"I'm done for Orwell, it's over. I'll give you what you came for … but I do have some pride left.""

"Keep going…

"There's something yet you can do for me," Roberts' says, his head bowed in shame, never looking up.

"Tell us what we can do for you, and maybe we'll do it Roberts. Just call it our gift to you… for this moment of pleasure!"

"Roberts looks up at him pitiful like, "My only hope is you let bygones … be bygones, Orwell."

Orwell moves even closer … while Roberts pulls a key from inside his vest; unlocking the case … handing it over to him, smiling.

Orwell doesn't wait … moving quickly across the room where Duncan stands, handing him the case… "You're the one who settled our score with these guys Duncan: have the honor of removing the cell phone and recorder!"

A smile appears. A quick glance at the case … turning the key and … Boom! … an explosion so loud it can be heard far and away.

The large room is gutted in a second. Walls fall, like dominoes … one upon one; blocking the door from with-out.

Smoke begins to show …while broken pipes send water spewing high into the air above them.

Mike still lies on his back bleeding, his arms hang limp shattered, dangling.

Roberts' lies close to him no better; legs shattered, bleeding from his side; while Duncan and Orwell lay in pieces ... beyond recognition.

"Can you hear me Mike?" Roberts asks...waiting.

"Hear you well--- Colonel."

"I've got something to tell you-----something important!"

"What's important at a time like this Colonel?" a weak voice mumbles.

"I want you to know something Mike ...

"Something about what sir?"

"Moments of hesitation and ... "You were one hell of a marine! I never liked the way you wouldn't listen to me ... but I was always proud of you when it was over Mike!"

Mike tries to laugh, but useless ...barely mumbling, "You mean Phu Bai, where blood flowed like water in a storm ... Colonel?"

"I do Mike ...

"But now, I've a question for you Colonel."

"Let it fly ... time's wasting Mike."

"Do you believe in predestination; like what the Bible teaches us sir?"

Roberts' grits his teeth trying to speak, "Never really thought about the subject ... but it sure is beginning to look like we're about to leave this place!"

"I wouldn't be so sure Colonel," Mike barely can mutter.

"But ... it's different this time Mike ... it's different for sure!"

"How different Mr. Roberts?"

"I see someone coming ... coming closer and closer. And she's beautiful Mike ... so very ... very beautiful ... Mike! And now ... she's dancing upon water! And the sun ... it's shining so brightly...so heavenly ... Mike ...

Roberts' shattered body remains lying on the concrete floor

covered in blood: when from a short distance away a white shadowy figure moves closer and closer toward Mike.

The pain subsides … gone in a moment … Friend is here!"

He reaches down to Mike, pulling him closer, while his fiery eyes dance … sparkling as diamonds.

"It's time to go home … He's waiting for you Mike!" Friend says, soft and tenderly.

Outside the concourse the welcoming delegation from the church, stand gazing toward the massive amount of destruction … when suddenly their faces brighten!

They're gazing upward toward heaven, beginning to realize: *life isn't over … It's just beginning!*

CHAPTER 42

Predestination

For whom he did foreknow, he also did dedestinate to be conformed to the image of his Son, that he might be the firstborn of among many brethren.

Romans 8: 29

Cries ring out throughout! Calling people's names go unanswered. Hundreds stand in shock observing death and destruction. Suddenly out in the middle of the crowd a policeman stands tall upon a platform, addressing the crowd with a Bull Horn.

"Attention everyone! It's necessary you comply with my instructions for your own safety. I've taken the necessary measures to keep the situation from spreading further, but I'll need your full cooperation getting this under control again!"

"But what about the ones inside … the dead, the injured?" Someone yells from the center of the crowd.

"My men are about to reach those trapped inside…we will need time to see where to begin."

"Injured bodies are everywhere, so please stay back and away," he tries, to explain over the screaming and yelling from all directions.

The mounting crowd of persons grows even larger, and the Captain decides to act immediately.

"I want everyone to move out quickly… unless your loved ones are inside the damaged area. Security personnel stand ready to take your name and phone number…please move forward."

Doug moves toward a couple of people from the "Intelligence Department." offering his credentials, and they walk quickly to a nearby undamaged office.

A tall thin looking agent about sixty or sixty-five sits looking up to him, "Step inside Doug … I'm William Reynolds, in charge of this operation." He says, never hesitating.

Doug looks up at him surprised, "And I'm Doug Cutler … associated with Mr. Roberts as his aide sir"

"Sit here beside me and have a seat Doug … I'll brief you on some matters. A dozen of our own will be sitting next to us."

"Thank you, sir."

"I'm aware you're not up on everything Doug, so I'll bring you up to date on some things"

"Sounds great…"

Reynolds douses a cigar he's smoking … throwing it into a nearby empty trash dispenser, looking back to Doug, "Bad habit … I'm trying to quit, Doug," he says, looking over at his friends, grinning."

"Doug looks up to him grinning, "I know all about it Mr. Reynolds, forget it!"

"Suppose we get down to business Doug. You begin the

conversation by telling me what you know … starting at the beginning with Marla. When you're finished I'll brief you on what we know!"

"That's great! I've been wondering about some things."

"But in the mean-time, gather your thoughts and mind together; it might take us a while to come up with everything Doug." He says, removing his coat ready for business.

Doug sits gathering his thoughts. He's thinking about "Operation Un-Holy Ground" and the part his uncle played in it. Perspiration begins to show upon his forehead.

He's thinking back to Marla, De Marco, the secret meeting of De Marco: other leaders gathering in Bali.

He continues onward, reviving memories of the information they turned over to the department.

When he comes to the part of meeting Orwell and Duncan, he wipes his eyes and takes a break…beginning again.

He tries to visualize traitors as ones to speak about in the same tone as persons he loved so well, but hopeless.

Finally, he's able to bring his words together without paying the price of crying. He finishes it up with their words of betrayal.

"It was Orwell and Duncan from Military Intelligence sir. Roberts knew them from way-back. He told me just before we met them," he mutters, holding back, a tear or two.

"He knew them back-when… Doug?" Reynolds asks.

"Years ago, while serving in the Far-East. He told me he never trusted a lot of people, but when we watched them coming to us… he seemed pleased; as if they were some of our own," Doug tries, to explain.

Reynolds looks up at him, shaking his head, "It's a sorry story for me to tell you this Doug …but it's no fault of you or Roberts!" He says, rising from his desk, slamming books around, in display of anger.

Doug watches in silence, as Reynolds walks in circles... cursing the names of those that once served him.

Doug can take it no more! He rises from his chair confronting him. "But to me Mr. Reynolds ... the whole affair is very simple!"

"What are talking about...this is serious as it gets; no other way I can say it Doug!"

"Then I'll say it for you, sir...we've been had by some of our own!"

"Reynolds looks up at Doug shouting, "Whatever you know that I don't know; let it all out ... I'm listening Doug!"

"Roberts and I oversaw delivering some secretive information back to Headquarters here in Washington. At the end of the journey we were taken by two of our very own!"

Carry on...tell me the rest of it----

"We did our job and we did it well, but when it was over... it carried a price: a very heavy price, Mr. Reynolds."

"Carry on ..."

"We made the switch with Marla and delivered the tapes as expected... ahead of the two guys coming later."

Roberts knew the two guys coming in the limo: he talked to them earlier, but I didn't know it. It was the only thing that kept them getting away with it sir."

"You're right! His plan was brilliant Doug. Roberts was one of the old war-horse type of guys ... a step ahead of everyone."

"But what bothers me more than anything Mr. Reynolds, is the fact Duncan and Orwell had credentials as good as mine. Roberts knew their history after serving with them for years in the Middle East."

"And what else Doug!"

322

"If Roberts hadn't asked for the code-word they would have pulled it off for sure, Mr. Reynolds!"

Reynolds stops, looking again at him...shouting, "Code-word hell, there was no code-word Doug! This gets crazier by the moment: nothing was ever mentioned about a code-word!"

A long moment, staring at one another, and... Reynolds begins to chuckle.

"Now, what's so funny Mr. Reynolds" Doug asks; while around them sit other agents grinning."

Reynolds stops ...getting his breath facing Doug, "Think about this Doug-----

"Now what...

"That sly old fox just put it to the ones that killed him. They didn't have the slightest idea what he was doing. It was Robert's way of giving them a place in hell for sure, Doug!"

Doug is speechless ... staring at Reynolds shouting, "No this can't be ... that double-dealing old fox, the guy I thought I really knew actually pulled one on me ... his closest confident!"

Standing close, other agents join the laughter heading to the door, while a couple of agents remain, shaking their head ... still chuckling.

Doug and Reynolds continue, occasionally wiping a tear or two when nobody is looking.

"Doug looks up at Reynolds beginning again,

"Roberts explained to me the possibility of traitors within our own government. He worried about others, but never these two. But something still bothers me...

"Bothers you-----tell me about it Doug."

"There's only one way I can say this Mr. Reynolds... why did something like this happen by two of our best ... our very own sir?"

Reynolds becomes speechless. He looks out and away, searching for an answer.

"This isn't easy, but there's only way of saying it: we here at Headquarters slipped up bad! Orwell and Duncan were let go two years ago; but for some unknown reason you weren't notified. That's the only way I know how to say it Doug."

He looks up at Reynolds… stunned again! "You failed to notify us … is that what you said?"

"We did … it happened Doug!"

"But … these two guys had credentials. I checked them over and over … this is impossible!"

Reynolds can only listen…waiting, while Doug continues.

"I checked them over just before Mike grabbed me from behind: they had credentials as good as my own. They were our friends … Roberts best friends from way back!"

Pity begins to show upon Reynolds' face. He wants to make Doug understand, but can't find the words.

He moves next to him, placing his hand upon his shoulder.

"This is hard for me to say, but they were no longer our people Doug … I can't put it to you any other way!"

"Their love and loyalty they once felt for our country was turned to De Marco!"

Doug looks up at him, dropping his head … "What's next on the menu sir?" He asks, waiting.

"You'll be briefed on what's taking place in this country you and I love and adore. It's getting scary … real scary, Doug!"

"When I try explaining the situation to others; everything goes silent. They only want to talk about politics: who said this and who said that!"

"Trouble's ahead of us for sure Mr. Reynolds. Roberts and I been preaching it."

Reynolds takes his time studying Doug over and over…

till, "I made a mistake Doug … a terrible mistake! I believe everyone has made a mistake… except Roberts and you. That's the only way I can say it. Is there something you might want to say Doug?"

Doug takes his time thinking back to the time he first met Roberts.

"There is something I'd like to say. I learned a lot serving with Roberts! He treated me as one of his own, always there when I needed him. He told me what I must do just before the switch and I did it…I've no regrets, sir."

A long pause and, "You've learned a lot from Roberts Doug. I see it in your eyes. It's time we talk about private matters … between you and I only: our thoughts, our beliefs … our faith!"

"Carry on sir."

"I've under estimated our enemies; the whole world has. Now, it's time we come to our senses!"

"Keep going…

"We're playing with fire and people can't recognize it: we're in trouble as never before Doug!"

Doug hangs his head thinking back … reminiscing his times talking the same with Roberts… looking up at Reynolds, waiting.

"I wish I knew the answer to the problem Doug. We lost one of our best, and you lost an uncle willing to give his life for you."

"By all reports coming to us from Bali: we knew the relationship you shared with Roberts was greater than just boss and aide: it was more like father and son!"

"We were close sir; very close. Uncle Mike was one of the best. I remember how he shoved me away … giving his life for me."

"And … Mr. Roberts, how can I better describe him. He was man of his own, a man of honor … Mr. Reynolds?"

"Shut the door and lock it Doug. It's time I tell you why I went to pieces… when I heard about Roberts!"

Doug sits across from him at the desk waiting, while Reynolds hesitates to look casually around, seeing the other two agents have departed.

"I'll begin with this Doug. Roberts was close to me, much closer than anyone knew. We served in Nam together back in the late sixties and early seventies."

"I was a young Second Lieutenant, just out of West-Point assigned to the 101st Airborne. I was under the command of then… Colonel Nathaniel P Roberts.

"Things were happening fast and furious all around us… hardly anyone knew where we were at most of the time.

"Our unit helped evacuate most everyone left alive at an airport---a place I'll never forget."

Doug can't wait … reaching across the desk stopping him. "Stop—please, Mr. Reynolds; don't go further!"

"You sound as if you know something Doug…keep going."

A wide grin appears upon his face, "The airport you speak of … could it possibly be near the village *Phu Bai*?"

Reynolds pulls back, staring at Doug shouting, "It was Phu Bai … but how in the hell do you know about Phu Bai… you're not half the age to know about what happened at a place nothing but hell on earth, lad!"

"You're right Mr. Reynolds … keep going …

"I left Phu Bai ahead of the Colonel on a chopper back to De Nang, but Roberts always insisted on being the last chopper out. But this time for some reason … it was a little different.

"What does a little different mean Mr. Reynolds?"

"Before he could get away something bad happened; bringing Roberts and some of his own under fire."

"When, Roberts finally arrived at De Nang he had a couple of wounded marines along with him. One was shot all to hell. The pilot told us how the Colonel was about to shoot the other one he called … "one crazy-ass marine if there ever was one!"

Doug waits … listening.

"Later there was a board of inquiry set up at De Nang, with a couple of Naval Officers present, wanting to press charges for your Uncle Mike's action disobeying orders."

"What was the end of it," Doug asks, innocent like.

Reynolds begins to laugh. "This will kill you, Doug … it's unbelievable! I was there with Roberts and got the shock of my life."

"They questioned Roberts about Mike's refusal to leave the place; still wanting to kill everyone in sight. But the Colonel just sat there…looking up at him listening and grinning. It was hilarious Doug. When they asked him if Mike deserved to be, court-martialed…

"What was his answer?"

"How can I ever forget! He looked up at the jury and said, "Court martial, hell! This crazy ass marine is a hero. I watched him kill a dozen of the enemy and loved every minute of it. And then he said----

Doug can't wait, "and then what…

"I'll never forget. He shouted "Hell … General, If I had a hundred like him… I could have won this stupid ass war in no time! I hereby recommend him for the Silver Star, and that's my final, General!"

"And then what?"

"He got up from his seat, looked over at the General and left along with everyone … including the General."

"Anything else----

"Oh yes, I still remember the day, the time and the look on every marine's face hearing Robert's statement. And-- oh brother … how they loved him."

"I can't help but laugh Mr. Reynolds. This has to be one for the books."

Reynolds looks at him perplexed …" Now what are you talking about Doug?"

"It's simple sir. The crazy ass marine you so easily describe was my uncle… Mike Cutler … the one who gave his life for me!"

Reynolds rises from his chair staring down at Doug… "You're joking of course-----

"It's true Mr. Reynolds. They met only three times during their lifetime, but there was something greater directing their movements. Something I believe strongly; something called predestination!"

"I've always wondered about predestination Doug. Come and see me at headquarters tomorrow. After you make your report, someone will brief you on what's going on within. You're welcome anytime, Doug."

"Thank you, maybe I'll be seeing you sooner than you think sir!"

"I believe you need some time off Doug. Time to get your thoughts together."

They shake hands, and Doug moves out looking satisfied.

He begins thinking back to a time he sat across from Mike wondering if he was going make the grade for something called *"Mission Un-Holy Ground."*

He remembers Friend telling him he was "One of His Chosen."

He remembers how often he wondered what it meant, something he found out later, at "Kennedy International Airport... **"Predestined," is something you can't get away from----no matter how hard you try.**

CHAPTER 43

A Man to Remember

**He will swallow up death in victory; and the
Lord God will wipe away tears from all faces.**

Isaiah 25: 8

Ailene writes a stirring memoir of Mike's life appearing
in the Star newspaper. It tells of his love, hatred, and
forgiveness. She tells of his life on the battle-field with
Roberts ... their death together at Kennedy; his long-sought
search for a place called Shangri-La.

Her newspaper days are ended ... their plan for marriage
over; all in an act of betrayal by some of his own.

"When you read between the lines; her story isn't just a
story of heroism, but maybe a hidden note of love and devotion.

Body-parts gathered from the floor of the rest-room arrive
home unnoticed; on burial day hundreds gather to pay Mike
honor.

Ailene sits with family members along with Ethel ... as
Brad stands tall before them, beginning his eulogy.

"I'm heart-broken as many of you. But this I know for sure----Mike...ended up where he always wanted to be!"

"Mike came to this church a couple of years ago and made a difference. We became friends: more like father and son might be a better way to describe it."

"Recently he made a personal request to me. He asked me to have someone sing a couple of his favorite songs… if he should depart this world soon after."

"But Mike was different! He was always talking about being someplace like the "New Jerusalem" … or meeting people like Peter, Paul, and Mary; or maybe like someone he met when things looked bad … a guy he called, *Friend!*"

"Mike had no fear of death: matter of fact he kind of looked forward to it. But today … thinking back again; I believe maybe it was because his best friend, Ethel. She told him about a place called … "The New Jerusalem, and he fell in love with the place like nobody ever."

"We talked aboard the plane to Kennedy and he expressed his hidden desires. We talked about his unending desire to serve the Lord."

"Mike was ready to meet the Lord if anyone ever was. Today, I ask myself the same----am I ready to meet the Lord as Mike was!"

"Miss Jackson will you please do us the honor of singing Mike's song … *"On Eagles Wings"*

Coming from behind the pulpit a very lovely lady appears dressed in a beautiful long black gown ready to perform. She opens her arms looking skyward … her voice resounding throughout---*"He will raise you up on Eagles Wings …*

Tears appear from young and old alike, but only Ethel sits near the casket smiling.

Miss Jackson finishes her powerful song and Brad tells the

biblical story how the *Prodigal Son* came home to his father and began his life anew. He tells of personal things … their friendship.

"Mike and I talked about what heaven might be, and I remember his statement well. He said, "Well, Brad … it's time for me to confess. I asked him what he must confess, and I'll never forget his answer."

"He looked at me and said, "Well--- it's like this, my friend: if my day should come before yours … this is my wish. Keep my eulogy short and sweet. Sing no sad songs for me. But more than anything … tell them how He removed my sin *as far as the east to the west … at a place called, Calvary!*"

"Today … I will honor Mike's request … "good-by and God bless you… till we meet again tomorrow, my Christian friends!"

Mike's family moves slowly to the casket with Brad leading the way.

One after one, they touch his casket; *seeing a young man dressed in white linen standing next to Ethel holding hands, touching his casket.*

A sound of taps from an honor guard … and Ethel stands alone, looking upward smiling.

She moves close to Ailene looking up into her eyes saying so pleasantly, "Please darling, stop your crying. Don't you know He's just around the corner waiting for the two of us," she says, giggling.

"But where around the corner, Ethel?" Ailene asks, quickly

"The New Jerusalem, darling … the place Jesus built for people like us. Mike and I have it all planned to meet there; but please don't worry … you'll be there, too Ailene; the three of us together… forever and ever, darling!"

"But there's something else I must tell you Ethel …

"What is it, my darling?"

"You're one foxy old gal for sure Ethel, no wonder Mike loved you as his mother."

"I know! I know! I loved him, too, darling," she says, ever so pleased, giggling again.

The funeral is over, and Doug and Martha return home seeing the message light flashing.

"Doug, this is Colonel Robert Poindexter with Military Intelligence. I know this isn't a good time to talk business, but I need you in my office soon as possible. Bring Martha with you if she desires."

Doug doesn't wait, seeing Martha raising her thumb pointing upward. "Martha and I will be at your office at one-p.m. tomorrow, count on it, sir!"

"But hold on a moment Doug... another matter needs to be discussed."

"Yes, Colonel ..."

"Well ... it's like this Doug; we've been trying to locate our friend Joshua Bernstein, but so far, no luck."

"He could be in hiding out someplace, but always welcome with us. He's a good man ... a trustworthy man for sure."

"He is, no doubt about it. I'll get some rest and we'll talk about it tomorrow, sir," Mike says, hanging up satisfied.

The following morning Martha and Doug leave for Washington wondering what's so important. They arrive at Poindexter's office on time-- anxious to begin.

Colonel Poindexter greets them cordially, pointing to a couple chairs across from him.

"I believe I have some news for you Doug, good news for a change."

Doug looks up at Poindexter and back to Martha, "I haven't the slightest idea what you mean, Colonel ... but good news is welcome, anytime."

"Pull your chair closer and listen to what I'm about to inform you about, Doug!"

A moment or two later they're sitting across from his desk staring at him … waiting.

Poindexter begins to smile, looking up at Doug smiling, "You, Doug Cutler are the designated heir to Mr. Robert's entire estate!"

Doug sits in moment shock… saying nothing, waiting.

"I talked to him before the two of you left Bali. He sent me his "Last Will and Testament. He explained how you and he were like father and son. He cared for you deeply, Doug."

"He worried about your safety, making the delivery at the Airport: today … we know he had reason to worry."

"But this is hard for me to understand, Colonel. I knew him only a short time, but we confided with each other."

"I knew he trusted me, and I did the same. He taught me things; made me think and understand life, and what it's all about, sir." Doug tries, to explain.

"You've just given a good description of Roberts, Doug. *He was truly a man for all seasons,*" Poindexter adds.

Doug moves closer to Poindexter, taking his hand, looking up to him.

"But … when I look back and add it all up, there was one thing I'll always remember him for---

"Explain it to me, Doug."

Doug looks across to Martha and back to Poindexter.

"I found his feelings, sir, his heart and soul. He was guided by his faith in God and country; the two most important things in his life. He was like a father I never knew before, but there was something else …

"Tell me about it Doug."

"It's something I'm sure about, sir. For Roberts and me ... life isn't over. We talked about the hereafter and then what ...

"What does ... then what, mean, Doug?"

Doug looks him over again ... "I don't need telling you the answer, sir ... I can see it upon your face: you're one of us... waiting to hear the sound ...

Poindexter looks at him smiling, "The sound of what Doug?"

"You know what I'm talking about; the sound of a bugle high in the sky ... and Him, riding a white horse, ready to take us home forever and forever, sir!"

Poindexter gazes up at Doug, thinking seriously ... admiringly. He's beginning to see him as a young vigorous, challenging young man.

"There's more of this kind talk later, Doug. This isn't the end of our relationship, we're together; there's a lot more of this kind of talk coming later."

"And I'll be ready, sir."

"Roberts was smart ... real smart. He let me know a couple of months ago you were informed about everything true Americans fight and die for; that's the way I am, Doug."

"Doug only sits listening, while Poindexter carries on.

Slowly he rises from the table, walking around where Doug sits next to Martha grasping his hand... "Would you like to carry on the same policy Roberts did, beginning this very day, Doug?" He asks, bluntly.

Doug looks up at him with a smile upon his face showing... "I told Roberts my feelings then; my commitment hasn't changed... nothing could please me better sir."

Poindexter places his left-hand upon his shoulder facing him... "You've met the test Doug. From this moment forward, you're one of one of our own … believers in God and country more than anything!"

Doug studies his words, and again a smile appears, "It's an honor and a pleasure, sir … I'll give it my best; believe me I will."

"Later you'll meet our group here in Washington. Go visit his grave at Arlington and come back when you're settled. There's a lot going on across the globe, and it isn't letting up, Doug!"

"Roberts stated the same to me before his death, sir."

"But there's another matter Doug …

"Another matter …" he asks surprised.

"What do you know about Joshua Bernstein…the Jew' he's missing?"

"He was with us at the airport during the exchange. He told me his followers in Israel were waiting to see what takes place after the seven-year treaty is signed. He seemed to be in good shape as always … but I could tell he was worried, Mr. Poindexter."

He looks up at him shaking his head. "I don't blame him for being worried: he has a lot to be worried about once the Palestinians move beside the Jewish people in Jerusalem."

The meeting is over and Doug and Martha waste no time heading for Roberts grave at *"Arlington National Cemetery."*

They stand gazing upon the head-stone … seeing an inscription in big letters reading-----*Nathanial P Roberts, Colonel, U. S. Army---West Point—Sgt. Major---Class of 1965"* *"Member of "The Long Grey-Line: Lover of God and Country."*

Next to his grave is his father's grave, another West Point cadet. Next to his father's grave is his grandfather's grave … all West Point years ago.

Martha becomes emotional, a tear appears … thinking *back*

how it all happened ... "Three generations of Roberts served our country, hero's all: today they rest with God!

Doug stands alone, as moments of sorrow begin to cloud his mind.

He remembers their time together; causing him to come to attention ... saluting before his grave respectfully.

He turns away pondering again, thinking back to their conversation before arriving at Kennedy: tears fill his eyes as he walks away, his head hanging downward.

Suddenly his face begins to glow, and a smile returns. *He remembers his friend's proudest moment; telling him his name is written in the Book of Life forever and ever!*

Six weeks go by, and Doug and Martha sit at home having breakfast, and the phone rings.

He picks it up the phone and a business only type of voice says, "This is the law firm of, Johnson and Pratt ... I wish to speak to, Mr. Doug Cutler."

"This is Doug Cutler, sir,"

"We're ready to read you the settlement as stated in Nathanial P Robert's last will and testament. Can you be here tomorrow at ten a. m. Mr. Cutler?"

"My wife and I will be with you at ten a. m. tomorrow sir," he replies... wondering.

Early the next morning they're on their way, and ten minutes till ten they're seated in the attorney's office: seeing an elderly well-dressed gentleman standing before them... waiting.

"I'm, Robert Johnson Doug; Attorney for your late friend, Nathaniel P Roberts. Suppose we get down to business with facts and figures: is this agreeable with you Mr. Cutler? He asks, smiling friendly.

"It's agreeable with me Mr. Johnson."

"I'll proceed with the reading of Mr. Roberts' "Last will

and Testament. My secretary will make notes of our meeting in detail."

"Within a week, you will receive a complete report of this entire procedure. Are there questions you might like to ask before we go further, Mr. Cutler?"

Martha and Doug begin to look at one another, wondering what's taking place.

"No questions needed sir."

"Good! Now we can move on Mr. Cutler."

Mr. Roberts is a very plain and simple will ... easy to understand---

"Understand what, sir?" Doug asks lowly...waiting.

"You, Mr. Cutler ... are the sole heir to all assets bearing the name *Nathanial P Roberts*. The six-thousand-acre ranch in Montana is yours Mr. Cutler. That includes cattle, barns, any type of structures—etc. The only thing that isn't yours ... is the air above surrounding you Mr. Cutler!" He says, chuckling.

"The last notation of the will reads as follows ... "*Doug ... only Doug ... will understand the* "case."

Doug looks over at Martha, and back to his attorney, glaring at him waiting ...

"But yet today, we're still trying to determine his intentions, but... the case is yours, Mr. Cutler!"

A flare of mystery suddenly takes place, while they sit gazing upon a small case lying in the middle of a large desk.

Doug opens the case and enclosed in fine silver wrapping is the biggest, blackest Cuban cigar he has ever seen. He wants to laugh all out ... but remembering where he is at...holding back.

Lying beside the cigar is another small package with two musical recordings. They read, "Julie Andrews sings, *The Sound of Music. And the other reads, Judy Garland sings "Somewhere over the Rainbow,*""

Doug lowers his head thinking back...fighting tears dripping downward. He alone knew the Colonel and all his earthly pleasures.

Long moments of reminiscing ... beginning to smile again. He stands gazing upon a big Cuban cigar sitting next to the recording...beginning to mutter to himself," *Thanks again Mr. Roberts...for being the father I longed for, but never knew ... till you came along, Mr. Roberts!*"

The End